# Taxed To Death
## Pine County Mysteries book #10

### Dean L. Hovey

**Print ISBNs**
Amazon Print 9780228625148
BWL Print 9780228625179
LSI Print 9780228625155
B&N Print 9780228625162

BWL Publ
Books we love to
Authors around the world.
http://bwlpublishing.ca

## *Acknowledgement*

As always, there is a group of people who deserve credit for helping mold my manuscripts. Julie reads the first draft of each book, offering opinions and correcting medical situations and terminology. Deanna Wilson willingly reads isolated chapters and out of context fragments while correcting errors and urging me on. She's also my police and horse consultant. Kathryn Nelson offered a plot twist that was too tasty to pass up. Andy Flagge and Andrew Kava helped me nail down some computer/Wi-Fi details. Mike Westfall, Clem MacIlravie, and Fran Brozo read early drafts, offered opinions that steered me to this final version. Anne Flagge and Natalie Lund proofread and remove my myriad typos and grammatical errors.

Thanks to Jude Pittman and Susan Davis of BWL for their editorial help and support.

## *Dedication*

To Bill and Mavis Wesley

# Table of Contents

# Chapter 1

Pine County Sheriff's Department Sergeant CJ Jensen was sleeping fitfully when the phone woke her. After glancing at the clock, which showed 2:37 AM, and checking the caller ID, which displayed PCSD, she answered, "Yeah."

The dispatcher's voice was more excited than usual. "Kerm Rajacich has requested an incident commander at the Pine County Historical Museum."

Through the haze in her mind, CJ tried to recall where the museum building was located. "Where?" she asked, searching for a location in Pine City, the county seat.

"It's on the south end of downtown Askov."

Throwing her legs out of bed, CJ shook her head to clear the cobwebs. She pictured Askov's old brick school. The building had been converted to an antique-filled museum and café. "What kind of incident occurs at a museum at two in the morning?"

"Kerm reported a fatality and that a pickup had driven into the side of the building."

While holding the phone against her ear with her shoulder, CJ pulled on a pair of jeans. "The driver died in the crash?"

"Kerm wasn't sure."

Grabbing a uniform shirt with her badge already pinned to it, the dispatcher's words made CJ pause. "He couldn't tell?"

"I guess there's a body there, but it's not inside the truck."

CJ ended the call, as she pulled on socks and shoes. Bailey, her basset hound, looked up from her bed in the corner of the room but made no effort to move. "Behave until I get back." After that admonition, CJ jogged to her cruiser. Flipping on the flashers but not the siren, she raced through the empty Pine City streets until she turned toward the interstate. On I-35, she accelerated, checking the speedometer as it approached 130 mph.

Passing a convoy of northbound semis, CJ tried to make sense of the dispatcher's comments. *There's a dead person, but not in the pickup. The only thing that makes sense is that some drunk must've been on his way home after the bars closed. He ran off the road and hit the building. Wow! The building is half a block off the road, with its own driveway. He must've mistaken the museum's driveway for the road.*

After passing a wayside rest with three idling semis in the parking lot, CJ approached the Kettle River bridge, which was partially shrouded in foggy mist.

Turning off the interstate, she drove east on Highway 23, toward downtown Askov. A billboard on the town's outskirts announced dates of the upcoming Rutabaga Festival. Immediately past the sign, CJ turned right, toward the old downtown. Ahead, she saw the flashing lights from the Askov fire department trucks and the lone Pine County Sheriff's Department cruiser.

Kerm Rajacich, a huge deputy known to relish breaking up bar fights, hustled toward CJ's car before it stopped rolling. "It's the craziest thing I've ever seen," he said, leading CJ toward the brick building.

As the dispatcher had said, a pickup was smashed against the brick wall near the entrance. Firemen stood ready to douse flames, but only a cloud of steam rose from the truck's engine. The smell of hot automotive antifreeze filled the still night air. A blue blanket was spread over a lump laying on dewy grass crisscrossed with tire tracks and human footprints.

Without hesitation, Kerm lifted the blanket, exposing the naked body of a young man. "Isn't that the craziest thing you've ever seen? I'm not sure if he was the driver, a passenger, or if he was out jogging, but here he is."

CJ knelt next to the body and made a cursory inspection. "I don't see any bruising or broken bones. It's as if he just laid down here and died."

"I know!" Rajacich replied. "It's like aliens dropped him out of a UFO or something."

CJ looked up at Rajacich, who seemed completely oblivious to the sad death of the young man. "Please don't repeat your comment about the UFO, Kerm, or you'll be quoted in the newspaper."

"Cool!" he replied, dropping the blanket over the dead man as CJ stood.

A fireman wearing the white chief's helmet approached them. "It doesn't look like there's any danger of the truck erupting in flames. Is there anything else you need from us?" he asked, his breath making small clouds of steam in the cool, damp morning air.

The Askov volunteer firemen, having been rousted from their beds by the call, looked tired. One man's coat was open, exposing his striped pajama shirt. Another was in wet moccasins, having rushed to the fire station without his boots. The firemen were gathered in a group by the fire truck, their collective breaths causing a small cloud of fog to form around them.

"Do you have lights to shine on the scene, Chief?"

"Sure. I can make it look like daylight, if you want."

"Do it. And ask your crew to walk the perimeter of the building to make sure there isn't another victim lying beyond the truck."

A smile creased the chief's face. "Do you want us to look for his clothes, too?"

"Sure. I'd like to find his clothes, ID, cell phone, and anything else that might identify him."

The Chief turned and yelled, "Hey, Randi! Come over here for a second."

The lone female firefighter trudged over in her heavy fireman's bunker outfit. While most of the firemen appeared to be in their twenties and thirties, Randi appeared to be old enough to be their mother. "What's up?"

"The sergeant wants to ID the victim."

Staring at the blanket, Randi drew a breath. "That's Nick Carlton."

"He's local?" CJ asked.

"He used to be. I wasn't close to his family."

"You said he used to be local. Did he stay in touch with anyone in town?"

"I can't really say. The family moved on a couple of years ago."

"Was he into drugs?" CJ asked, her thoughts directed to the recent rash of fentanyl overdose deaths.

"I thought he was a clean-cut kid." Randi paused, then added, "But I thought that of the kid we couldn't revive last week. He was on the high school debate team."

A fireman called to the chief from near the pickup, waving for him to walk over. "We can see wet footprints inside the building."

After walking across the dewy grass that had been criss-crossed repeatedly by the firemen, CJ pulled out a flashlight and shined it through the glass front door onto the tile floor. "Someone wearing shoes made those footprints. Either our victim took his shoes off before he died, or there was another person here. He went in and walked back out again."

CJ looked at Kerm. "Call the curator, or historical society president, and ask them to open the building. We need to know why someone was inside."

Randi was at CJ's shoulder. "There's a lot of old stuff in there, but I wouldn't call any of it particularly valuable. It's not like they owned a Rembrandt or Van Gogh."

Kerm perked up as a thought hit him. "The Little Mermaid Café is inside. Maybe someone broke in for the cash."

Shaking his head, the fire chief said, "The workers empty the cash register and take a deposit to the bank every night."

"Just the same, they probably leave enough to make change the next day. I'd like someone to check the museum inventory and displays, too." Stepping away from the firemen, CJ dialed Eddie Paulson's phone.

A sleepy voice answered on the third ring. "What's up?"

"I've got a guy's naked body next to a pickup truck that crashed into a museum."

"That sounds like the opening scene of a British mystery."

"I wish it was in Britain. I'm in Askov, standing outside the Pine County Historical Museum."

"A naked drunk crashed into the historical society?"

CJ walked to the blanket and lifted a corner. "I wish I knew what happened. The naked body is twenty yards from the crash site."

"Maybe he was thrown free by the impact."

"That's as good a theory as I've got."

"Wait a second. You called my cell phone, not the office. Have you already spoken to Tony?" he asked, referring to Tony Oresek MD, the medical examiner.

Staring at the boy's unseeing blue eyes, CJ drew a breath. "I needed to talk to a friend before calling your office."

"Sorry. Of course, you did. Are you okay?"

"Not really. I'm staring at a handsome kid's body and am about thirty seconds away from breaking into tears."

"Cover the body. Take a deep breath. Step away."

Standing and breathing deeply, she walked away from the scene. "Thanks. I've got myself together."

"I'll call Tony, and we'll be there in an hour or so. Will you still be around?"

"I'm the incident commander. I'm here until I'm relieved or the scene is cleared."

"Good. I'll give you a hug when I get there."

"You will *not* give me a hug when you get here. Geez! I don't need another rumor flying around about my personal life."

"That's what you need—a mental break from the scene."

"That's fine, but don't ever hug me when there are other cops around. Okay?"

Laughing, Eddie replied, "Sure. No hugging around cops. Got it."

* * *

As promised by the fire chief, the area around the crashed pickup was lit up like daylight when the medical examiner's van arrived at the museum. The volunteer firemen, aside from the chief, had departed to catch a few hours of sleep before going to their daytime jobs.

Tony Oresek, the ME, wasted no time socializing. "I assume that one of you checked to make sure the victim was actually dead before calling us."

The fire chief was speechless for a moment. "It was pretty obvious that he was dead when we arrived."

"So, you checked for his pulse, right?"

"Um, no," the chief said, taking off his helmet and rubbing his bald scalp. "He was white as a ghost, there was no steam coming from his mouth, and, well, he was *dead.*"

He glared at CJ who shook her head, indicating she hadn't checked for a pulse, either. Pulling on surgical gloves, the ME approached the corpse and pulled back the blanket. He stood back, taking in the scene, before kneeling down and touching the victim's skin and poking at his abdomen. Attempting to lift the victim's wrist, he was met with resistance.

"What time was the accident reported?" Oresek asked, as his assistant took pictures of the body from various angles and heights.

"I was called out just before three o'clock," CJ responded.

"He's in full rigor mortis, so he was dead before your call. Was the accident reported immediately by a witness, or was it discovered some time later?"

The fire chief cocked his head. "We were dispatched at 2:30 when Frank Fabin drove his bulk milk truck past. Steam was rising from the pickup's coolant leak when we arrived, so the engine was still hot. The truck couldn't have been here long before Frank called it in."

"Did the milk truck driver check the wreck for victims?" Oresek asked.

"Like I told Sergeant Jensen, he saw the body, then checked the cab. It was empty. He thought maybe the dead guy had been driving and had staggered away before collapsing."

Deputy Kerm Rajacich stepped up to the group, catching the last of the chief's comments. "I'm sticking with my theory that aliens dropped the kid from their UFO and kidnapped the driver."

The UFO theory froze the ME, who looked at CJ, "Sergeant, is an alien abduction the official view of the sheriff's department?"

CJ glared at Kerm before answering. "Um, no. I'm keeping an open mind."

Eddie Paulson, the ME's assistant, turned his face aside, hiding his smile.

The ME relaxed a bit, relieved to note that not all the members of the department were delusional.

Knowing it was too early to have a definitive time of death but wanting to move to more solid footing, CJ asked, "Dr.

Oresek, can you estimate how long the victim has been dead."

The ME stared at the naked victim. "Sergeant Jensen, you've been around enough death scenes to know that it's unreasonable to ask for a time of death before we do a full post-mortem exam."

Eddie's eyes crinkled as he smiled, anticipating CJ's next comment. "But Dr. Oresek, you often speculate on the time and cause of death before the autopsy."

Oresek looked at her, obviously annoyed. "And every time I do that, some smartass cop quotes me, and the newspaper reports my preliminary *best guess* as God's honest truth."

"Humor me."

"Fine," Oresek snapped. "Based only on the state of rigor mortis, I'd say the victim has been dead at least four but no more than eight hours."

"I didn't notice any obvious cause of death," CJ said, knowing that the ME hated having others, especially cops, speculating on the cause of death.

"That's very observant of you, Sergeant. I don't see an obvious sign of death, either." Oresek stood, his knees cracking as he rose. "Since he doesn't appear to have been stabbed, shot, or beaten to death, would you care to speculate on which of the other ten thousand causes might've led to his demise?"

Smiling at Eddie, CJ replied, "Nope. I'll leave that to professionals like you and your assistant."

Having seen the exchange, Oresek shook his head. "Are you two planning a comedy improv act?"

Eddie turned away. "I'll get the gurney."

"He didn't die in this position," CJ noted as the M.E. turned the body. "I see some livor mortis blood pooling on his back."

Oresek, having said his piece, nodded. "One might speculate that the pattern of lines in the pooled blood was due to his body laying on the pickup bed immediately after his death." He looked at the pickup. "I assume his body was ejected from the pickup bed when it ran over the curb or by the impact with the building."

"It seemed unlikely he was driving."

Oresesk pushed his glasses up his nose with the back of his plastic-gloved hand. "Well, he wouldn't have been the first naked driver I've encountered at an accident scene."

"Really? I'd think that was rare."

"Not as rare as you might believe. My first was a carload of teens fleeing the police after being caught skinny dipping. The second was an amorous couple—it appeared the driver lost control when he became distracted by…the events in the car."

CJ shook her head. "Useless deaths."

"Other than people dying in their beds, far too many of the others are useless."

"Well, I doubt this guy was in the throes of passion, nor was he skinny dipping in the middle of town. Do you have any observations about a *possible* cause of death?"

Oresek watched his assistant push the gurney across the museum's parking lot. "The victim expelled water when I probed his abdomen. Don't announce this to the press but I think he drowned." A hint of a smile twitched at the corner of the ME's mouth. "Don't rule out skinny dipping yet."

"When will you do the autopsy?"

Oresek nodded at Eddie. "Ask your boyfriend what's on the schedule. I just cut whomever he delivers to me."

"Eddie's not my boyfriend…" Seeing the slightest hint of a smile and knowing how closely he and Eddie worked, CJ stopped. "Yes, Dr. Oresek."

Eddie lifted a black body bag from the gurney and unfolded it while the ME knelt down to look at the body's underside. "Tony knows we're just friends," he whispered. "He's getting even with you for pushing him for a time and cause of death."

Helping Eddie unfold and unzip the bag, CJ nodded. "It's just a little creepy being kidded by the medical examiner."

Without looking up from the body, Oresek said, "I may have gray hair, but I'm not deaf."

"Good," CJ said. "I didn't want to waste that comment on Eddie."

Oresek took one end of the bag from Eddie and looked at CJ, "You may be the most disrespectful and outspoken smartass the Pine County Sheriff's Department has ever hired."

Helping roll the body into the bag, CJ nodded. "That's the nicest thing you've ever said to me, Dr. Oresek."

"If I thought you could tell a liver from a spleen, I might consider hiring you."

Helping lift the body bag onto the gurney, CJ snorted. "I wouldn't like spending my days cutting up dead bodies."

"There's more to the job than that," Eddie replied. "I spend endless hours filling out paperwork, too."

"Gee, you make it sound so exciting. I don't know how I could pass it up."

Oresek stretched after lifting the body. "Listen, Sergeant. No one has punched, shot at, or threatened me. I wouldn't switch jobs with you, either." He looked at Eddie. "What's on our schedule?"

"We've got one PM requested by a family who thinks their mother's doctor misdiagnosed her metastatic cancer. Other than that, I've got nothing else but a couple hundred toxicology reports to review."

"Are you going to join us for the PM if I schedule it for tomorrow afternoon, Sergeant?"

"Gee, Doc, how can a girl refuse an offer like that?"

Oresek chuckled. "If you play your cards right, you may be able to convince my assistant to take you out for dinner."

"Won't you join us?"

Oresek exchanged glances with both CJ and Eddie. "My wife says that I am a fun sponge; capable of sucking the fun out of any situation. I'll pass."

* * *

The sun shone brightly and had burned the morning dew off the grass. It was nearly six by the time the historical society president arrived at the museum. Surveying the scene, Agatha Perkins stood next to her car with her hand over her mouth. "Oh, dear."

Pam Ryan, the Pine County Sheriff's Department investigator, searched the truck's cab. With gloved hands, she carefully removed items and placed them into evidence bags that she sealed, labeled, and signed.

"Can you tell us if anything is missing?" CJ asked.

"I don't know if I can do that quickly," the curator said. "There are thousands of items on display. It will take days to compare the displays with the inventory list."

Handing Agatha a pair of purple nitrile gloves, CJ replied, "Let's take a quick look to see if any display cases have been broken or if there's anything obviously out of place or missing."

"Um, certainly," Agatha responded. Taking a keyring out of her purse, she unlocked the front door. "But some of the most valuable pieces are small and easily removed."

CJ followed Agatha from room to room as the historical society president turned on lights and perused the displays. Peering into glass cases and inspecting shelves, they found no broken glass, vandalism, or missing displays. After turning off the lights in the last room of the museum, they entered the auditorium. Their footsteps echoed in the large open space often used for wedding receptions and meetings.

"I really don't see anything out of place," Agatha said as she turned off the lights."

"Let's check the Little Mermaid Café and offices," CJ suggested.

The café seemed undisturbed, but the cash register drawer was open. "The café manager leaves the drawer open," Agatha explained. "She doesn't want anyone to break it open to verify there isn't any money inside. She takes the cash to the bank every day, after closing."

"Let's look in the offices," CJ suggested.

Just inside the front door, the offices that had once housed the school principal, nurse, and secretary, were dark behind a counter. Agatha verified that each door was locked, then turned to CJ, "I think everything is intact."

Looking around the outer office at the copier/scanner/fax and assorted office supplies, CJ asked, "Is everything as it should be, here?"

"I think so. The copier is the most expensive item in the office, and it seems untouched. The spare ink cartridges are here, as are the extra reams of paper." Agatha turned slowly, pointing to items as she mentally ticked them off. "Stapler. Tape dispenser. Cup of pens. Post-it notes. Events calendar. Clock. That's all…"

"What's the matter?" CJ asked.

Pointing to an empty hook, Agatha said, "The van keys are gone."

"Is there a chance someone forgot to return them to the hook after they were used?"

Stepping to the front windows, Agatha shook her head. "The van's missing from its parking spot."

"Can you give me a description of the van and its license number?"

"I think Toni, our secretary, probably has the paperwork with the license number somewhere. We'll have to get it from her."

Taking out a notebook, CJ instructed, "Describe the van."

"It was a big white one, with the museum logo on the front doors."

"What brand?"

"Um…it was either a Ford, Dodge, or Chevy…I think."

Suppressing a grin, knowing that virtually all vans were one of those three brands, CJ asked, "Was it a full-sized van or a minivan?"

"It was a big van. We sometimes pick up groups of eight or nine people from local care centers and bring them here for tours and lunch." Agatha stared at CJ, "Aren't you going to use your radio to put out an all points bulletin?"

"I need a better van description for that to be effective."

"You should call Francine Gustafson, she'd be able to describe it better."

"Is she one of the historical society leaders?"

Making a scoffing sound, Agatha waved her hand. "Heavens no. Francine donated the van to the historical society. She used it for deliveries until the bakery closed."

"Does the van have windows?" CJ asked, thinking of other delivery vans with windowless rear compartments.

"Of course, it does! How else would the driver see the road?"

Biting her lip and wondering if Agatha was mentally slipping, CJ asked, "In the rear, does the van have windows so the passengers can see outside?"

"Oh. That question makes more sense. Yes, it has side windows."

After thanking Agatha, CJ radioed the vague van description to the dispatcher, then checked on Pam, who was packing up the items she'd collected from the pickup. "Did the driver leave behind a wallet or cell phone to make this a short investigation?"

"No such luck," Pam said. "There's a bunch of food wrappers and other crap inside." She held up an envelope containing a white piece of paper. "This is probably our best lead. It's a gas receipt from the station at the Highway 11 exit. We should be able to get the driver's ID from the credit card slip and possibly a security camera photo."

# Chapter 2

Although there wasn't usually any trouble at the Hinckley horse show, the sheriff liked the deputies to walk the grounds and show goodwill. As the sergeant/shift supervisor, CJ Jensen passed the usual Sunday patrols to the other deputies and seized the opportunity to walk around the show rather than spending eight hours driving the 1,400 square miles of mostly rural Pine County. She'd done the same thing on Saturday, walking through the flea market on the other side of Highway 45 east of Hinckley.

Leaning on the crossbeam of a portable fence, CJ watched a mother and daughter groom their red-coated gelding for the competition. The mother, Anna Weise, walked over, smiling. "CJ Jensen, how are you?"

"Talking to horse people beats the heck out of patrol duty."

Anna, dressed all in black with a black Stetson, tipped her head back, looking at the sky. "Days like this make it worth staying in Minnesota through the miserable winters."

"At least you have the option of staying inside if there's a March blizzard. I'm expected to show up for my shift whether it's sunny or snowing."

"Kins and I work the horses in the indoor arena if the weather is too bad. The horses don't like being out in a blizzard any more than we do. How's Bailey?" Anna asked, reaching down to scratch the dog's ears. Bailey was referred to as *the fart machine* by the other deputies.

"She's becoming less of a puppy."

"So, Bailey isn't chewing up everything in sight?"

"She stopped chewing up my underwear. My chairs aren't faring as well, which is why she's with me and not alone at home."

Surveying the quiet crowd and people preparing their horses, Anna asked, "Are you expecting trouble, or are you just making the rounds?"

"I'm being a conspicuous presence and building bridges with the community."

Kinsley looked up in annoyance. "Mom, stop talking to CJ and help me wrap Cash's tail."

After glancing over her shoulder, Anna leaned close. "You'd think she'd never done it by herself."

CJ laughed and walked on, past the row of temporary corrals set up next to the horse trailers and living quarters of the horse owners. Drawn to the aroma of fresh baked goods, she approached a small seating area near the show ring. A few people were in line at each of the food booths. CJ and Bailey stepped into line behind Bob Olsen, the county tax assessor.

"Hi, CJ, are you here for the show or in your official capacity?"

Reaching up with her left hand, she touched her badge. "I don't usually socialize in my uniform with my dog."

"I've got two horses in the show. I'm really pumped this time after being beat out by a teenager and a woman from Finlayson last year." Reaching the front of the line, Bob studied the chalkboard menu behind the woman whose hair was put up under a kerchief. She wore a long-sleeved blouse and ankle-length denim skirt that the locals called Amish attire. "How hot is your chili?"

The woman was about to respond when a man wearing a white apron and a baseball cap embroidered with a cross stepped in front of her. "Bob wants the Norwegian chili, Karen."

"Norwegian chili?" CJ asked, curious about the unusual description.

The apron-clad man reached behind a row of steaming chafing dishes to a small crock pot. "Every year Bob asks if our chili is spicy. We always say no, because the seasoning is very mild. Bob tastes it and always complains that his mouth is on fire.

This year, I set aside part of the batch before I seasoned it." He passed a steaming Styrofoam bowl to the tax assessor and smiled. "The only seasonings in this are salt and brown sugar."

Stifling a gag, CJ choked out, "You put brown sugar in chili?"

"Just like my mother used to make. Nothing but tomato soup, hamburger, celery, and kidney beans." Reaching for his wallet, Bob asked, "How much?"

"It's free for you, our favorite tax assessor."

After setting his bowl down, Bob set a $5 bill on the table. "I can't take any gifts, especially from you while we're arguing about the tax status of your property."

The server looked past Bob and smiled at CJ, "I don't believe we've met. I'm Brother Eugene Palmquist of the Congregation of the Holy Resurrection."

"Sergeant CJ Jensen of the Pine County Sheriff's Office. This is Bailey."

Taking a homemade dog biscuit from a tin, Brother Palmquist bent down and fed it to Bailey, whose tail circled like a propeller in excitement. "What would you like today, Sergeant?"

"What do you recommend?"

Palmquist stood, squirted sanitizer on his hands, and turned toward the menu board. "Everything we serve is raised in our commune. I personally like the grass-fed beef hamburgers on homemade bread. The chili is a big seller. It's made from our own tomatoes, onions, beef, beans, and peppers."

"The burger sounds good. What are your beverage options?"

"Chokecherry tea sweetened with honey, or homemade root beer from a secret recipe."

The thought of drinking root beer made from heaven knows what seemed unwise. "I'll try the tea."

A young woman, wearing a white headcover and long dress, set a burger on a slice of bread while Brother Palmquist drew a cup of tea from a coffee urn. The woman, who appeared to be barely out of her teens, averted her eyes when she handed the hamburger to CJ, "Here you are, ma'am."

Palmquist stepped beside her, his smile beaming. "I hope you enjoy your burger and tea."

CJ looked at the chalkboard for the prices. "How much do I owe you?"

"I'd be pleased if you'd accept it as a donation to a dedicated first responder. We appreciate your service."

"Like Bob, I can't accept your kind offer." CJ took out a $10 bill and put it into a tip jar.

"Thanks. If you're ever around our compound near mealtime, we'd be happy to have you join us at our communal table."

Hopefully unknown to Brother Palmquist, the congregation was under investigation for income tax fraud, and harassment of members who were trying to leave the commune. CJ smiled, "Thanks. I'll take you up on that offer, sometime."

CJ led Bailey to a folding chair next to the tax assessor. She tied Bailey's leash to her chair and said, "I'm surprised you bought lunch from the religious sect."

"Everything they make is organic." He glanced at a more popular vendor who was dispensing sausages and hot dogs. "I can't handle all the preservatives and nitrates in the sausages." Nodding the other direction, the assessor wrinkled his nose. "George's burgers are dripping fat and the buns he serves will survive fifty years in a landfill."

Wiping her mouth after taking a bite of burger, CJ asked, "How's your brown sugar chili?"

"The beans are a little firm, but the flavor is good. How's your burger?"

"The meat is a little dry, but the bread is incredible. The tea could use another teaspoon of honey."

With a knowing nod, the assessor said, "It's hard to offset the tartness of the chokecherries. Mom used to make them into jelly. The recipe used five pounds of sugar in a pound of chokecherries."

"I'm sure I'll be healthier tomorrow because of this fine lunch."

Bob tipped his head down and leaned forward. "It won't offset all the doughnuts you eat at Tobies."

"Cops eating doughnuts is an urban myth."

Snorting, Bob shook his head. "Sure, I see your cruiser parked at Tobies because you've stopped for the salad bar, right?"

# Chapter 3

Strolling near the stands with her basset hound, CJ watched people's faces. Most everyone focused on the horses being shown in the ring. One young man, dressed like a cowboy, leaned against the fence while checking out women who walked past. His leer made CJ's skin crawl. Slipping alongside him unnoticed while he ogled a teenage girl wearing short shorts, CJ leaned close. "Are you a sex offender or just a pervert?"

The man's face was angry until he noticed CJ's uniform. "Just watching the horses," he said.

"The girl you're ogling is only about fifteen. Show me your driver's license."

"I'm not driving anywhere."

CJ held out her hand. "Your license, please."

Still resting his arms on the top fence rail, the man asked, "Why do you want my license?"

Hearing the change in CJ's voice, Bailey sat down and stared at the man.

"I'm going to see if you're a registered sex offender or if you have any outstanding warrants."

"There's no law about watching people at a horse show, is there?"

CJ leaned close. "That depends on your legal status. If you're a pedophile, you might have to stay away from children under eighteen. If there's a protection order against you, you have to stay away from whoever you've been harassing. If you have an open warrant, I have to arrest you. Hand me your license."

With obvious irritation, the cowboy removed his wallet from his back pocket. He extended the wallet to CJ.

"Remove the license from the wallet. I don't want to be accused of losing something from your wallet while it is in my possession."

"Fine," the cowboy said, removing the license. He reached out, letting the license slip from his fingers a few inches from CJ's hand. Smiling, he said, "Oops. I guess you'll have to pick it up."

Sliding the license with the toe of her shoe, CJ looked down. "Robert Barr, from Braham." Turning toward her shoulder mounted mic, she read Barr's name and date of birth to the dispatcher. "Please check his sex offender status and for open warrants."

Barr's face colored as people edged away from him. "I'm no pervert!"

Glaring at him while waiting for the dispatcher to reply, CJ said, "You're a pervert. The question is whether you've ever been convicted in court."

Barr glared as a gust of wind flipped his license onto a damp piece of horse manure— where it stuck.

"Oops. It looks like some manure got smeared on your license. That's probably going to stink for a while." The dispatcher replied that Barr had been ticketed for reckless driving, a DUI, and speeding, but all his fines had been paid. CJ acknowledged that and smiled at Barr. "Have a nice day."

While the cowboy used the railing to scrape the horse manure off his license, CJ walked over to a group of young teenage girls. She introduced herself, nodded toward Barr and advised the girls to keep an eye on him because he'd been visually undressing them. "Warn your friends, too."

Moving on and talking to a young couple with a golden retriever, CJ heard emergency tones for the Hinckley Fire Department over her radio, followed by the dispatcher's announcement, "Medical emergency at the Hinckley horse show near the contestants' trailers."

CJ excused herself and edged through the crowd until she got free of the congestion, then ran toward the trailers. Jogging with one hand on her Glock and the other holding Bailey's leash, she neared the trailers as the first siren sounded at the firehall across the freeway. Ahead of her, two EMTs in orange vests knelt inside a ring of onlookers.

"Step back, please," she said as she walked through the people surrounding the first responders. After turning Bailey over to a familiar woman at the rear of the crowd, CJ pushed forward. Kneeling beside the EMTs, she saw the tax assessor's ashen face. Spittle dribbled from his mouth, and he clutched his belly while writhing in pain. "What's going on?"

Bob turned his head and vomited in the grass. The female first responder looked at CJ, "He's got stomach pain, his pulse is racing, and his blood pressure is 173 over 104."

"Stomach, not chest pain?" CJ asked.

"It's more like food poisoning than a heart attack. But I've never seen anyone with this much pain from a bad meal."

"I have," CJ responded. "We were on our Mexican honeymoon and a guy staying near us got bad shrimp from a street vendor. He was doubled up in pain like this within a couple of hours."

The male first responder glanced around the crowd. "I hope it was something he ate somewhere else. We're not staffed to deal with dozens of people who ate bad bratwurst."

The female EMT groaned. "Like the bad tuna salad at Johnsons' July 4$^{th}$ picnic. By the time we got there, twenty people were puking into the bushes. Grandma Helen lost her teeth in the marigold flower bed."

The tax assessor groaned and clenched his knees to his chest. "I'll never eat another egg cooked sunny side up."

"Where did you eat those eggs?" CJ asked as a siren stopped in the driveway and two firemen ran carrying more first aid equipment.

"At home. My wife told me to throw the eggs away, but they were barely past their expiration date."

Standing to clear a path for the firemen, CJ considered the expired and undercooked egg scenario. She'd eaten dozens of eggs with runny yolks, never considering their age. *How many cases of 24-hour flu have I had that were really food poisoning?* Pausing, another thought came to her. *Bob had chili from a special crock pot. He said the beans were undercooked; I wonder if that batch wasn't kept hot enough?*

Another siren whined west of the show ring as the ambulance announced their ETA in four minutes over CJ's radio.

* * *

After the ambulance departed, the crowd dispersed, and the firemen packed up their first aid kits. They used a garden hose to rinse down the vomit, then loaded their remaining gear back on the firetruck.

CJ retrieved Bailey from the Good Samaritan and led her to the fire truck.

The female EMT walked to CJ, looking uneasy. "Do you think he really ate bad eggs?"

"I'm not a microbiologist, but people's views about eggs have changed over the years. I used to eat cookie dough as a kid and never got sick from the raw eggs in it. Now, moms won't let their kids touch a cookie until after it's baked. I suppose it's possible his undercooked eggs were bad."

Bending down to pet Bailey, the EMT wrinkled her nose. "Every menu has a warning printed across the bottom warning about the risk of eating undercooked eggs, fish, and meat. People continue to order eggs with runny yolks and hamburgers that are pink in the middle."

Finding a quiet corner in a barn, CJ convinced Bailey to sit, then dialed her friend, Eddie, at the medical examiner's office. "What's up?" Eddie asked.

"I'm at a horse show, and we had a guy puking with stomach cramps. The ambulance just left. The patient speculated that he'd eaten expired eggs, cooked sunny side up, this morning. Does that seem like a reasonable cause?"

"Eggs sometimes have Salmonella bacteria, but if they're stored in the refrigerator, they're usually safe for weeks past the sell by date. If they're left on the counter for too long, they sometimes go bad before that date. It all depends." Eddie paused. "What symptoms was he having?"

"He had severe stomach pain, and he was vomiting."

"Those are two of the classic Salmonella poisoning symptoms. The others are diarrhea and an elevated temperature."

"One of the EMTs was fearful that there would be an outbreak among more people because of something eaten at the food trucks and booths here at the show."

"That's unlikely. Salmonella poisoning usually shows up twelve to twenty-four hours after consumption of the contaminated food. In some cases, it doesn't show up for days or even weeks."

"The victim said he'd eaten runny eggs for breakfast."

"That's a pretty quick response to Salmonella. Other bacteria act more quickly, sometimes in as little as 30 minutes, but they're usually found in seafood. I assume none of the vendors are serving raw oysters or clams."

Chuckling, CJ replied, "No, not even Rocky Mountain oysters."

"Nearly two thirds of all food poisoning cases are from uncooked shellfish, and a lot of the rest are due to raw or undercooked fish. I'd check to see if the victim had sushi or undercooked seafood before considering his undercooked eggs."

Reflecting on her lunch discussion with the tax assessor, CJ frowned. "I ate lunch next to the victim. He ate chili while sharing his concerns about eating greasy foods or processed meats. I can't see him eating sushi or raw fish."

"Those are my only thoughts."

"Have you ever examined someone who died from food poisoning?"

"Whew. There have been a couple cases, but the only ones I recall were either elderly or immunocompromised. Healthy people may get miserably ill from food poisoning, but they don't usually die from it." Eddie paused, "Since you're a cop, I'll share an anecdote from 'Nam. I got dysentery from slogging through rice paddies fertilized with night soil. I thought I was going to die. After a while, I was so miserable I hoped I would die."

"I've never been quite that sick," CJ said, thinking she'd rather have not heard that story. "What's night soil?"

"That's a euphemism for human excrement."

"You were wading through…"

"Yes, and it wasn't pleasant. Do you have supper plans?"

"Nice segue, Mr. medical examiner's assistant. You go right from dysentery and night soil to asking me out on a date."

"Sorry. I've become calloused and sometimes ignore the norms of polite society. Back to dinner plans, are you up for a burger at the microbrewery in Canal Park?"

"Sure, Eddie, as long as my burger isn't pink in the middle."

"I'll meet you there at six."

Ending the call, CJ looked at Bailey. "Eddie and I are going out for supper. Will you behave yourself if I leave you alone in the apartment?"

"She can stay at our house."

CJ turned as Floyd Swenson, the sheriff department's newly appointed interim chief deputy, and his wife, Mary, approached. "Bailey should be okay in the apartment."

Floyd handed CJ a bag. "Bailey should wear this while you're on patrol."

Opening the bag while Mary petted Bailey, CJ looked at Floyd skeptically. "Really? You think Bailey should wear a K-9 vest embroidered with a Pine County Sheriff's Department badge?"

Grinning, Floyd nodded his head. "It'll give her street credibility."

CJ released the snaps and fit the vest around Bailey's front legs and under her chest. She adjusted the straps and stood, considering the new vest on the dog.

"I think Bailey likes it," Mary said, watching the dog's tail wag.

"She likes any kind of attention."

CJ stepped back and two children raced up and petted Bailey. "A police dog!" the girl said.

The kids' mother followed with a child harness strapped to her chest. "Really? Your department has a basset K-9?"

Floyd jumped in before CJ replied. "She's more of a department goodwill ambassador."

The mother nodded. "Yeah, I can't see a basset hound chasing down a suspect."

Mary laughed. "He'd be covered with slobber if she caught him."

When the mother and children left, Mary took the leash from CJ, "We'll watch her."

"Take her to doggie daycare. I'll pick her up after my shift."

# Chapter 4

As she watched the riders lead their horses through patterns of white poles laid out in the arena, CJ felt a tug on her pants legs. A young girl with platinum blonde hair, about five-years-old, stared up at her with tears in her eyes. Kneeling, CJ asked, "What's wrong, honey?"

"My mommy is lost."

"What's your name?"

"Ashley."

Assessing the girl's situation, CJ determined that Ashley looked neat, healthy, and well dressed. Her jeans had worn knees but were clean. Her pink "My Little Pony" t-shirt looked nearly new, as did her white cowboy hat. "I'm CJ. What's your last name?"

"Peterson. Ashley Peterson."

"Where did you last see your mommy?"

Tears streamed from Ashley's eyes. "I don't know. That's why she's lost." She reached up, and CJ lifted the girl into her arms.

"Look around. Do you see your mommy anywhere?"

Ashley gripped CJ's neck as if she were going to fall off, then she scanned the crowd in the stands. "I don't see her."

"What's your mommy's name?"

"People call her Heather."

Patting the girl's back, CJ clutched Ashley tight. "Let's talk to the announcer."

After explaining the situation to the public address announcer, Ray Stevens picked up the microphone. "Ashley Peterson has misplaced her mother, Heather. If anyone knows where Ashley's lost mother is, please come to the announcer's booth."

CJ bent to set Ashley on her feet, but the girl tightened her grip on CJ's neck. "NO! I want to stay with you until you find Mommy."

"Do you and Mommy have a horse in the show?"

Nodding emphatically, Ashley explained, "We're showing Pinto. His real name is Pinto Bean Guacamole, but we just call him Pinto. He's a gelding. That means the vet cut off his nuts so he's not as wild as a stallion."

"That must've hurt."

"I don't think so. Mommy says he's a eunuch, just like Daddy."

Stifling a laugh, CJ smiled. "Your Mommy says that?"

"Not to me, but that's what she tells her friends."

"Is your daddy here too?"

Ashely shook her head. "He's not a horse person like Mommy and me. He stays home and drinks. Beer makes him fart, so Mommy and I go to the barn when he's drinking." Looking sincere, Ashley stared at CJ, "Does beer make you fart?"

"I'm more of a wine person," CJ responded. Commotion in the crowd caught CJ's attention as a frantic woman, wearing western-cut show clothes, pushed her way past people. "Is that your mommy?"

Ashley's head spun around, searching the crowd for a familiar face. Seeing her mother, Ashley wriggled herself free of CJ's grip. "It's her!"

"Please hold my hand until we talk to your mommy, Ashley." They met the frantic woman who scooped the child into her arms. "Could I see your ID, please."

The young woman dug in her back pocket and pulled out her cell phone and driver's license. "I've been so worried."

After glancing at the driver's license, CJ handed it back. "Do you have custody of Ashley?"

"Or course I do. Why would you ask?"

"Ashley said her last name was Peterson. Your license says Heather Broadus."

"I've remarried. Kevin Peterson is my ex-husband. We share custody."

Apparently bored, Ashley squirmed in her mother's arms. "Can we go now?"

Turning toward her shoulder-mounted mic, CJ asked the dispatcher if anyone had reported Ashley missing. She gave the dispatcher Heather's name and birthdate.

"Is there a problem, sergeant?" Heather asked.

"I'm just making sure there isn't a custodial issue. You'll be able to return to Pinto in a minute."

Ashley turned her mother's chin, so they were nose-to-nose. "I told CJ that Pinto is a gelding, like daddy."

Heather's face turned red. "We don't talk about Daddy like that."

"Why not? You tell everyone he's a gelding and that he farts."

Staring helplessly at CJ, Heather was speechless. "I think we need to have a discussion about language and boundaries."

Raising her eyebrows, CJ replied, "Or you could watch your language around the child with big ears."

Heather turned to Ashley. "Daddy isn't a gelding. It's just something I tell people when we're kidding around."

"He's not a gelding. Is he still a eunuch?"

"He's not that either."

The dispatcher responded that there were no missing persons reports filed for Ashley Peterson, nor were there any open warrants for her mother.

"You guys are free to go," CJ said, smiling at Ashley. "Try not to lose mommy again. Okay?"

Heather and Ashley were walking away when a series of pops that sounded like gunfire, echoed over the arena. A woman screamed from somewhere near the horse trailers, and the crowd surged away. Pushing herself through the oncoming throng, CJ mulled the possible scenarios as she keyed her radio mic, "Officer needs assistance at the Hinckley show arena."

People shoved and elbowed their way past her. As she neared the arena entrance, the sound of laughing teenage boys preceded another round of popping sounds. At the railing, CJ saw a smoky haze in the show ring, where a teenage rider attempted to control her spooked horse. A string of smoking firecrackers arced over the railing and into the ring, landing near the horse's hooves. The rider reined her horse away from the commotion. They trotted to the opposite side of the show ring seconds before the firecrackers started popping.

Huddling together as they lit another string of firecrackers, the boys were oblivious to CJ's approach. She grabbed the nearest boy's shoulder, causing him to drop the lit string of firecrackers at their feet. More concerned with jumping away from the firecrackers than anything around them, the other three boys didn't react until CJ had two of them in her grip. She pushed the two into the others, pinning them against the railing.

The announcer tried to calm the crowd. "Some juvenile delinquents are throwing fireworks into the show ring. The sheriff's department is dealing with them."

Nearly frothing at the mouth, a middle-aged man rushed to CJ's side and grabbed the collar of a boy holding a cigarette lighter. "What in hell is the matter with you? My daughter, Maddie, is on that horse. She could've been killed!"

The kid grabbed the man's arm and sneered at him. "Let go of me, old man. We're just having some fun."

Using the element of surprise to her advantage, CJ snapped her handcuffs on one boy, then pulled his arm around a fence post before snapping the other cuff on the boy with the lighter. Snatching the lighter from his hand, she inserted herself between the angry father and the boy. "I've got this," she said, gently using her body to back the angry father away from the boys before fists started flying.

Leaning around CJ, a man yelled, "Arrest them! They could've killed someone, and they're still laughing about it."

Putting up her hand to hold the angry dad in place, she extended her other hand to the boy holding a paper bag. "Give me the firecrackers."

"No way! We paid good money for these!"

"And they're illegal in Minnesota. Hand me the bag."

The boy turned, preparing to run. CJ grabbed his belt and yanked it up, nearly lifting the boy off the ground. He howled and dropped the bag.

"The cop just gave Speedy a wedgie," one of the other boys laughed as he reached for the dropped bag.

Placing her foot firmly on the bag, CJ pulled what appeared to be an expensive cowboy hat from the head of the kid reaching for the fireworks. "All of you listen carefully," she said, as several people from the crowd moved closer to offer her assistance. "You're all getting tickets for possession of illegal fireworks. 'Cigarette lighter boy' is getting an additional ticket for being a public nuisance and assault. The county attorney can decide if he only gets fined or if he'll also have to go to jail. I assume all of you will be picking up litter along the highway for the rest of the summer."

The tallest kid, his complexion dotted with blemishes, pushed himself nose-to-nose with CJ, "Don't you know who I am?"

A smile creased CJ's face. "If you don't know who you are, we may have to put you on a psych hold until your memory returns."

The gathering crowd laughed, and the boy's face turned crimson. "My father is a lawyer."

"Then, you should call him. Tell him that you're in police custody at the Hinckley horse arena and explain that you're being held for assault."

The boy pulled out his cell phone, then hesitated when his friend leaned close. "Your dad won't be happy about being dragged off the golf course because we were throwing firecrackers at the show horses."

Locking his phone, the zit-faced kid turned to CJ, "Fine. Give me a ticket. My dad can fight it in court."

"Since you've decided to escalate this, let's call your dad from the courthouse. You're under arrest."

"You said we were getting tickets."

"You're all getting tickets. We need to speak with Dad about your memory issue. Cops don't like being threatened."

"This is bullshit!"

The father of the rider stepped forward. "They'll have to do a body cavity search before they put him in a cell, right?"

The teen glared at the father. "I don't know what that is."

The man smiled. "A guard sticks his finger up your butt to make sure you're not bringing any hidden contraband into the jail."

With the color draining from the boy's face, he pulled his cell phone out of his pocket. CJ snatched it from his hand and put it into her pocket. "You'll be able to call him on a landline from the jail."

Deputy Sandy Maki pushed his way through the crowd. Quickly assessing the situation, he stepped in front of the zit-faced boy, holding his handcuffs. "Put your hands behind your back."

The boy tried to step away from Sandy, but CJ blocked his path. "I don't actually remember Dad's number. He's in the contacts on my cell."

Sandy pulled the boy's hands behind his back. "Maybe one of your friends can contact him for you."

CJ suppressed a smirk. "I'm sure your mother will bail you out if you don't want to interrupt your father's golf game." She handed the boy's cell phone to Sandy.

The boy who'd dropped the fireworks shook his head. "His mom will kill him."

Starting to look frantic, the zit-faced kid turned to Sandy. "Listen, that woman cop is overreacting. Let me go and this will all be fine. I'm sure my dad will cut you some slack on his next case."

"Gee, Deputy Maki," CJ said, "that sounds like bribery."

Realizing his situation, the kid shook his head. "I never said anything about bribing you."

"Too bad we're wearing body cams, and it's recorded for the judge." CJ looked at

Sandy. "Take him to jail. I'll hold the other boys here for their parents."

* * *

With Sandy and the apparent ringleader gone, the other boys were contrite. Aaron Brown, the boy who had the lighter, gave his name and address to CJ while they sat on folding chairs behind the stands. "Look, I'm really sorry. We didn't mean to hurt anyone; we're just messing around."

Not looking up from her citation pad as she wrote out a ticket for the boy, CJ said, "Aaron, your intentions were to scare the horses. Scared horses react badly. They could've thrown the rider, injured themselves, or hurt someone in the crowd. You're old enough to understand that."

Looking disgusted, Aaron said, "We were just messing around."

"You can explain that to your parents and the judge. 'Just messing around,' isn't a defense for stupidity."

Aaron hung his head. "Are they really going to do a body cavity search when Landon gets to the jail?"

Suppressing a smile, CJ said, "We'll hold him in the sheriff's office until a parent picks him up."

"I hope they call Landon's dad before his mom gets there. She'll beat the crap outta him."

52

"Landon's mother has anger issues?"

Aaron shrugged. "She gets worked up over stuff. The coach threw her out of a basketball game because she was swearing at the referee and the other team's coach. She apologized later, but she sometimes loses it."

CJ moved her chair to the next boy, then flipped her citation book to a new page. "Tell me your name and address."

"Bruno Mars, from Honolulu."

The other two boys sniggered. "Either you tell me your real name, or we'll hold you until you contact someone who gives us your name and pays your fine."

"Ben Bosworth. My mom has a PO box in Rutledge."

"What's the physical address of your house?"

"We live in an apartment. Mom says the building used to be a restaurant before they built the freeway."

CJ wrote both the PO box number and the apartment's street address on the citation. "Is your mom coming to pick you up?"

"She's probably working until six o'clock. She cooks at the Floppy Crappie Pub." The boy said the pub name with the rhyming name, pronounced Floppy Croppy. "Does that mean she'll have to pick me up at the jail?"

"Let's see what happens. Okay?"

"How much will my ticket cost? I don't have any cash and Mom… She only works during the summer."

"I don't know. I assume the fine will be fifty dollars plus court costs."

Ben leaned close to CJ and whispered, "My mom had to borrow money from grandma to buy gas for her car."

"But somehow you had enough cash to buy fireworks."

"I helped Swansons bale hay. I only made twenty bucks."

"Maybe you should've *given* your mother money for gas."

"But that was *my* money."

"Right."

Sliding her chair to the next boy, CJ asked, "What is your name and address?"

"Troy Johnson." He gave an address in Sandstone.

"Who's coming to pick you up?"

"I drove here. I can take the ticket and leave."

"No. I have to release you into the custody of an adult."

"My sister is eighteen. She's working at the taco place across the highway."

"Where are your parents?"

"Mom went shopping at the Mall of America this weekend. My dad lives in North Dakota. He's working in the oil fields."

"Let's call your mom and let her decide who will pick you up."

Troy grimaced. "She'll be pissed."

"That's the point, Troy. You're a minor who's in trouble. No matter how inconvenient, the problem goes to your parents." CJ paused. "Who owns the car you're driving?"

"Dad bought it for me last time he was home. He makes big bucks working oil. I'm moving out there as soon as I'm eighteen."

"Let me see your license," CJ said, putting out her hand. She called Troy's name and address into the dispatcher and handed the license back to the boy.

"Why'd you do that? This isn't a traffic stop."

"Let's say I'm curious."

Troy put the license back into his wallet and frowned. "My driving record has nothing to do with this."

"If you have an outstanding bench warrant for failing to show up for a hearing, I'll have to arrest you."

"That's bullshit!"

The dispatcher responded with Troy's driving history, then added, "His license was suspended June 11."

"Did you drive here?" CJ asked.

Seeing the problem, Troy shook his head. "Ben drove."

The other boys were in conversation behind them, so CJ leaned back. "Ben, please hand me Troy's car keys."

"What?"

"Pass me the keys to Troy's car."

"I don't have a license. He drove."

CJ turned to Troy. "Your mom can pick up your car from the Pine City impound lot." She radioed the dispatcher and asked her to have a tow truck transport Troy's vehicle to the impound lot.

"C'mon. Just let me drive it home. I'll leave it parked in the yard, really."

"I'd have to ticket you for driving without a license. You wouldn't be eligible to drive until you turn 18, then you probably wouldn't be able to afford the insurance."

A heavyset woman appeared behind the stands, looking frantically around until she spotted CJ. Ben saw her before the others. "Uh oh, Aaron. There's your mom."

After waving to the woman, CJ looked at Aaron. "It appears you're going to be the first one to have a parental encounter."

The woman stormed up to CJ. "What the hell has he done this time?"

Handing the citation to the woman, CJ said, "He was throwing firecrackers at the horses in the arena."

Not anticipating the woman's reaction, CJ was unprepared to stop the open-handed slap that knocked Aaron from his chair.

"You stupid, little shit! You don't have the brains God gave a duck!"

The woman was preparing to kick the boy, who was curled into the fetal position, when CJ jerked her arm back. "Ma'am, stop right now!"

The woman's face was red with rage, and she turned to CJ. "Stop now or what?"

"I'll arrest you for assault."

"You'll arrest me for kicking the shit out of my idiot son?"

"Kicking him won't solve whatever problems he has. Ground him. Take away his privileges, but don't lay a hand on him."

"He doesn't understand anything but the back of my hand." The woman paused. "You're skinny. You've never had any kids, so you don't know what it takes to get their attention."

"Ma'am, I've dealt with a lot of parents and teenagers. Hitting them is not the solution."

Another woman emerged from the crowd and went to Aaron. "Let's get you dusted off, and we'll get this sorted out."

"Who are you?" the woman asked.

"I'm Aaron's English teacher. We can deal with this."

Out of the corner of her eye, CJ saw another brown uniform walking toward them. "Knock it off, Maggie," Floyd Swenson said as he approached from behind the teacher.

Aaron's mother glared at him. "This is none of your concern, Floyd Swenson."

Standing between the mother and the teacher, Floyd glared at Aaron's mother. Although he was half her weight, he looked as if he could beat her in a wrestling match. "Maggie, after all the times I've arrested and ticketed you, you should know this *is* my business."

Aaron's mother relaxed and looked at Floyd. "He's acting up, Floyd. I need to knock him down a notch."

Floyd touched the mother's arm. "He's not in kindergarten anymore. You can't cut a willow switch and spank him behind the barn."

"That's what he needs!"

"It didn't work fifteen years ago, so it sure as hell isn't going to work now."

Throwing her arms into the air, the woman sighed. "Geez, Floyd. I'm at my wit's end with him."

"Go with his teacher and see what you two can work out. There's something you can do to discipline him, and it isn't putting him in the ER with broken ribs...again."

As they watched the mother, son, and teacher walk away, CJ said, "I'll never have the local knowledge to handle situations like this."

"Local knowledge isn't always an advantage. It's easier for you to ticket people around here. A number of them expect me to let them off with a slap on the wrist because we're high school friends." After looking at the other two boys, Floyd turned his back toward them and whispered, "Anything I should know about these two or have they just been making trouble?"

"They were throwing firecrackers into the show arena, spooking the horses. I'm trying to put the fear of God into them while we wait for their parents to show up."

"Let me try something." Floyd walked to the boys and moved a chair, so it was facing them. Sitting down, he leaned forward. "We're going to play, *let's make a deal*. If you can put me onto a crime I don't know about, I may ask Deputy Jensen to look the other way about your fireworks ticket."

The boys jammed their hands in their pockets and stared at their jeans.

"You don't know anything about people offering drugs at school, or someone who keeps a gun in their locker?" Their response was a barely noticeable head shake. "How about someone who's beating his wife or bullying the underclassmen?"

Again, he got no response.

After assessing the two boys, he stood and looked at CJ. "Troy and I are going for a walk." He bent down and put his hand on Troy's arm. "Let's talk."

Ben craned his head to watch them walk away behind him. He looked at CJ. "What's that all about?"

"Chief Deputy Swenson thinks Troy has some information about a crime. Troy signaled that he didn't want to talk about it in front of you. I guess he's more interested in making his fireworks ticket go away than you are."

Looking around the area nervously, Ben glanced at CJ. "I might know something."

Sitting down, CJ leaned close. "What do you know?"

"A girl is missing from class. No one knows where she went."

"We haven't had any missing persons reports recently."

"No one's reported her missing because her mother's gone too."

"Gone, as in moved away?" CJ asked, taking out a pen and notebook.

"Gone as in, gone. Their car isn't in the driveway. The drapes are closed, and the lights are never on. The homeroom teacher asked if anyone knows where she is, but no one knows shit."

"What are their names?"

"The girl is Molly Brady. I don't know her mother's name."

"Was something going on in her life?"

"She was really quiet, so nobody really knew her. I mean, she was nice, but it's not like she had any friends."

"It sounds like you were her friend."

Ben stared at his shoes. "We weren't *friend* friends. You know, we just talked sometimes."

"Did you date Molly?"

"I…don't drive, so I don't go on dates."

"Where do they live?"

"They rented a dumpy little house in Henriette since they left the commune."

CJ's mind swirled, thinking about an investigation the department was conducting about a family who'd reported ongoing harassment after they'd left a commune. They'd eventually moved to a Minneapolis suburb, but rumors still remained about harassment from commune members. "Do you know Molly's mother's name?"

"She was just Mrs. Brady to us."

"Tell me more about them."

"There's nothing to tell. They wore old-fashioned kind of clothes that looked like they'd made them at home. Molly couldn't do much in gym class because she always wore a long dress and couldn't wear tennis shoes."

Floyd was approaching, but CJ gestured for him to stay away. "Think hard, Ben. What else seemed suspicious in the days before Molly disappeared."

"There wasn't anything especially odd. I mean, Molly always brought her own lunch and sat by herself while she ate it. She never gossiped or anything, and I don't think she'd ever been on a date." Ben paused, then looked up. "There was something odd. She didn't take her books or homework with her the day before she disappeared. It's like she knew she wasn't coming back."

He watched as CJ made notes. "Thank you, Ben."

"Will you get me out of the ticket?"

CJ took the citation pad out of her back pocket and opened it. She marked "void" across the face of it and smiled. "Your ticket is gone."

"You're not going to tell the other guys, are you?"

"I won't tell the guys, but your parents will know about the firecracker incident. You'll have to deal with whatever punishment they dole out."

Sighing, Ben replied, "I suppose I deserve that."

CJ nodded to Floyd. "Ben says Molly Brady, a girl he knew from school, and her mother disappeared. Do you know anything about that?"

After glancing at the boys to make sure they couldn't hear, Floyd responded, "I'm not familiar with that name. I suppose someone might've reported them missing during my brief retirement."

"Molly apparently knew about the plan because she left her books and homework at school the day before they disappeared."

"I'll talk to the principal Monday. He might know something that Molly's classmates haven't heard."

Tapping the gold maple leaf on Floyd's collar, CJ smiled. "Don't you think the Pine County Chief Deputy will have more important things to do than chasing down a girl who may have moved away?"

"John didn't offer a lot of direction when he appointed me. I assume that means I can do whatever I want as long as I don't embarrass him."

"What did the previous chief deputy do? I never saw him around the bullpen."

Floyd looked around again, making sure no one could hear them. "I think he spent a lot of time drinking coffee with the county commissioners. I'm also sure he knew the hangout of every mayor in the county, and he attended every soil and water commission meeting."

"Why soil and water commission meetings?"

"I think the commission paid for his dinner after the meeting, and he liked hanging out with Jerry, the guy who sells culverts in Hinckley."

"I think you just defined the job."

"As much as I like Jerry, it pains me to sit through any meeting about manure runoff and shoreline erosion protection."

"I meant drinking coffee with the county commissioners and mayors."

Rubbing his face, Floyd grimaced. "I'd rather be involved in an investigation than talk about politics. I'll leave that to John."

With a sparkle in her eye, CJ said, "The sheriff might fire you."

"Don't raise my hopes."

# Chapter 5

With the delinquents picked up by their parents and the horse show winding down, CJ watched the horses being loaded into their trailers and the food trucks packing up. Wondering about Bob Olsen's food poisoning, she drove to the Sandstone hospital. The emergency room was empty except for a young receptionist doing a Wordle puzzle on her cell phone.

"Is Bob Olsen still here?"

The receptionist, apparently annoyed by the interruption, sighed and typed into her computer. "He's in exam room three." She nodded toward the double doors to her left. "Trish and Doc Mlankoch are back there."

Somewhat surprised by the apparent lack of security, CJ walked to the double doors, then had to wait while the receptionist released the lock. The door buzzed, signaling the lock release. Bert Mlankoch, MD was typing on a keyboard at the nurse's station.

"How's Bob Olsen doing?"

The doctor hesitated, then took in CJ's uniform. "Is this a police matter?"

"He got sick at the horse show. I called for the ambulance." CJ paused, realizing that the doctor was bound by HIPAA laws restricting the sharing of medical information. "It appeared he may have food poisoning, which makes it a public health issue."

Pushing himself back from the keyboard, the doctor weighed his words. "We've got him on an IV and some meds to ease his stomach cramps and nausea. The lab is culturing a stool sample, but we won't have the results until tomorrow morning. The quick test didn't show any Salmonella, which was my first guess based on his violent symptoms."

"Bob was blaming it on the runny eggs he had for breakfast."

"He told me that, too. Salmonella is the most common contaminant in eggs, but that doesn't usually attack until a day after the contaminated food is ingested. So that would eliminate his breakfast eggs as the cause. I took a history of what he's eaten over the past three days. He's had several restaurant meals. If any of those had been the source of his illness, I'd expect a number of people coming in with symptoms."

"Maybe they're curled up in front of their toilets at home," CJ suggested.

"The severity of Bob's symptoms would bring most people to the ER."

CJ chuckled. "Doc, we're in the land of stoic Scandinavians who suffer in silence."

"I know. And most of them are too cheap to hand over money for an ER co-pay unless they think they're actually dying. Bob's cramps were so severe, I think even the cheapest Swedes would come in, or at least call their doctor's office. I've called the local clinics, and no one is reporting an outbreak of cramps and diarrhea."

"So, what are you thinking?"

"I'm intrigued by Bob's symptoms. They look like food poisoning, but some things don't add up. I was searching on-line when you walked in."

"What does Google say?" CJ asked.

"I don't actually use Google. We've got a link to the Mayo Clinic and Johns Hopkins websites which give me factual information backed up by research. Most common search engines generate too much information supplied by people whose medical credentials are…questionable."

"Graduates of the Internet School of Medicine?"

Mlankoch smiled. "That's a kinder way of putting it than most of my colleagues use."

"What do they call it?"

"The Crackpot and Uneducated Schools of Medicine. It sometimes amazes me that smart, sane people are willing to accept questionable medical information just because it's posted on the internet."

"There are legitimate internet sources."

"Certainly!" Mlankoch replied. "But there are also charlatans and shysters who take great joy in spreading crackpot theories and false information. I'm amazed at the number of patients who walk in with an internet diagnosis of their condition, expecting me to accept it and provide the posted treatment."

"Every week, the sheriff's department hears about women who are taken in by a sexual predator who posted a picture of a cute guy. They sometimes get strung along for weeks by his great line of bullshit. Then, they agree to a meeting in a motel or some remote spot, only to find out that the cute guy who has been professing his undying love is actually a sexual predator who assaults them."

The doctor shook his head. "Back to Bob's case. I feel a little over my head with his situation. I spoke with an infectious disease specialist, and I'm going to have Bob transported to Duluth for treatment. Like I said, this is not a textbook case of food poisoning, and I'd like someone more experienced to treat him."

"You've treated dozens of people with food poisoning, and Bob's case is extraordinary?"

Mlankoch pointed to the computer screen. "I reviewed all the common bugs; E.coli, Botulinum, Salmonella, Campylobacter, Shigella, and Listeria. Then

I moved to parasites like Giardia and Cryptosporidium. It might be rotavirus or Covid-19. Bob's symptoms fit most of those infections."

"Is he in danger?"

"Healthy people usually recover after the bugs are eliminated from their systems."

"I sense a 'but' in your answer."

"There's always an outlier who is immunocompromised, or someone who is hypersensitive to a particular bug or parasite. Bob isn't responding to any treatment, so I want someone with broader experience to take a look at him. Tina called an ambulance for transport to Duluth."

CJ looked around the quiet ER. "Is Bob's wife here?"

"Tina called and told Fran we're transporting him to Duluth. She'll meet him there."

* * *

After checking in with the dispatcher, CJ drove to Pine City where Bailey was happily awaiting her arrival at the doggie day care. Bailey was the day's last dog at the hobby farm where Aggie, a middle-aged widow, ran a kennel and doggie day care. Bailey was lying next to the sofa, her tail thumping the floor, when CJ knocked on the screen door and let herself in.

Kneeling, CJ patted the floor. "Come on. It's time to leave."

Bailey looked up at Aggie who laughed. "She's been the only dog here for the last three hours. I think we've bonded."

"Enough with the poor abandoned dog act. Come here."

After hesitating another second, Bailey bounded across the living room and threw herself at CJ, sending them both sprawling.

"You goofball. First you pretend you're not ready to leave, then you bowl me over."

Aggie stood and took a leash off a hook by the door. "Is Bailey coming back tomorrow?"

"I've got a few more day shifts, then I rotate to afternoons for five days."

"I'll see you in the morning."

CJ spread a blanket on the back seat of the cruiser and urged Bailey to climb in. "I know you'd rather ride in the front, but there are too many things you can get into up there."

After much coaxing, Bailey struggled to pull herself into the car, then punctuated her displeasure by passing gas.

"Really?" CJ asked as she started the engine. "You had to wait until you were inside the car to fart?"

Bailey wagged her tail, then flopped down on the seat.

After arriving at home and changing out of her uniform, CJ walked Bailey, then poured dry dog food into a bowl. "I'm meeting Eddie for supper. You'll be on your own. Try not to chew up anything valuable."

* * *

The search for a parking spot in Duluth's Canal Park took longer than the drive from Pine City. After paying for two hours at a metered spot, CJ walked with dozens of tourists through the area that once had been devoted to manufacturing and warehouses, now transformed into a tourist mecca. CJ walked past two art galleries, a lakefront motel, and three restaurants before arriving at the micro-brewery. Eddie wasn't among the people waiting in line for a table, so CJ looked around inside and found him sitting in a rear booth with half a beer and two menus.

Sliding into the booth opposite him, CJ said, "It looks like you've been waiting a while for me."

"I'm avoiding the pile of paperwork on my desk."

A waiter with a nose ring and tattooed arms arrived, looking haggard. "My name is Erik and I'll be serving you tonight. The beer menu is on the back. There are a couple additions on the chalkboard behind the bar."

"Just Diet Coke, thanks."

"The specials are the BeerBQ and Tidehaus Burgers. They come with your choice of soup, fries, or a house salad. Can

70

I start you off with an appetizer? The roasted bone marrow platter is excellent."

CJ shook her head. "An appetizer would ruin my dinner."

"I'll get your beverage and give you a minute to look at the menu."

Leaning across the table, CJ said, "They have a bone marrow appetizer? Just the sound of it ruins my appetite."

"It's actually beef shanks with toast and dipping sauces. They're very good."

Wrinkling her nose, CJ said, "I suppose the millennials don't know what bone marrow is."

"The only foods they know come wrapped from a grocery store." He paused. "You know, bone marrow is a delicacy in some places."

"Maybe for wolves and cannibals. I think I've evolved past the point of finding bone marrow tempting."

Erik set the Diet Coke on the table and asked, "Have you found anything interesting?"

"I'll have the smoked salmon salad," CJ said, handing the waiter her menu.

"The smoked salmon BLT sounds good to me," Eddie said.

Eric entered their orders into an iPad and smiled. "I'll bring those out momentarily."

When the waiter left, Eddie asked, "How is your food poisoning victim doing?"

CJ sipped her soda, then leaned across the table to be heard over the noisy crowd. "No one but you, the medical examiner's tech, would bring up food poisoning over supper."

"I wouldn't have mentioned it to anyone else." He smiled. "We're kindred spirits, capable of discussing dead bodies and food poisoning while eating a bloody steak."

"Just because I *can do that* doesn't mean I *want to* have those discussions over dinner."

"Okay, what do you think of the Vikings' chances of winning the Super Bowl this year?"

Rolling her eyes, CJ shook her head. "That's hardly less depressing than the mortuary discussions."

"Okay. How is Bailey?"

"She's still a fart machine, but she's stopped chewing up my underwear."

"Progress!"

"I suppose those are small steps. How are things at work?"

"I thought you didn't want to talk about dead bodies?"

"I was being polite. I don't want to talk about dead bodies. What else is going on?"

"You know very well that there are only two aspects to my job. Talking about the paperwork is only slightly less disturbing than the autopsies. Do you have anything less disturbing going on?"

"I caught some kids throwing firecrackers into the arena during a horse show. I really hate teenage boys."

"Yeah, testosterone is coursing through their veins. It makes them disgusting and crazy for a few years."

"Some of them never outgrow it."

"Isn't that the truth? Last week we had a stabbing victim…"

CJ put up her hand. "There is nothing appetizing about the discussion of a stabbing victim."

"Okay, tell me more about your juvenile delinquents."

"One of them told me about a girl who disappeared from school. One day she didn't take her books or homework home, the next day she was gone."

"It sounds like she was planning to leave. What did her parents say?"

"She and her mother lived in a rundown house after leaving a rural commune. The house is apparently empty with the blinds still open, but all the lights are off."

"Did you check the house?"

"That's tomorrow's project."

Their dinners arrived, and conversation switched to Floyd's return from retirement and speculation on whether the sheriff would run for re-election. After dinner, CJ and Eddie walked to the lift bridge and watched an ore freighter pass through the canal. After the ship passed, CJ sighed. "I'd better go home and walk Bailey."

"Where are you parked? I'll walk you to your car."

A young couple passed, the man's arm over the woman's shoulder. "You've never made a pass at me," CJ said.

"It's not my place."

"That's never stopped any of the other men who've tried to get close to me. Some of them were married, and others were co-workers who shouldn't have tried anything."

After letting out a deep breath, Eddie looked out over Lake Superior. "You and I both need friends. Sex complicates things."

CJ nodded her agreement. "I overheard someone talking about friends with benefits. I don't see how that works."

"That wouldn't work for me. I'm old-fashioned, and there's a distinct line between friends and lovers. You're a friend."

CJ clasped his hand and intertwined her fingers with his. "Thank you."

At her car, Eddie released CJ's hand. "I suppose you're on the afternoon shift next week. I could meet you in Pine County for supper some evening."

"You'll be hard pressed to find a meal as tasty as your smoked salmon BLT."

"Trust me, a burger and fries beats the heck out of whatever I'd warm up in the microwave. Besides, I'm more interested in the company than the food."

"Let's plan on Thursday. Fridays and Saturdays often get busy. I think a lot of people get paid on Fridays, and they can afford to get drunk, which leads to stupidity."

# Chapter 6

Floyd was sitting in Pam Ryan's guest chair when CJ arrived at the sheriff's office. He looked behind CJ, then raised his eyebrows. "You didn't bring the dog along?"

After starting a cup of coffee, CJ replied, "I've got Bailey in doggie daycare."

"I heard she was quite a hit at the horse show. I'm sure the sheriff would be thrilled to have her as a department mascot."

Chuckling, Pam added, "It was really special when the head jailer came down to see if someone had died in the bullpen after one of Bailey's farting episodes."

Rolling her eyes, CJ nodded. "I'm not sure that *special* is the correct word for the jailer's response." Taking her coffee mug and sitting at a desk adjacent to Pam's, CJ framed her thoughts. "I've got a couple things going on today, and I could use some assistance from someone like Pam. Do I have permission from the chief deputy to borrow her for a few hours?"

"You'd be rescuing Pam from paperwork," Floyd replied. "For that matter, I'd be happy to be rescued from whatever undefined responsibilities a chief deputy is supposed to have."

"Uh, Floyd," CJ said, looking down the hallway toward the sheriff's office. "You might want to have a discussion about your official duties with the sheriff before volunteering to help with an investigation."

Making sure the sheriff wasn't listening, Floyd smiled. "What's he going to do, fire me? Then he'd have to find some other fool to take this appointment for a few weeks while he decides if he's going to run for re-election."

"Just the same..." CJ said.

Pam leaned back, smiling. Her youthful face and short blonde hair contrasted with Floyd's face, which was lined from years of worry and sunshine. His graying hair showed that he was twenty years older than Pam and a decade older than CJ.

Pam said, "Floyd, I prefer having you around the department, rather than having to buy you coffee and a roll every time I want to talk to you. I'm paying for daycare now, and my doughnut budget is gone."

Standing, Floyd smiled. "You do know I'd be happy to buy the coffee."

"All right, you two," CJ, now wearing sergeant's stripes reflecting her promotion to patrol commander, said, "I need to check on the Brady house. Would one of you like to come along as my backup?"

Pam, always patient and analytical, picked up a pen and nervously tapped it on the desk. "You've got several things that need follow up. There's the dead guy at the museum, the impending food poisoning outbreak, and the possibly missing mother and daughter, right?"

CJ nodded. "Why are you asking?"

Pam stood. "Because I deal with dirty diapers and a kid spitting up on me every night. I have no interest in dealing with food poisoning. I'll ride with you to the house in Henriette."

"Now wait one cotton-picking second," Floyd said, blocking the path to the exit door. "I'm the chief deputy, and I should decide who pursues which investigation."

Pam patted his shoulder as she walked past. "The view of the Duluth harbor is beautiful this time of year. I'd drive up I-35 rather than taking the Midway Road exit."

She stopped short of the hallway when the sheriff arrived alongside a baby-faced young man wearing a deputy's uniform. "I'm glad you're all here," the sheriff said. "This is our new probationary deputy, Riley Sanders."

Pam and CJ looked at Floyd, who seemed as surprised as they were. "I didn't know we were interviewing," Floyd said, offering his hand to Riley.

The sheriff waved off Floyd's comment. "You were all tied up, so I hired Riley to replace Pam."

CJ shook Riley's hand. She turned to the sheriff and asked, "Who have you chosen to be Riley's Field Training Officer?"

"I'd hoped to team him up with you or Pam."

Looking to Pam for support, CJ said, "We're going to Henriette to investigate a tip about a missing mother and daughter."

Pam nodded. "I spend most of my day at the computer or on the phone. Riley needs patrol experience, not time watching me making phone calls. Maybe he could ride with Floyd to Duluth to check on the food poisoning victim."

Floyd shook his head. "I don't think it'd be appropriate for the new deputy to be trained by the chief deputy. It would be better to put him on patrol. Call Sandy Maki in. He's got the qualifications."

Acting like he was unaware he was being manipulated, the sheriff nodded. "You're right, Sandy would make a good training officer. Follow me, Riley. I'll introduce you to the dispatcher, and we'll have Deputy Maki orient you to his cruiser."

Outside the building, CJ started laughing. "Floyd, did you know the sheriff was interviewing candidates for Pam's replacement?"

"No, but I've only been back a few days. Hasn't he asked either of you to interview anyone?"

Both Pam and CJ shook their heads.

Floyd raised his eyebrows. "Technically, John doesn't need anyone but the county board to approve of a probationary deputy. On the other hand, I'd expect him to involve a few people in the process out of courtesy."

Pam paused, like she expected someone to walk out. "Did you see Riley's face? He looked so excited about meeting us I was afraid he was going to pee on his shoes."

Floyd smiled and pointed a finger at Pam. "Be careful, Missy. That's what you looked like a few years ago."


* * *


CJ parked in front of the Brady house in Henriette. "Well, Pam, here we are. As reported, it's run down, the blinds are closed, and it appears to be unoccupied."

"No car in the driveway. The lawn hasn't seen a mower in months, not that much of the grass is alive," Pam observed as she flipped through a county plat map. "The listed owner is Henry Bedard. I wonder if he's one of the other seventy-one residents of this bustling town." After sliding her finger past each property listed in the tiny town,

Pam closed the book. "It appears this is the only property owned by Mr. Bedard. And no one else seems to be around to interview."

"I've heard the bar is bustling on karaoke nights," CJ replied as they continued to watch the windows for signs of habitation. "Henriette has seventy-one residents?"

"That's according to the 2020 census. After watching this house, my guess is that the population is down to sixty-nine. I don't think you need backup, unless you're afraid of mice."

CJ opened the cruiser's door and stepped out. With Pam behind her, CJ walked to the weathered front steps, prepared to knock on the door. "Not only did the residents forget to lock the door, but they also forgot to close it."

"Hang on," Pam said, reaching into her back pocket. "Let's put on gloves." She pushed the half-open door with the toe of her shoe, her hand on the butt of her pistol. "Anyone home?"

Pausing inside the door, to listen for a response, they stood in a tiny living room with a sagging couch and matching chair. When no one responded, CJ sniffed the air. "The house smells musty, like it's been empty for a while."

"I wonder if the residents chose the hideous green furniture to match the dirty gold carpeting and blue walls or if the house came furnished?"

"I've seen couches in better shape dumped in ditches," CJ replied.

"I think the interior decorator was color blind."

"It kind of reminds me of a college dorm room."

Pam sniffed the air. "The house smells musty with a hint of rotting food."

"The bedrooms and bathroom are to the left. Watch our backs while I check them."

Pam hesitated. "We should get a warrant."

"The door was open," CJ countered, "and we're doing a welfare check on the residents."

"Okay, but if we find evidence of a crime, or we determine that the house isn't empty, we're backing out of here and locking the door behind us."

CJ nodded. "Let's check the bedrooms first."

Looking past CJ who opened the closet, Pam said, "The bed is unmade, the dresser drawers are open but empty, and there's clothing strewn around the floor. It looks like someone was planning to return, or they left in a hurry."

In the bathroom, towels had been dropped on the floor, and the medicine cabinet door stood open. Pam lifted the wastebasket and looked inside. "Used tissues, a couple Walmart bags, and an empty container of birth control pills." She picked up the pill dispenser and flipped it over. "It's empty." She lifted a small white box from the wastebasket. "The pills were prescribed for Colleen Brady and were filled at the Walmart pharmacy. The prescription has three remaining refills. It's dated last month."

CJ watched from the hallway, keeping an eye on the living room and kitchen. "Why would a woman living in a commune need birth control pills?"

"She wasn't a nun. It appears the commune members don't take a vow of chastity."

CJ shut her eyes for a second. "I've never really thought about it."

Pam returned the box to the wastebasket. "I pictured the commune as a place like the hippie days of the '60s. Free love and lots of pot smoking."

"I've seen the commune women wearing Amish-looking clothing. I assumed they led a very simple life, one different from hippies in halter tops and short shorts worn by the women at Woodstock."

A smile crept across Pam's face. "And all the children in the commune are born by immaculate conception?"

"Let's look in the kitchen," CJ said, ending the conversation.

The stench of rotting food filled the air. The only kitchen sound was the humming of the refrigerator. Standing at the arch between the tiny dining area and the kitchen, CJ surveyed the scene. "There are dirty dishes in the sink, and it smells like they left without emptying the wastebasket."

Pam opened the refrigerator, releasing even stronger odors. "Spoiled milk," she said, quickly closing the door.

A glint of metal on the floor by the back door caught CJ's eye. She crossed the kitchen and knelt to inspect a paring knife on the floor. "There's blood on this knife and also on the doorknob." Without touching the evidence, CJ stood. "I've never seen a three-inch paring knife used as a murder weapon."

A drawer was ajar, and Pam gently pulled it open with her gloved fingers. "This drawer is full of knives, spatulas, and scrapers. If I was being threatened, I wouldn't dig through the drawer to find a big old knife. I'd grab the first sharp item I put my hand on."

"I wonder whose blood is on the knife?"

'Leave everything as it is. I'll call the Bureau of Criminal Apprehension to request a crime scene team and then get a search warrant."

CJ nodded. "The basement door is next to the stove. We should look downstairs."

Pam felt goosebumps as she recalled a previous incident involving a killer who'd hidden in a basement. Steeling herself, she pulled her pistol. "Give me a second."

"What's wrong?" CJ asked.

"Let's say basements aren't my favorite places."

"Spiders and cobwebs?"

"Crazed killers behind hidden panels."

Acknowledging Pam's reluctance, CJ drew her Glock and opened the door. "I'll go first." She flipped the light switch, casting a weak yellowish light on the steps.

To augment the dim light, CJ pulled out her flashlight and held it in her left hand, shining the beam where her pistol was pointed. The wooden steps creaked as CJ descended the first few steps. Halfway down the stairs, she squatted and swung her flashlight from side to side, focusing on the shadowy corners of the room. "Clear!" she shouted.

Pam followed into the unfinished basement, its gray cement blocks, with cracked mortar lined the walls. An aging washer and dryer sat alongside a wash basin, water pump, and a sump. Holstering her gun, Pam surveyed the small space occupying the square footage under the kitchen. "If I lived here, I'd spray the whole space with bleach and scrub it with a brush."

CJ crossed the room to a gap in the upper blocks. "The pipes running to the bathroom go through here. There must be a crawlspace under the rest of the house." Flipping over a wicker laundry basket, she stepped up and shined her flashlight into the dark beyond the gap.

"Any dead bodies in there?" Pam asked, rubbing her arms to warm the chill accompanying her goosebumps.

"Nothing but spiderwebs and mildewed blocks," CJ responded as she stepped down off the basket. "This place is wreaking havoc with my mold allergy. Let's go upstairs."

"Hang on for a minute," Pam said, walking across the basement toward a fuse box. "There's sawdust on the floor here."

Shining her flashlight on the box, CJ traced a line of wires running from the top of the fuse box to the ceiling. "Most of the wires are black. I've seen this style in houses of this vintage; before the electrical codes required wires to be enclosed in conduit. Here's one white cable running through a newly bored hole between the basement ceiling and the floor above. The owner must've replaced a faulty wire. Any licensed electrician wouldn't have run a bare wire here."

"It looks like something my dad would've done on the farm," Pam said as CJ walked to the stairs. "He was always doing electrical work. I assume none of Dad's work would've passed an electrical inspection."

After exiting the front door, CJ circled the house while Pam called the BCA. The backyard was as sparse as the front, the only green plants were dandelions that had gone to seed, the white puffs ready to be blown away with the first wind. Stopping next to the back steps, CJ found a trail of blood droplets leading from the back door. She followed them to the gravel driveway where they stopped abruptly next to a set of dusty tire tracks.

After ending her call. Pam came around the corner of the house and found CJ kneeling next to the driveway. "Did you find something interesting?"

"There's a blood trail from the back door. It ends here, suggesting that someone got into a car and drove away." Standing, CJ straightened her pants legs. "There's a car somewhere with a puddle of blood inside it."

"I called dispatch. Colleen Brady owns an '86 Buick. I put out a BOLO. Maybe we can locate her and ask why Molly isn't in school."

* * *

After getting directions to Bob Olsen's room in the Duluth hospital, Floyd stopped at the nurses' station. "Can you update me on Mr. Olsen's condition?"

The woman at the computer looked at Floyd over her reading glasses. "Are you a family member?"

"I'm the cop who's investigating a food poisoning incident in Hinckley. I need to assess Mr. Olsen's condition and question him about where he's eaten over the past three days."

"You need to speak with Dr. Pradeep. She's been treating him."

Floyd waited while the nurse paged the doctor. A few moments later a dark-complected woman walked out of the elevator and approached Floyd. She was tiny, almost bird-like. with flecks of gray in her dark hair. Everything about her demeanor said she was a no-nonsense person who commanded respect despite her short stature and lean build. A stethoscope peeked out of the left pocket of her white smock.

"Are you the officer inquiring about Mr. Olsen?"

"I am," he said, offering his hand. "I'm trying to determine if we're expecting a food poisoning outbreak or if something else is happening."

Offering her hand horizontally so Floyd shook only her fingertips, the doctor glanced at Floyd's stripes. "Sergeant, I'm afraid Mr. Olsen's medical details are subject to HIPAA laws. I can't discuss his condition without permission."

"We believe he has food poisoning. In that case, the public health laws come into play, and you're obligated to divulge details of his condition so we can prevent a larger outbreak."

After a moment of consideration, the doctor nodded to a small office behind the nurses' station. The space was crowded with a copier/fax machine and a desk. Closing the door, the doctor frowned. "In addition to your sergeant's stripes, you have an oak leaf on your collar. Those don't agree and make me suspicious of your claim to be an officer. Could I please see other identification?"

Floyd removed his wallet from a back pocket, slid out a laminated ID card, and handed it to the doctor, who compared the picture to his face. "This identifies you as the Pine County Chief Deputy. Why are you wearing sergeant's stripes?"

Returning the ID to his wallet, Floyd drew a breath. "I retired as a sergeant. Last week, I was invited to fill in for the retired chief deputy until the sheriff's election."

"Ahh, you failed retirement."

With a sheepish grin, Floyd replied, "I suppose you could look at it that way."

"You're the first uniformed officer who's investigated an apparent food poisoning outbreak. I usually have a phone interview with the Minnesota Department of Health."

"One of my sergeants was the first responder who came to Mr. Olsen's aid. She called for the ambulance, and later spoke with the ER doctor in Sandstone. He expressed some concern that Mr. Olsen's condition wasn't a typical food poisoning case."

Burying her hands into the pockets of her white smock, Dr. Pradeep stared at Floyd's badge. "I've seen thousands of food poisoning cases. This is…challenging. I've been able to rule out bacterial and parasitic causes, which leaves me with something viral, and most of them don't fit his symptoms or something else."

"Something else?"

"I suspect Mr. Olsen has been poisoned."

"Poisoned?"

"In the famous words of Sherlock Holmes, 'when all clues lead to dead ends, we're left with the obvious, no matter how unlikely.'"

"Sherlock Holmes was a fictional nineteenth century detective."

Smiling, the doctor said, "Arthur Conan Doyle was as brilliant as his characters. I've quoted him many times. As for Mr. Olsen's condition, I was in my office researching obscure poisons when you paged me."

"I don't want to appear overly skeptical, but Pine County is hardly a place I'd expect to find a sophisticated poisoner. My county is poor and rural. I think you could count the number of people with science degrees in the dozens, most of them being teachers."

"Ah, Chief Deputy Swenson, you've fallen into the trap of assuming that because something is rare, that it's also sophisticated. Hemlock, for example, has been a known poison for thousands of years. It's extremely rare, but deadly and easy to acquire."

"Bob was poisoned with hemlock?"

"It's a possibility I've just eliminated."

"What else have you eliminated? Rat poison?"

"Rat poison is most often a variation of warfarin that interrupts the blood's ability to clot, causing the rat to die from hemorrhaging. Bob's symptoms are not caused by warfarin."

"Okay, it's not warfarin. What poison fits Bob's symptoms?"

"If he'd been exposed to any neurotoxin, he'd already be dead. And those usually cause convulsions. Many poisons, like hemlock and strychnine, cause frothing of the mouth, muscle pain and spasms, not vomiting and diarrhea."

"You've ruled out a number of things. Is it a farm chemical or pesticide?"

"As I said before I was interrupted by your urgent page, I was researching the possibilities. Most toxic farm chemicals are carcinogens, not acute poisons. He'd have to ingest gallons of them to cause an intestinal response. His symptoms are consistent with nicotine poisoning, which is sometimes used as an insecticide. In that case, he would've noticed the off flavor of a food or beverage laced with enough nicotine to make him this ill."

"How quickly would these unusual poisons act?"

Chuckling, the doctor shook her head. "It depends on which poison is involved. Some, like strychnine, act in minutes. Others take hours or days to exhibit symptoms."

"How are you treating him?"

"We usually empty the stomach. By the time he arrived here, it appears that nature had taken care of that. We had him drink activated charcoal to absorb whatever may have been left in his system, then we put benzodiazepine into his IV to relax his muscle spasms. Not knowing which poison we're dealing with, there's little else I can do. It's now in God's hands."

Floyd clenched his eyes shut and crossed his arms. "How soon will we know if your treatment has been effective?"

"At the rate his body is declining, I expect he'll be on a respirator in a few hours. He'll either respond soon, or he may not see tomorrow."

"What can I do?" Floyd asked.

"Get samples of everything he ate over the last two days."

"Two days?"

"Focus on his most recent foods and beverages, but the poison may have been slow acting. It may have been in something he ate last Friday."

"Will there be an outbreak if this is something from restaurant contamination?"

"If there haven't already been any other reports of similar symptoms, probably not. It's possible, but unlikely, that Mr. Olsen was particularly susceptible to the toxin. He seems generally healthy. I think we'd be treating many more cases if this was from something eaten in a restaurant."

"Should we be checking his house? I'm thinking of the painkiller contamination from back in the 1980s. Should we be checking his medicine cabinet?"

"It's certainly possible, but unlikely. There are many more safety seals on every type of bottle since the '80s. We'd be seeing more ill people if someone had tampered with food or medicine in a store."

Floyd ran his hand over his thinning hair. "So, we've got a guy who was probably poisoned but we don't know which toxin. Because we don't know which chemical is involved, we don't know how long ago it was ingested. Does that cover it?"

"I don't mean to be flippant, but he may die in a few hours, or he may pull through."

"Is there anything I can do?" Floyd asked.

Shaking her head, the doctor took out a pen and wrote a telephone number on the back of a business card. "Until we know what poison Mr. Olsen ingested, there isn't a lot any of us can do. Stay in touch with your local clinics and hospitals in case similar cases arise. Aside from that, stay in touch. This is my personal cell phone number."

Floyd patted his pockets. "I don't even have a business card for you. If you need me, the Pine County dispatcher will know how to reach me."

Dr. Pradeep took another business card from her pocket and handed it to Floyd along with a pen. "Write down your cell phone number. I'll continue my research, and I'll call if I have a great revelation."

"Or if he dies," Floyd said as he returned the card and pen.

"Sergeant, I don't know what faith you believe in, but St. Jude is receiving my prayers."

"I'm Lutheran, but I think St. Jude, the patron saint of lost causes, is universal."

"Mrs. Olsen was in her husband's room. A few words of encouragement from a friend might be appreciated."

"We're more acquaintances than friends, but I can say hello and let her know that Bob's case is being actively pursued."

The doctor put her hand on Floyd's arm. "I learned to never underestimate the value of prayer and kind words."

"Is that all Bob has left?"

"I'm not out of ideas, but let's say the bucket is nearly empty."

# Chapter 7

Fran Olsen looked up when Floyd walked into the hospital room. Her eyes were bloodshot, and her pink shirt and khaki pants were wrinkled. The room felt sterile and impersonal. There were no flowers, cards, or personal touches, just the regular beep of the overhead heart monitor. "I thought you'd retired, Floyd."

"The sheriff caught me in a weak moment, and I agreed to return to the department until the election." At a loss for words, Floyd froze. "Would you like to walk to the cafeteria for a cup of coffee?"

Fran looked at her husband, whose eyes were closed, then nodded. "Coffee would be nice."

"How long have you been here?" Floyd asked as they walked to the elevator.

"Since yesterday afternoon. The doctors said things were unstable, and they wanted to be able to contact me if there was a sudden change in Bob's condition."

"I can sit with him for a while if you want to go home for a nap and change of clothes."

The elevator arrived, and they rode in silence to the lobby with three other people. Following signs to the cafeteria, Floyd walked in silence. He offered to buy her a sandwich or sweet roll, but Fran declined anything other than black coffee.

At a table away from the few hospital workers taking their breaks, Floyd sat across from Fran. "The last time I was here, Mary was convinced she was going to die."

As soon as the words were said, he realized that they might sound insensitive. He was about to backtrack when Fran reached out and touched his hand. "Did you feel numb? I mean, I'm upset and confused, but mostly, I just feel numb."

"I felt helpless, Fran. My world was spinning out of control, and there was nothing I could do."

"Maybe that's it. I don't know what to do or say. I don't know what's expected of me, except that I need to be available for…whatever. I'm lost." Fran sipped her coffee, then cocked her head. "Why are you here? I mean, I appreciate the coffee and a shoulder to cry on, but you're neither my minister nor a grief counselor."

"One of our sergeants was at the horse show when Bob got sick. She suspected he had food poisoning. CJ asked me to follow up."

"I heard there was a female deputy who took control of the situation. No one mentioned her name."

"She's CJ Jensen. We stole her from the Cloquet Police Department."

"Isn't she the deputy who was attacked by that kid last year and left for dead? How is she?"

After taking a sip of coffee to compose his thoughts, Floyd said, "CJ is a survivor. She's struggled a bit, but I think she's recovered from the trauma. CJ is one of the best officers in the department."

"I'd like to thank her when we're through with whatever happens."

"She'd be touched by your thanks. She might also be able to offer you some coping tips."

"Coping tips?"

"CJ is a widow."

Searching Floyd's face, Fran asked, "Is Bob going to die?"

"You probably know more than I do, Fran."

"I really don't. The doctors come in and say technical things that I don't understand. Most times I'm too confused and tired to question them about Bob's situation. None of them give me a straight answer when I ask if he'll recover."

"They're not sure. I spoke with Dr. Pradeep, and she's baffled by Bob's situation. She's in her office researching symptoms and poisons."

"Food poisoning?"

"They've ruled out most food poisoning causes. She thinks Bob ate or drank something with an unusual poison in it."

"What? When?"

"They don't know, Fran."

"If they don't know, how can they treat him?"

"There are apparently generic treatment options that can help. Once they know which poison they're dealing with, there may be more specific treatments."

"Why don't they do more blood tests or something?"

"They're doing all they know how to do."

Fran squeezed the paper cup, and coffee spilled on her hand and the table. "Geez, I'm sorry. Not knowing is so frustrating."

Mopping up the spilled coffee with paper napkins, Floyd nodded. "Trust me, I've been in the chair where you're sitting. This isn't any easier for you than it is for Bob."

"Can't they fly him to the Mayo Clinic or somewhere with more experienced doctors?"

"I think Dr. Pradeep is one of the top people in her field. Doc Mlankoch was talking with her before Bob was transported to Duluth. If he thought there was a better doctor available elsewhere, I'm sure Bob would've been sent there."

Fran leaned forward. "But she's from India or Pakistan. She's not even American."

"She speaks with a Midwestern accent, so I assume she's just as American as you or me. She told me that she's treated thousands of food poisoning cases, which puts her into the top one percent of doctors in her field, and Dr. Mlankoch said she was the infectious disease specialist he relied on."

"I'm sorry. I didn't mean to insult her credentials."

"Just because her name doesn't sound Scandinavian doesn't mean she's not from Minnesota. Nor does it diminish her medical credentials." Floyd paused. "Think of her as a Swede with a deep tan."

Fran shook her head. "I take your point."

"Is there someone I could contact to be here with you?"

"I've contacted our daughter in Oklahoma and our son in San Diego. They're checking on flights."

"Do you have a friend who could bring you a change of clothes?"

Fran sighed. "Being the tax assessor doesn't lend itself to friendships in the community."

Floyd was suddenly engaged. "Was there someone in particular who was unhappy with Bob's property valuation?"

"He got a few irate calls at home, but I don't think any of them were threatening. He usually said it was just someone who wanted to vent their displeasure. I don't even know who called. I tried to stay uninvolved."

"Had he been physically confronted by anyone?"

"Who, besides Donald Trump, confronts the tax assessor? Even the people who don't agree with their property valuation just vent. Bob explains that property valuations are rising, and he sometimes even gives the complainers examples of comparable properties that have recently sold. That's all there is to it!"

"Bob never mentioned feeling threatened by something in his job?"

"There were things that disgusted him, but he never mentioned being threatened..." Fran stopped as a thought arose. "Actually, Bob had confronted a guy who lived on an old farm in Arlot Township. He was living off the land and walked out of his house with a shotgun when Bob pulled into his driveway. There was a 'no trespassing' sign next to the driveway, and the guy, not too politely, told Bob that he, 'shot all trespassers and shot the survivors again.'"

Taking out a notepad and pen, Floyd asked, "Do you remember the guy's name?"

"I don't know that Bob ever mentioned the guy's name. He only referred to him as a 'jack pine savage.'"

"Obviously, the guy didn't shoot Bob."

"I guess Bob talked him back from the brink. I understand the house was so run down that Bob accepted the man's assertion that no improvements had been added since the previous assessment."

"I wish Bob had reported that. We like to keep an eye on the crazier residents."

"Bob mentioned it to one of the deputies. Whoever he talked to knew about, 'the crazy guy with the shotgun.' I guess he's shown up on your radar because he regularly sends threats to his legislators, congressmen, senators, the governor, and the president."

Floyd pushed the notepad aside and tipped his head back. "That'd be Ed Holcomb. The Secret Service asked us to accompany them to the Holcomb place the last time the President flew to Minnesota. They had a talk with Ed, and he agreed to stay home instead of being jailed the entire time the president was in town."

"Will you talk to him?" Fran asked. "He seems like a threat."

"Sure," Floyd said, writing the name in his notepad. "Ed's more likely to fire off a letter than to actually act on his threats."

"You're sure of that?" Fran asked.

"I like to use a guard dog analogy when I talk about people like Ed. If I walk up to a house with a barking dog, I feel threatened, but it's unlikely that dog will bite me. Real guard dogs don't bark a warning, they'll latch onto your arm without making a sound."

"Ah, the people you worry about aren't the ones who send threatening letters."

"I'm more concerned about someone like Ted Kaczynski, the Unabomber, who sat in his rural shed and sent letter bombs to the people he didn't like."

"Do you think there's someone like that in Pine County?"

"We won't know until the bombs start going off."

Fran's eyes went wide, and she froze. "Bombs? In Pine County?"

"Sorry, I was using the Unabomber as an example of someone who was unobtrusive, but dangerous."

Fran relaxed slightly. "I thought…" Floyd let her gather her thoughts without interruption. That sometimes gave people a moment to consider things they'd held back or overlooked. "Have you spoken to the people in the commune?"

Floyd wasn't surprised by the question. The commune, near Finlayson, was located on a property that had been a dairy farm for decades. A religious sect purchased the land and moved in. Because of their old-fashioned dress and unusual habits, many people in the community distrusted them. "Do you have a specific incident in mind, or are you just talking about them in general?"

"Bob referred to them as communists." Fran shook her head as if she was pushing aside a thought. "I'm not sure if he was talking about their practices or politics. I know he was upset when the tax court ruled that their property qualified for a religious tax exemption."

Grinning, Floyd responded, "I haven't heard them referred to as communists, but I suppose that *commune* is the root of the word *communist*."

"I don't know what denomination they claim to be," Fran said, nervously fingering her crumpled paper cup. "Do you think they'd give you a new cup for a refill? I'd like another cup of coffee."

After paying for two more cups of coffee, Floyd returned to the table. "I hope black is okay."

"Thank you, I usually drink my coffee with a dollop of cream. The doctor told me to cut back on cholesterol, so I've been skipping cream and butter." Fran blew on her steaming coffee. "Bob's situation makes me less concerned about dying of a heart attack in twenty or thirty years."

"I understand," Floyd said. "Most cops are fatalists. My job could put my life on the line occasionally. There's nothing like having bullets flying past you to cause you to rethink your long-term plans. I live by the motto, 'plan for tomorrow, but live for today.'"

"I get angry with our daughter when she does stupid things. She says, 'YOLO.'" Seeing Floyd's confusion, Fran translated, "You only live once. Gabby says it's better to live with regrets about things you did, than wishing you'd done things."

"I can think of a few exceptions to that," Floyd said, flashing back to arrests he'd made of drunks and drug users, and the bodies he'd pulled from the cars of distracted drivers and drunks.

"Yeah, I have a problem with some of that too. Gabby told me her goal was to have her adrenaline pumping weekly. I've spent my life trying to stay in situations that don't require my adrenaline to rise."

"Years of experience have revealed that our bodies make adrenaline when they think we're going to die. It's most often part of the 'fight or flight' situation."

After a sip of coffee and some thought, Fran leaned back. "Thanks."

"For what?"

"You've taken me away from my miserable vigil and given me resolve to have a stern conversation with my daughter."

"Stern conversations with teens tend to stiffen, rather than soften, their resolve."

"Gabby is twenty-three and still expects financial help with her graduate school tuition. I have a lever. I can choose not to enable her lifestyle."

"I hope that works for you."

Fran took another sip of coffee, then wrinkled her nose. "Was cream available?"

Pointing to a kiosk with cream and sugar, Floyd said, "You've given up on your cholesterol concerns."

"What was it you said? 'Plan for tomorrow but live for today.'" Fran stood, then paused. "When Bob recovers, we're going on an Alaskan cruise. We've talked about that as our retirement gift to ourselves. Screw that! We're going to spend a little money now."

Floyd watched the woman pour cream into her coffee and thought, *I hope he lives to experience that adventure.*

# Chapter 8

Back at her desk in the sheriff's office, Pam searched county records to find the owner of the rental house. The plat map listed the owner as Henry Bedard. A search of the driver's license database revealed an expired driver's license for him with the Henriette address. His birthdate was June 23, 1939. "If he's driving, his car isn't stored at the house he owns."

Henry's driving record listed two tickets for inattentive driving in the previous five years before his license expired. Beyond that, he'd never been arrested. An online search of his name showed his residence as Henriette with three additional names, Agnes Bedard age 81, Justine Bedard Juntunen age 55, and William Bedard age 52. There were dozens of William Bedards in the Midwest, none showed a relationship to Henry. Justine Bedard Juntunen lived at an address in Finlayson, which wasn't far from Henriette.

Pam typed the Finlayson address into the tax assessor's database. She sat back, contemplating that the Church of the Holy

Sepulchre owned that property. *How ironic that Henry once owned the rental house, and his daughter lives at the commune that Molly and Colleen Brady were fleeing.*

The sound of a coffee pod being popped into the coffeemaker distracted Pam from her thoughts. The sheriff looked over at her. "How is my best investigator doing today?"

"You know how Floyd says there are never coincidences in police work? I just discovered that the missing mother and daughter were living in a rental house. The owner's daughter's recorded address is the commune the missing women fled."

Picking up his steaming coffee cup, the sheriff sat in Pam's guest chair. "I suppose the daughter suggested that they rent the house."

Suddenly struck by Floyd's admonition not to seek the sheriff's input on investigations, Pam nodded. "I'm sure that's the case." She turned back to the computer, hoping the sheriff would take the hint, and leave.

"Draft a search warrant and take it upstairs for a judge's signature. You said the mother and daughter are missing. I think that's plenty of justification."

"We were responding to a tip from a high school student. CJ and I found a bloody knife when we did a welfare check. That's justification for a search warrant."

The sheriff stood. "Perfect. You did a welfare check based on a tip."

"That might be challenged if we go to court."

"Cross that bridge when you get to it," the sheriff said, as he walked away.

*Right. You're not running for re-election, so you're not worried about a future court case being thrown out.* Pam leaned back and stared at the ceiling. *Floyd, why aren't you here when I need to pick your brain? Okay, reason through this. The tip from the kid was sufficient justification for a wellness check. CJ found blood in the driveway during the wellness check, which provides justification for a search warrant.*

Five minutes later, Pam handed the search warrant to Judge Albertson's clerk and explained the situation. She waited impatiently for the judge to take a break from the trial, then met in the judicial chambers, explaining the background of the missing mother and daughter, their tip, the wellness check, the discovery of the bloody knife, and the blood trail in the driveway.

The judge listened to Pam while holding the warrant. "Did you search while you were in the house?"

"Sergeant Jensen and I made a sweep of the home. Discovering the blood and knife, we verified there was no injured party in need of immediate medical attention. Then we secured and left the residence in order to obtain a search warrant. I called the BCA for crime scene assistance."

After spending a moment rereading the search warrant, Judge Albertson picked up a pen and signed it. "Let my clerk make a copy of that before you leave." Pam had taken a step toward the door when the judge added. "Find them before..."

Looking over her shoulder, Pam replied, "That's my top priority." She stopped, sensing that the judge had something more to add.

"Was there a lot of blood? I mean, do you expect to find them alive?"

"There was a bloody paring knife on the floor, with dribbles of blood. The kitchen didn't look like a murder scene."

"Good," the judge said. "Get after them."

* * *


Pam stuck her head in the dispatcher's cubicle. Jodi, surrounded by computer monitors and radios, turned her head when she sensed Pam's presence. "What's up?"

"Is there a deputy near Henriette who is available to assist me with a search warrant?"

"Two deputies are assisting with an accident on Highway 23, near the Kanabec County border, and Sergeant Jensen is 10-100 at the Speedway station on County Road 11."

Pam smiled at Jodi's use of the informal 10 code for a bathroom break. "When Sergeant Jensen is 10-8, ask her to meet me in Henriette." She was turning to step away when she paused. "Where's the chief deputy?"

"He was in Duluth an hour ago. I haven't heard anything from him recently, but it's not like I'd call him for anything short of a nuclear war."

"A nuclear war?"

"You know what I mean," Jodi said, smiling. "His role is ceremonial. Mike Smith, the previous Chief Deputy, told me he was unavailable for anything that might ruin his retirement."

"Floyd is more hands-on than Mike was the last few months. I think he'd be happy to respond to a call that might get his uniform dirty. He told me the only reason he's wearing his uniform is to wear them out rather than wait for moths to eat them in his closet."

"I'm not quite sure how to deal with that information. It's traditional for the senior sergeant to be the incident commander if something arises. The last few years, the chief deputy was never available, so having him take over a shooting scene or an accident was never an issue. Wouldn't Floyd be stepping on CJ's feet if I dispatched him?"

The sheriff's voice startled Pam. "I don't think you need to worry about that. Floyd groomed CJ for the sergeant's job. He won't do anything that would undermine her authority." He paused. "Do you have that search warrant yet, Pam?"

"There's a copy loaded on my phone."

Shaking his head, the sheriff said, "Is that legal? I mean, don't you need to have a paper copy in your possession?"

"The county attorney said as long as I can show the affected party a copy of the search warrant, I'm covered. If they demand a paper copy, I can have one printed."

Jodi turned back to her console as CJ announced that she was "10-8," back in service. Jodi spoke into the mic mounted on her headset. "Investigator Ryan requests that you meet her in Henriette."

"I'll see her there."

* * *

Arriving in Henriette, CJ noticed a car in the driveway of the neighboring house. She parked behind it and announced her location to the dispatcher. The yard was slightly greener than at the rental house, and it had been recently mown. The house was better maintained than the rental, and the concrete steps looked new. CJ's knock on the door was answered by a woman in khaki pants and a golf shirt with a logo CJ didn't recognize.

The woman didn't look surprised to see a deputy on her steps. "Can I help you?" she asked, in an east coast accent.

"When did you last see your neighbors?"

The woman leaned out of the door and looked toward the rental. "I haven't seen anyone around there in days. If you find them, would you tell them if they're not going to mow the grass, ask if they would at least cut down the weeds?"

CJ smiled. "We're not the dandelion police."

"Fine, just tell them the weeds are disgusting."

"How many days has it been since you last saw them?"

"How in hell would I know? It's not like I'm their keeper." She paused with a disgusted look on her face. "I haven't seen that shitty green car since Saturday. It rumbled out of here, and never came back."

CJ took out a notebook and wrote Saturday's date. "What's your name, ma'am?"

"Listen, I'm not a busybody, and I have no interest in getting involved in whatever is going on over there. They buzz back and forth with that noisy car, wearing their Amish-long skirts and their heads covered. It's none of my business, but I wouldn't have been surprised if they'd shown up in a horse-drawn carriage."

"There really aren't many Amish people in this area."

"I don't *know* that they were Amish. They just dressed kind of like the Amish people I've seen on television. I suppose they could belong to some other cult that doesn't believe in wearing shorts or…whatever."

CJ's thoughts flashed to Palmquist's religious sect. "Your name, please."

The woman blew out a breath. "Jennifer Morse."

"How long have you lived here?"

"My husband dragged me to this shithole town fourteen months ago."

CJ focused on her notepad, trying not to smile. "Where did you live before?"

"I sold insurance in Quincey, Massachusetts." The woman paused. "I used to entertain my customers on the golf course. Did you know that the only golf course near here is only nine holes, and they allow people to play in jeans and t-shirts?"

"I'm not a golfer, Mrs. Morse."

"There was a woman teeing off wearing a scoop-necked t-shirt." Jennifer rolled her eyes. "That's right, a scooped-neck t-shirt. She leaned over to tee off and I swear I could see her navel."

"You said the people in the rental house wore Amish-style clothes?"

"They were the other extreme. There weren't even any ankles showing below the skirts of those two, much less a belly button."

"There were just the two of them living there?"

"Most of the time. Every once in a while, a guy or two would show up carrying what I assume were Bibles…or phone books. Always wearing white shirts with their jeans, On Sundays they wore dark suit coats. Not that they were fancy, and they never smiled. I swear their faces would've cracked if they'd smiled."

"Did you recognize any of the men?"

"Nope. None of them looked like potential customers."

CJ continued to make notes. "Did the men ever spend the night?"

"Ha! Most of them never got inside the front door. Mom kept them on the front porch. It looked like she was blocking the door with her body."

"Do you know the women's names?"

"I know their last name was Brady, but that's only because the mailman delivered one of their bills to my house. I took it over to them and had to slip it into a crack in the door because Mom wouldn't open it enough for me to see inside." Jennifer snorted. "There was none of that rumored *Minnesota nice* being offered up there. I don't think she even thanked me for the effort."

"You said there were two female residents?"

"A girl caught the school bus every morning. Mom stood by her in the driveway and met her there when she came home. That girl never had a friend over, and no one ever picked her up for a date. I suppose they sat in the house reading the Bible by candlelight."

"They had electricity, right?"

"Yeah, the candlelight comment was more judgement than fact. They kept the blinds closed tight all the time, day and night, but I could see light leaking between the slats."

"Can you tell me anything else about them?"

"They weren't neighborly, they didn't mow the grass, the house needs a coat of paint, and their car needs a muffler. Other than that, they were perfect neighbors."

CJ closed her notebook and smiled. "Thanks for your time."

"If you've got a minute, I could write up a quote on your car and homeowner's insurance. I could probably save you a couple hundred dollars a year."

"I'm on duty, so I can't sit down with you right now."

Jennifer looked at what appeared to be an expensive watch and sighed. "Yeah, I've got to meet someone in ten minutes at the feed store." She paused. "I didn't know what a feed store was before I moved here. Not that it's information I felt I'd missed."

"It's a different world from Massachusetts."

"I need to buy some clothes, and it appears the nearest Nordstroms is in Minneapolis. Is that right?"

"I wouldn't know. I'm not much of a shopper."

"Yeah, I suppose you wear uniforms all the time."

CJ was about to explain that her off-duty attire was often jeans and a t-shirt purchased at the Farm and Fleet store but decided not to offer that information.

Pam pulled into the rental house's driveway as CJ stepped away from Jennifer. "You interviewed the neighbors?"

"I met Jennifer Morse from Quincey, Massachusetts. She's an unhappy woman. I swear if she was living in the garden of Eden, she'd complain that the apples were too high on the trees."

Pam grinned and said, "I've met a few people like that."

CJ chuckled to herself. "I have a sister-in-law like that. She's the reason I volunteer for weekend shifts when there are family reunions."

"You're kidding?"

CJ shook her head. "Nope. She whines about everything and expects my brother to make it right."

Glancing at her watch, Pam looked down the road. "The BCA forensics team should be here in a few minutes. I'm torn between waiting for them or going back inside the house. The more I think about that new wire coming out of the circuit breaker box, the more intrigued I become."

"The wire is probably just some amateur DIY project. I'm more interested in the bloody knife. Does the blood belong to one of the Bradys, or is it from someone who dragged them out?"

The question about waiting for the Bureau of Criminal Apprehension became moot when the BCA's travelling crime lab turned into the driveway. Two gray-haired men stepped out. Both Jeff Telker and Sonny Carlson were known to Pam and CJ, having collaborated with them on several investigations. Sonny was having an emphatic discussion with Jeff, who seemed to be ignoring him.

"Listen to me, Jeff," Sonny said, talking as they walked toward the house. "This is going to be as big as Enron was."

"Enron went bankrupt, Sonny."

"I mean before they went bankrupt, when their stock was climbing like the sky was the limit."

"It was skyrocketing because Enron executives were cooking the books."

"I was just using Enron as an example of a hot stock," Sonny said. "I'm sure this company is legitimate. I read about it on the internet."

Jeff held up his hand to interrupt Sonny when they reached Pam and CJ. "If it isn't my favorite Pine County investigator and sergeant. How are you two?"

Pam smiled while they shook hands. "Am I your favorite investigator because I'm the only Pine County Investigator?"

Jeff's eyes twinkled. "I'll never admit that."

Sonny pulled CJ aside when they shook hands. "I'm onto something really hot. Jeff's ignoring me, but maybe you'd like to get in on the ground floor of a new company that's boring test holes in Mahtowa. A smart, young geologist found information about a depression-era gold mining operation south of Mahtowa on what used to be the Peterson farm. Back then, gold was only worth $35 an ounce. With gold eventually pushing $1,500 an ounce, the payout could be huge! He's looking for a few investors to get in on the ground floor."

Jeff turned away from Pam. "Ignore him, CJ. The guy who's trying to raise the money is one of Sonny's Finnish relatives. I don't want to cast aspersions on the guy, but he's only been out of prison for a few months after serving time for operating a Ponzi scheme."

"Torry is on the straight and narrow now," Sonny argued. "He finished his geology degree and did lots of research while he was in prison. He's found some really lucrative mining locations. He just needs the capital to bore test holes."

CJ gestured toward the house. "Let's talk about your cousin's mining dreams after we've finished our search."

"Okay," Sonny said, "But he may find other investors while we're searching, and we might miss out on the chance to get in on the ground floor."

"He's meeting with potential investors?" CJ asked as they all pulled on surgical gloves.

"Well, he's not meeting with investors as much as talking about the mine with the afternoon crew sitting in the Mahtowa Bar."

Grimacing, CJ held the screen door open, "He's looking for investors in a bar?"

Sonny explained, "It's one of the three Mahtowa social centers."

Pam mouthed "*Social centers, in a bar?*" to Jeff, who shrugged.

"What are the other social centers, Sonny?" CJ asked, trying to remember anything in the tiny town of Mahtowa besides T.J.'s sausage store and the bar.

"The Covenant and Lutheran Churches," Sonny replied, in complete seriousness.

Pam interrupted the conversation inside the door. "CJ and I were here earlier, doing a welfare check. We found a bloody knife in the kitchen, but we were unable to locate the residents. Once we determined no injured people or dead bodies were inside, I called your office and obtained a search warrant."

Nodding, Jeff took out his phone, unlocked it, and handed it to Pam. "Text or email a copy of the search warrant to me for our files."

"I had Sonny's email from earlier investigations, so I sent a copy to him."

Sonny retrieved his cell phone from a pocket inside his non-linting Tyvek coveralls. Flipping through screens he nodded. "Here it is, right after the five emails from our boss reminding me to send him input for my annual performance review."

CJ raised her eyebrows and asked, "You don't respond to emails from your boss?"

"Well," Sonny said, returning his phone to a pocket in his coveralls, "I prefer to meet with him and give verbal input. For some reason, he wants a written summary of the past year's investigations."

Pam and CJ could tell from Jeff's grin that there was more to the story. "The problem is," Jeff explained, "that our boss wants a succinct recap of the number of investigations we contributed to, the number of resulting arrests, the conviction rate, and the resulting sentences."

Wrinkling his nose, Sonny responded. "I hate digging through our old work to find those numbers. I prefer sitting down with him to expand on our contributions that made those arrests and convictions possible."

Sonny was about to expand on that when Jeff cut him off. "How long did you spend with the boss the last time you recapped our contributions, Sonny?"

With his head tipped back, Sonny started mentally counting. "I think it was two and a half days. Yes, he gave me twenty bucks at noon the third day and asked me to pick up lunch for us while he returned phone calls. He apparently got called away, because his office was dark, and his coat was gone when I got back from the deli."

Pam covered her mouth, but she couldn't contain her laughter.

"What?" Sonny asked. "He's a busy man."

Without responding, Pam waved her hand. "We should get started." She led the BCA agents to the kitchen. "Here's the bloody knife."

Jeff took pictures of the knife as Sonny made measurements of its location relative to other kitchen landmarks. Then Sonny dropped the bloody knife into an evidence bag. "A paring knife is an uncommon murder weapon."

CJ pointed to the open drawer. "It looks like someone grabbed whatever knife was handy to fend off an attack. I suspect the blood belongs to the attacker, or the attacker and victim."

Jeff was already swabbing the dried blood droplets and placing each swab in a different container. "I can see your theory, CJ. But, as you know, we prefer to let the evidence lead us to conclusions rather than fitting the evidence to our theories.”

“I agree. On the other hand, my first impression of a crime scene often leads me down lanes of investigation I might have dismissed.”

Sonny opened the basement door. “It appears the blood trail goes out the back door, not into the basement.”

“Correct,” Pam said, stepping around Jeff’s blood collection effort. “There *is* something interesting in the basement.”

After turning on the lights, Pam, CJ, and Sonny walked down the steps to the small basement. Sonny sniffed the air, “There are no windows, so this is technically a crawl space, not a basement. It’s musty, like there’s no air turnover down here.”

CJ removed her flashlight from her belt and illuminated the floor under the circuit breaker box. “There’s sawdust on the floor.” She redirected the flashlight beam to the circuit breaker box. “It looks like someone replaced a faulty wire.”

Sonny removed a penlight flashlight from his pocket and shone it on the ceiling. “Whoever ran this wire bored a new hole. There’s no space alongside the other wires, so I think this was an addition, rather than a replacement.” Holding the flashlight in his teeth, he took out a multi-tool and unscrewed the breaker box cover, exposing the wires and connections inside. “The amateur electrician added the wire to the bedroom circuit breaker."

"What makes you say an amateur made the connection?" CJ asked.

"It's only a 15-amp breaker and a 12-gauge wire, like the one that was added, would require a higher amperage circuit breaker to meet the electrical code. This looks like wiring for an entirely new circuit. No professional electrician did this wiring job."

"Can you tell where it leads?"

While he replaced the cover, Sonny said, "It appears to run inside the wall. Maybe there's a new plug-in receptacle in the kitchen."

Upstairs, Sonny walked to the approximate location over the breaker box. "I think the wire runs here, behind the refrigerator." Checking the adjacent countertop he announced, "There's no new plug." Unable to reach the cabinet over the refrigerator, he stood on a chair and examined the cabinet above the refrigerator. "Well, look at this. There's a lock on the cupboard door." Using his multi-tool screwdriver, he pried the hasp off the door.

Jeff walked over with the camera and photographed the computer modem located inside the cupboard. A row of green lights indicated it was connected to the power and was operating. "There's nothing else in that cupboard, so I suppose the residents never used it."

CJ cocked her head. "I suppose the owner didn't want the renters tampering with or stealing the modem."

Sonny stepped down from the chair, then looked at the blinking green lights on the modem. "Why are the lights blinking if the television is off and no one is logged onto the Wi-Fi?"

"Maybe the neighbors are piggybacking on this modem," Pam suggested. Seeing Sonny's skeptical look, she stepped back. "You're thinking there's something else going on."

Jeff looked at CJ, "What do you think?"

CJ gestured at a heat vent over the living room entry. "Big brother is watching."

Bringing a chair, Sonny climbed up and removed the screws securing the vent to the wall. Removing the vent cover exposed a cable with a shiny end. "CJ wins the prize. It's a camera lens the size of a pencil eraser."

Jeff took another chair down the hallway and removed a vent cover in the nearest bedroom, exposing another camera. A third and fourth camera were found behind vents in the second bedroom and the bathroom.

"I've got to find the guy who owns this house. I suppose he's a pervert who gets off watching his female tenants."

After taking photos, Jeff reinstalled the vent covers. "A few years ago, we would've found a recorder of some kind in the attic or crawlspace. Now, the images are probably broadcast to an account in the cloud and are on a remote server somewhere."

CJ clenched her fists and watched silently. Surprised by her sudden change, Pam asked, "What's wrong?"

"The images may be in the owner's personal account. Or they may be all over the internet. The renter's daughter isn't eighteen. If someone is sharing images of her, it's child pornography."

"Maybe the owner is just trying to monitor the care of his rental house," Sonny suggested.

CJ glared at him. "With two female renters and a camera aimed at the bathtub. I don't think so."

Putting up his hands, Sonny said, "Hey, I'm just throwing out thoughts. Don't kill the messenger."

CJ stared at the bathtub. "I've become a cynical cop who looks for the bad in everything. The problem is, I'm usually not far off the mark."

Jeff pulled the chair out of the small bathroom. "Let's continue to collect information before reaching conclusions. I'll call St. Paul. We have people who specialize in electronic surveillance and Wi-Fi security. I'll ask one of them to look at the modem. Maybe he can tell us where the images are going."

* * *

The missing mother and daughter, the blood in the kitchen, and the discovery of the hidden cameras had CJ's mind swirling. The Henriette neighbor described the Amish-looking men who'd visited the empty house. She'd said they wore dark-colored clothes and appeared to be carrying Bibles. That look didn't mesh with the surveillance cameras and the electronics. *I might be profiling, but Amish men seem unlikely to have the tech skills to set up the surveillance system in that house. I think the cameras were installed by the owner who is a nerdy guy without a girlfriend.*

A lightning bolt flashed in CJ's mind, remembering Brother Palmquist's followers wearing head covers and long skirts, but using electric crock pots to serve hot meals at the horse show. CJ decided to check out the Palmquist compound.

Locating the address on a dusty gravel township road, CJ noted the new barbed wire fence enclosing a pasture. Inside the fence were a mixture of dairy and beef cattle. Near the house, women appeared to be tending a large garden, while a young man swung an ax, splitting firewood. A trail of smoke rose from the house's chimney, spreading the scent of burning oak through the air.

As much as the house and inhabitants seemed to be old-fashioned, the fence posts were new, green-treated wood. The gate across the driveway was painted steel, like the ones for sale at the co-op store. The gate was secured by a chain and padlock.

Parking with her cruiser blocking the driveway, CJ got out and leaned on the top rail of the chest-high gate. She waved at the people working around the house. Although one of the women glanced at her, none of them acknowledged CJ's waves. After a few moments, a dusty, but new pickup drove toward the gate.

Brother Palmquist stepped out, his smile broad and apparently genuine. "Sergeant Jensen, did you decide to take me up on my offer of a communal meal?"

"I can't today. Maybe you can help me solve a mystery."

"Certainly, what mystery is vexing you?"

"A woman and her daughter disappeared from a house in Henriette. The daughter hasn't been to school, and we're concerned that they may not have left the house willingly."

Palmquist cocked his head. "I'm not sure how I could help with that."

"The neighbor reported that they dressed like the members of your…congregation, and she said that men, dressed conservatively and apparently carrying Bibles, had visited in the days before the woman and girl disappeared."

"That's quite a mystery, Sergeant. I can't offer any solutions for you. Sorry."

"It was a longshot. I thought they might've been members of your congregation."

"All of my flock are present and accounted for." Palmquist paused and gestured toward the house. "You're welcome to come in. Everyone is working right now, so you'll be able to easily see if they're around."

"Thanks. I'll take your word for it."

As CJ walked toward her car, Palmquist called out. "Be sure and come by at mealtime. We'd happily break bread with you."

CJ turned onto the road and drove away. In her mirror she noted that Palmquist continued to watch her until she was out of sight. *You invited me in. But you never made a move to unlock the chain or open the gate. I'm welcome, but only if I don't really want to come in.*

# Chapter 9

The search of the Henriette house caused Pam's mind to race. Although Henry Bedard's expired driver's license listed his residence as the rental house, Pam knew he was living elsewhere. Staring at her computer screen, Pam contemplated other searches. A thought formed. *He was born in 1939, maybe he's dead?* She searched for obituaries including the name Bedard and found Agnes Bedard's 2003 obituary, listing Henry and Justine as her living heirs. Henry's name was never mentioned in any later obituary.

Accessing a county database of welfare recipients, Pam found Henry. The listed address was unfamiliar. She keyed the address into a Google search and *Minnesota Masonic Home* popped up with an address in a south Minneapolis suburb. A call to the listed phone number was answered by a perky female voice. "Masonic Retirement Residence, how may I help you?"

"I'm an investigator from the Pine County Sheriff's Department. Is Henry Bedard a resident there?"

"May I ask the context of your inquiry?"

"Mr. Bedard owns a rental house in Pine County, and there's been a police-involved incident there. I need to speak with him about the recent renters."

The woman hesitated. "Mr. Bedard lives in our memory care unit. I can connect you with the nurses' desk there. Mr. Bedard doesn't have a phone in his room."

The transferred call rang nearly a dozen times before a breathless male voice answered. "I'm an investigator with the Pine County Sheriff's Office, and there's been a possible crime at a rental house owned by Henry Bedard. Could I speak with him?"

After a derisive snort, the man replied, "You can talk to him, but it's going to be a monologue. Henry's not…conversational."

"How is his long-term memory?"

"It's hard to tell. Most of our communication is non-verbal."

"I don't understand," Pam said.

"If he likes the food, he eats it. If he doesn't, he throws it. If he likes what's on television, he watches it. If he dislikes a show, he looks for someone to change the channel."

"You don't let the residents use the television remote?"

"Ma'am, he can't figure it out. The last time he used the remote, he pushed buttons until it was broadcasting in Spanish with French subtitles. It took us a day to get it back to English because the only person in the place who speaks Spanish was off."

"Does Henry have visitors?"

"He used to, but there's really no point anymore. He doesn't recognize them, and they can't converse. He's happy to see people, but it really doesn't matter if the visitor is a volunteer or his granddaughter."

"His granddaughter has visited him?"

"She used to come with Henry's daughter, but they haven't been around much since…"

"Since what?"

The man sighed. "They used to be normal people. I mean, normal in the sense that they wore clothes like everyone else. About two years ago, they showed up in head covers and long dresses, kinda Amish-like, with a guy who acted like their bodyguard."

"Why did they need protection?"

"I'm not so sure they needed protection, as much as he was there to make sure they returned to their home. I heard that he drove them, and he hovered over them the whole time they were here. It's almost as if he was afraid they were going to run away. He even stopped them from making a phone call—saying it wasn't their custom. It looked more like it was against the rules."

Pam processed what she was hearing. "They had a man with them who looked like he was minding them more than protecting them, and he stopped them from making a phone call?"

"That's what I saw."

"Henry wasn't able to converse with them?"

"They tried a bit, but Henry was spacey. I'm sure he didn't know who they were. They hung around a while, had Henry sign something, then they were gone."

"Whoa!" Pam said. "Henry signed something. Is he competent to sign a legal document?"

"They said it was for his medical insurance. They had me witness Henry's signature."

"Did you read any of it?"

"Not really. I signed on the second page and all that was there were signature blocks for Henry, his daughter, and two witnesses."

"Who was the second witness?"

"The guy who drove them signed the other witness line." The man paused. "You know, I did see the front page before they flipped it over for the signatures. It was a power of attorney."

"Henry, who isn't communicative and living in a memory care unit, signed a power of attorney form? Didn't that seem odd?"

"Most everyone here has granted one of their children power of attorney so they can sign checks and legal documents. They all have living wills, too. You know, so it's clear what end of life medical care they want, or don't want."

"Do you keep them on file?"

The man chuckled. "I imagine so. You'd have to check with the business office about that."

"Think back to the power of attorney you witnessed. Who was assigned to act as Henry's advocate?"

"I didn't see that. I just signed below..." The man paused. "You know, it's odd, but I think Henry transferred his power of attorney from his daughter to his pastor."

"Do you recall the pastor's name?"

"Nah. It was some typical Swedish sounding name. That's all I remember."

"Could it have been Brother Palmquist?"

"It could've been. I don't remember."

"Can you transfer me to the business office, or do I need to call back through the switchboard?"

"Could you call back? I've got call lights blinking all down the hallway."

Instead of calling back, Pam walked upstairs to the county attorney's office. His office was dark, but Pam found Alissa Preston, one of the assistant county attorneys at her desk. "Hey, Liss, do you have a second?"

The new law school grad looked up from a stack of papers. "What's up, Pam?"

"I just spoke to a guy at the Masonic Home, where the owner of a Henriette rental property lives. The owner is in a memory care unit and is non-communicative. A year or so ago, his daughter and an unknown man showed up with a power of attorney form for the resident to sign. Is that legal?"

"It depends."

"That's not helpful, Liss."

The attorney smiled. "I know, but it's the truth. For a legal document to be valid, the signatories have to be sane, uncoerced, and functionally literate. If this guy was mentally sharp, but unable to speak, his signature is most likely valid. If he's no longer a competent adult, then any document he signs can be challenged and the court would probably rule that it's invalid."

"I think he assigned Brother Palmquist of the commune his power of attorney."

"That's not terribly unusual. We've had people give their bartenders power of attorney. Personally, I'd prefer a minister to a bartender."

"Is there any way to determine if Brother Palmquist is acting in good faith?"

The attorney leaned back. "I'd have to ask someone about that. Theoretically, we could look at his bank account and see if the rent is going to places that seem inappropriate."

Pam's eyes brightened and she stiffened. "Can you see if his property taxes are being paid?"

"Sure!" The attorney turned and keyed information into her computer. "What property are you concerned about?"

"Henry Bedard owns a rental house in Henriette."

"The taxes haven't been paid in two years, and the county assessor filed a lien against the property." The attorney paused. "Uh oh."

"What's wrong?" Pam asked, sliding close to the computer monitor.

"The Masonic Home had Henry declared indigent, and the county is paying for his care."

"When did that happen?" Pam asked, peeling a Post-it note off a pad.

"About eighteen months ago. Henry's assets were the Henriette house and a bank account with $43."

"I suppose that's not surprising. People go through their savings quickly when they move into a care facility."

"What's surprising is that Brother Palmquist tried to sell the house first. The sale was held up because of the property tax lien. That's when the county was asked to take over Bedard's care."

"I don't suppose you can see what Henry's bank account looked like before that?"

The attorney turned. "Not without a court order. Do you have probable cause that a financial crime or fraud has been committed?"

"I'd love to know how much money Henry had when the church took over his accounts."

Tom Bakken, the county attorney, stepped into the office, apparently ready to ask a question. He paused when he saw there was a visitor. "Pam Ryan, are you socializing or is this business?"

"Pam stumbled across an interesting situation." Alissa nodded to Pam, who retold the story about Henry Bedard's mental state and the power of attorney.

Bakken nodded toward the door. "Let's move this discussion to my office. Alissa, can you join us?"

Closing the door as the two young women sat at his meeting table, Bakken removed his suit coat and hung it behind the door. He unlocked a cabinet and removed three files that he set on the table. He slid them across the table. "I'm assigning these investigations to you, Alissa. Work with Pam on them." Looking at Pam he said, "Be careful, one of these may be your potential murderer."

Opening the first file, Alissa read a few lines, then looked up. "Bob Olsen brought this to your attention the week before he got food poisoning?"

Bakken sighed. "Bob brought all three of these to me in the past month. With the trial, I haven't had time to deal with them."

Pam slid the first file over so she could see what Alissa had read. Holding her finger on the spot where she stopped reading, Pam looked at Bakken. "We're waiting for the results of the toxicology testing on Bob's blood. The doctors said whatever he's got is not a common food poisoning bug."

Bakken sighed again. "Bob was especially concerned about the commune ownership and the lien on Henry Bedard's property. He'd also had confrontations with the other two people as well."

Pam read a few more lines of the first file, then passed it back to Alissa. "Floyd says the hair stands up on the back of his neck when he senses a crime in progress." Pam held out her arm, exposing the goose bumps. "Every hair on my body is standing on end. This reeks of fraud, manipulation of a vulnerable adult, and possible assault by food poisoning."

Alissa blew out a breath as she read the second file. "This guy built a pole barn behind his house, then opened a small engine repair business. He was upset when Bob Olsen reassessed his property from residential to commercial, doubling the estimated value. The changes tripled his property taxes."

The county attorney leaned back in his chair and said, "Bob explained that the tax classification is based on the highest and best use of the property. A business operation makes the whole property, including the house, a commercial property. In this case, adding the pole barn made the property worth more than $500,000 and changed his base property tax from the 1% residential rate to the commercial 2% rate. That's in the Minnesota statutes."

After passing the second file to Pam, Alissa opened the third file. "I read about this in the newspaper. A guy from Illinois bought a house on Sturgeon Lake, remodeled it into four apartments, and is renting them out through an online rental agency. Bob determined that it's now a multi-unit rental apartment. The owner never notified the neighbors or the township and failed to request a zoning change from single-family residential to multi-family apartments. An apartment building is in a much higher tax category. The Illinois guy is arguing that the rental situation is temporary. He plans to retire in the house. Bob's notes indicate that the house has four separate entrances with four bathrooms. That's more bathrooms than the on-site septic system is designed to handle. Bob turned it over to the county code enforcement people. Here's a copy of a letter sent by the code officer demanding that the homeowner submit a plan to replace the septic system, or they're going to condemn the property." Alissa flipped through the remaining pieces of the file. "The owner hasn't responded."

Scanning the documents and holding the transcript of a phone message, Pam said, "Bob recorded a threatening message from the owner. The Illinois guy sounds like a nut case with anger management issues. I'd say he's a pretty good suspect in Bob's poisoning."

Gathering the files, Alissa licked her dry lips. "Tom, I'm not ready for anything this big. I've only been here a few months, and I've spent most of that time prepping for the Ogden case."

Bakken leaned on his elbows. "Alissa, I'm up to my eyeballs, as are the other assistant attorneys. Pam can handle the investigative part. When you have questions about our department's role, and I assume you will, leave a note or catch me after court."

Alissa smiled. "Really?"

"It's all yours." Bakken stood and opened the office door. "You two get out of here so I can look at today's defense motions."

Pam stopped outside Alissa's office. "You've got your first solo cases, and I have three possible suspects in Bob's murder attempt."

"Tom said you were handling the investigations. What are your plans?"

"I'm going to leave the Bedard property issues to CJ. I'll drive out to the small engine repair place and talk to the owner. After that, I'll call the guy with the apartments in Illinois."

"Do you think a guy from Illinois would drive up here to poison Bob?"

"His threatening voicemail shows that he's a hothead. Even if he didn't drive here himself, he may have contracted someone local to act on his behalf."

"What should I do?" Alissa asked.

"Start the condemnation of the house that was remodeled into apartments. It doesn't appear that the guy responded to the code officer's demand for a new septic system."

Alissa nodded. "I have to check the statute and determine exactly how to start a condemnation." She paused, then asked, "Do you have a few minutes for a cup of coffee or a glass of wine at the end of your shift?"

Pam smiled. "After last Friday's gab session with you at the Rock Creek Cafe, I had to give Travis the whole weekend off."

"It wasn't that bad, was it?"

"We got going, and I lost track of time. Travis was sure I'd been killed in a car accident or something because my cell phone battery was dead, and he couldn't reach me."

"Call him first and warn him that I'm kidnapping you to talk about these cases."

"One cup of decaf coffee, and then I'm gone."

"It's a date!"

Pam looked around, then whispered, "Shh. Do not say things like that around here. The walls have ears and the last thing either of us need is a rumor that we're dating each other."

"You are so…small town."

Pam smiled. "Welcome to Pine County where no rumor is too small or unbelievable to repeat."

* * *

A sign next to the driveway read SMALL ENGINE REPAIR. The gravel driveway wound past a house to a steel-sided pole barn. The adjacent yard was covered with shaggy grass, dotted with yellow dandelion blossoms. Beyond the house was a fenced field with two cows and their calves grazing in pasture. A car and pickup were parked in front of the pole barn next to a row of lawnmowers, garden tractors, and a snowmobile.

After announcing her location to the dispatcher, Pam walked through a door into an unoccupied dusty office. Crude shelves made from 2x4s and plywood were covered with dirty engine parts, catalogs, and repair manuals. The metal desk was covered with a mixture of invoices, bills, and unopened mail.

Voices from beyond the office led Pam into a large workspace filled with push lawnmowers in varying states of disassembly and a green garden tractor with a tilted mower deck. Two men stood in the back of the room talking to a third man seated on a stool next to a workbench. They all stopped speaking when Pam walked in.

"Can I help you?" the seated man asked.

"I'm looking for Jim Asmus."

"That's me," the seated man responded.

The two other men nodded to Asmus, then walked past Pam toward the office.

"I heard you had a disagreement with the tax assessor," Pam said, approaching the workbench.

Asmus, who was in his middle-30s, looked disgusted. "Yeah, I've got a beef with the tax assessor. That jerk tripled my property taxes. What about it?" Suddenly aware of Pam's uniform, Asmus' eyes narrowed. "Don't tell me he called the cops on me."

"You verbally assaulted a county official in the course of his job."

Abruptly standing, Asmus towered over Pam. His face turned red, and he pointed his finger at Pam's chest. "I gave that shithead a piece of my mind. That's all."

"What happened after that?"

Looking confused, Asmus asked, "What do you mean?"

"What happened after Bob left?"

"After he left?"

"Yes, what happened after the tax assessor left?"

"I guess I went back to work." Asmus gestured around the space. "I'm backed up for weeks. I don't have time to do anything else. Hell, it takes a month's profits to pay my new real estate taxes. THEN, I can think about paying the two mortgages and the grocery bill. Don't get me started on putting a little away to cover the slow times in the fall and spring when nobody's lawnmower, snowblower, or outboard is broken."

"Were you angry enough to hurt the tax assessor?"

"Hurt him? You mean like take a poke at him?"

"Sure. Were you mad enough to punch him?"

Asmus sighed. "Let's be clear, he's a pompous ass who likes to wield his power. I would've walked away from him if I saw him in a bar, but there's no way I would punch him. At least not anywhere but in my dreams."

"Did you know he's been poisoned?"

Snorting, Asmus said, "There is a God who answers prayers."

Pam scanned the assortment of chemicals, oils, solvents, and greases lining the shelves in the shop. "You didn't slip any…mineral spirits in Bob's coffee?"

"You've got to be kidding. I might throw a cup of coffee into his face, but I wouldn't poison him. That'd be plain stupid."

"I agree. But people do stupid things in a fit of anger."

"Listen, I've got a wife and two kids who rely on me to pay the bills…" Asmus paused. "Well, I pay part of the bills. My wife is a checkout clerk at the store in town. She gets benefits, pays for daycare, and covers half the mortgage. I may get mad, but I'm not crazy enough to pour something into the tax assessor's coffee. No way."

Watching Asmus go from anger to being a concerned husband and father made Pam discount him as the poisoner. "I'm sorry about your taxes, but you can't threaten the tax assessor. If it happens again, I'll be back to arrest you."

Asmus ran his fingers through his hair. "If he shows up here again, I'll give him another piece of my mind, but I won't punch or threaten him. Okay?"

"Keep your temper under control. I don't want to return."

"Fine. If we're done, I've got a guy coming to pick up the John Deere in an hour, and I'm only halfway through the repair."

* * *

Back in the bullpen, Pam made a cup of coffee and pulled Rocco Halston's phone number out of the apartment/sewer complaint file. The listed number was answered by a woman on the second ring. "Rocco's Construction."

"This is Investigator Pam Ryan from the Pine County Sheriff's Department. Is Mr. Halston there?"

The woman apparently held the phone aside when she yelled, "Hey, Rocco. There's a cop calling for you on line two."

A moment later, a gruff male voice answered, "This is Rocco."

Pam repeated her introduction then said, "I have complaints about your remodeling project on Sturgeon Lake. It appears that you converted a single-family house without getting a variance from the neighbors and township, you built without a building permit, the work wasn't inspected by the building, electrical, or plumbing inspectors, and the septic system is inadequate for the new use."

"Are you from that hick Minnesota town?"

"I'm from Pine County."

"Yeah, that county with all the lakes. What do you call your state, the land of 50 million lakes or something?"

"Mr. Halston, the lakes are irrelevant to my inquiry. You've violated the building and sewer codes and threatened a tax assessor."

"Listen, little lady. I tried to get a building permit, but that hick town's office was closed. I left a message and they said they're only open on Friday mornings. I had a crew there sitting on their asses on Monday morning, and I wasn't going to pay for the workers to sit around until some hillbilly showed up on Friday morning to issue a building permit."

"I'm sorry that the building permit process was...cumbersome for you. Regardless of your inconvenience, a permit is still required before you start construction. Besides that, they wouldn't have given you a building permit to turn a single-family residence into an apartment building without a zoning variance, and that would've required permission from the neighboring properties."

"See! That's just what I mean. Your hick county is full of people who are only around on the weekends. I've only seen my neighbors like twice, and there's no way I was going to ask their permission after the..."

"After what, Mr. Halston?"

"Never mind. What's the problem with the sewer?"

"There isn't a sewer. The property has a septic system that was built to accommodate a single-family home. The system is outdated and undersized. It has to be replaced."

"You're joking. You want me to replace the sewer?"

"The county sent you notice that the septic system has to be replaced. It would've been part of the building permit requirement if you'd applied for a building permit."

Halston blew out a breath. "So, what will it take to make this go away?"

"At this point, it's going to be a painful process. Because you made uninspected modifications to the structure without a building permit, you'll be required to open the walls and show the inspectors that you've met the building codes. The septic system has to be replaced regardless of what else happens. And, you'll have to talk to the township and county about possibly rezoning the property as a multi-unit apartment. All that will take time, and the county is proceeding with condemnation pending your compliance with the requirements."

"No."

Pam froze. "No?"

"I asked you what it will take to make this go away."

"And I explained the process."

Halston blew out a breath. "What will it take? I can have a case of your favorite booze delivered discreetly to your house. Give me your home address."

"Are you trying to bribe me?"

"Let's say I'm just trying to grease the skids. What's the issue? If you're not a booze hound, I can make it a case of very nice wine. You women sometimes prefer wine to booze. Am I right?"

"Attempting to bribe a public official is a felony punishable by up to ten years in prison and a $10,000 fine."

"Hey, I'm not trying to bribe you. I'm just trying to ease these issues out of the system. Just lose the file, and you might receive an envelope with ten $100 bills inside. Would that work better for you?"

"Mr. Halston, I'm recording this conversation, and my next stop will be the county attorney's office."

"Call me Rocco," the man said with a chuckle. "Jeez, don't get your undies in a bunch, honey. You can't record this because I never gave permission."

"I can record a conversation if one party is aware of the recording. This call is over."

"Wait! Chicago is a nice town. Why don't you and your boyfriend come down for a long weekend. I'll send you a couple first-class tickets, set you up in a hotel suite overlooking Lake Michigan, we'll have a couple nice dinners while we talk through the details of resolving your concerns. What do you say?"

"Should the cops arrest you at your office or your home?"

“What?”

“The county attorney is going to draft a criminal complaint warrant and send it to your local police department. They’ll arrest you and hold you for extradition to Minnesota.”

“Listen, bitch. This is all bullshit, and you know it. I already told your hick taxman to stuff this all up his ass.”

“You spoke with Bob Olsen?”

“I don’t remember his name. He called whining about the remodeling and wouldn’t listen to reason. I told him to…”

“Did you meet with Mr. Olsen in person?”

“Naw. I wouldn’t drive all the way there to argue about stupid building code shit. I told him that I’m a licensed contractor and all the work was done to code. He started whining about permits and inspections and wouldn’t listen to reason. I hung up on him.”

“Did you, or your representatives, ever meet face to face with Bob Olsen?”

“Nah. We talked on the phone a couple times, but it was like talking to a brick wall. ‘Wah. Wah. Wah. Rocco, you’ve got to correct this or that.’ I got tired of his whining and hung up.”

“Thanks for explaining it in such great detail. I’m sure the jury will love hearing your attempts to bribe me and the tax assessor.”

“Send it to my attorney. He’ll talk to your attorney, and they’ll sort it out.”

Pam was about to ask for his attorney's name when she realized she was listening to a dial tone. Hanging up the phone she thought, *you might think about this issue differently from behind bars.*

* * *

Pam was sitting in a back corner of Nicolls Café when the assistant county attorney walked in. Other than a pair of old men arguing about the poor price of beef cattle—something they couldn't control any more than the weather, Nicolls was empty.

Alissa took a chair across from Pam and signalled the waitress for Mountain Dew. "What did you find out about the engine repair shop and the remodeled apartment building?"

"The repair shop guy is just trying to eke out a living. He's no threat to anyone." Pam paused when Alissa's soda pop arrived. "The Chicago builder was another matter. I've got a recording of him trying to bribe me. I'll forward it to you tomorrow, and you can draft a criminal complaint warrant and find a judge to sign it."

"Really? He tried to bribe you?"

"Yep. He went from booze, to cash, to an all-expense paid weekend in Chicago."

"Do you think he might've poisoned Bob Olsen?"

"I don't think so. He seems more like someone who'd break your legs than poison you."

Alissa leaned forward. "Holy shit. I didn't think people like that existed outside of television movies."

"They're out there."

"I need to talk about something else. Tell me about your baby."

Pam, whose son was nearly nine months old, smiled. "Noah is crawling and getting into everything. We had to put locks on all the cabinet doors and the drawers."

"I'd like to have kids someday." She paused while the waitress topped off Pam's cup. When the waitress was out of earshot, Alissa leaned closer to Pam. "I haven't dated since I moved here. I've met a couple guys at the bar, but somehow, they seemed…"

"Rural?" Pam suggested.

Sighing, Alissa nodded. "I grew up in a Minneapolis suburb where there were a dozen entertainment venues within a fifteen-minute drive. Here, there's the casino and bars. To be honest, I'm not big into drinking or gambling."

"There aren't the entertainment options you're accustomed to, but there are things to do and places to meet guys who aren't drunks or looking for a hookup. There was a horse show last weekend and I'm sure some of the women there would welcome you to ride with them. Join a church and get into their social activities. There's a country theater in Sandstone. If you'd like to try acting, there's a community theater in Cambridge. Think outside the box."

"Tom warned me about dating too close to town. What did he mean by that?"

Smiling, Pam leaned close. "Remember what I said about no rumor being too small to repeat? If you're seen on a date in town, or even in a nearby town, the news will be back to the courthouse by morning. Even if it was an innocent cup of coffee with a guy at Tobies, the rumor mill will report that you spent the night with him."

"Why would someone start a rumor like that?"

"It's like playing telephone, Liss. Someone tells their friend she saw you with a guy at Tobies, and each retelling gets juicier, because it's more interesting to say the new attorney is sleeping around, than to say you had a cup of coffee and left in separate cars, going different directions."

"How did you and your husband get past that?"

"We'd have supper somewhere, leave at different times, in our own cars, driving different directions." Pam leaned close. "Even if I was spending the night at Travis' house, I'd drive south and loop around before driving toward Carlton."

"That's nuts."

The waitress came back to top off their coffee and soda. "The dinner specials are a hot roast beef sandwich with mashed potatoes and gravy, or a chef's salad. Would you like to see the menu?"

Pam put $10 on the table. "We're just having coffee. Keep the change, Wanda."

Pocketing the bill, the waitress smiled. "Ladies night out?"

"We're just talking over a case," Pam replied.

Wanda gave them a conspirator's smile. "I heard about the drug operation in Sandstone. I won't tell a soul."

Alissa watched the waitress walk away. "There's a drug operation in Sandstone?"

"Apparently. That's the rumor."

"Are you going to investigate it?"

Pam leaned back. "Are you kidding? We don't go chasing after rumors overheard in restaurants."

"But..."

"I don't know where or what she's talking about. For all I know, it's some kid vaping behind a barn. His neighbor saw him and assumed he was doing something illegal because he was hiding from his parents. That probably morphed into a story that there was a drug party behind the barn. The next retelling moved it to a meth cooking operation..."

Alissa grinned. "No rumor is too small or illogical that it can't be twisted and improved."

Pam pushed her coffee cup aside. "Read the files Tom gave you. We'll talk about how we want to deal with it tomorrow."

"You're leaving?" Alissa asked.

Pam nodded to the farmers who'd ended their beef price discussion and moved on to the upcoming elections. "Don't leave until five minutes after I'm gone and drive south."

Alissa looked confused. "Why?"

"If we leave together driving in the same direction, there'll be a rumor that I'm leaving my husband to have a lesbian relationship with you."

Alissa stared at the farmers and said, "You're kidding."

Pam stood up and replied, "Not entirely."

# Chapter 10

After booking a driver who'd failed a breathalyzer test, CJ sat in the bullpen filling out the arrest report. Looking up when the coffee maker gurgled, she saw Floyd and smiled. He made a second cup and carried it to her. "Was Kerm right?"

Cocking her head as she sipped, CJ asked, "Was Kerm right about what?"

"His suggestion that aliens had experimented on the dead guy at the museum and kidnapped the pickup's driver."

"I can't believe he says things like that out loud. Did you ever coach him about keeping his goofy thoughts to himself?"

Floyd blew on his coffee to cool it. "Nope. Kerm says whatever goes through his head. There's no filter between his thoughts and his mouth. On the other hand, he's always the deputy I trusted to have my back. At least until Pam and you came along."

CJ wrapped her hands around her coffee cup, then quickly released the hot mug. "I can see that. I'd want Kerm by my side if I got called to a bar fight."

"Regardless of the situation, he'd be fearless. You'll more often have to hold him back than urge him on."

"Has that caused you problems over the years?"

Floyd looked behind himself to make sure no one was listening in. "Kerm sometimes makes more wake than a Lake Superior ore freighter. I spent about ten percent of my career smoothing over things he stirred up. His heart was always in the right spot, but his judgement was sometimes lacking."

Taking a sip of the hot coffee, CJ nodded her understanding. "He speaks and acts before he thinks. That has surprised or offended a few people."

Floyd chuckled. "Thinking before speaking is not Kerm's strong suit."

"But he'd save your butt in a pinch."

"CJ, Kerm would take a bullet for any deputy in the department. I can put up with a few hurt feelings knowing that I've got a brave, caring deputy beside me."

"Yeah, but saying things like the dead guy was dropped by aliens…"

Floyd paused, shifting mental gears. "Was anything stolen from the museum?"

"It took a while for Aggie to look through the exhibits and to check the café. The museum was undisturbed, but she eventually realized that their van keys were missing."

Floyd was surprised. "The museum had a van?"

"Apparently it was a donation from a baker who used it for deliveries. When he retired, the van was given to the museum. It became part of their outreach, driving senior citizens to doctor appointments, and bringing in small groups from nearby nursing homes and the group home in Sandstone."

"Has it been located?"

"It was parked at the Pine City Walmart."

Frowning, deep in thought, Floyd stared at the wall. "I'm surprised anyone noticed it there. Hundreds of cars move through that parking lot daily. It's the perfect place to hide something in plain sight."

"One of the guys who collects shopping carts noticed that it was parked in the back corner of the lot for a long time. He mentioned it to the Walmart manager, and she called it in. I assume the driver was picked up by a nearby friend."

"Who owns the pickup that smashed into the museum?"

"It was stolen from the Beroun Bar two nights ago."

Sipping his coffee, Floyd shook his head. "Let me guess, the owner left the keys in the ignition and was surprised when he walked out, and the pickup was gone."

"That's part of the story. Jerry Johnson was too drunk to drive, so his friend drove him home from the bar. The next day, with a terrible hangover, Jerry didn't remember how he got home, or where he'd been drinking. When I knocked on his door, he thought he was in trouble because he couldn't remember what had happened, and seeing my uniform made him assume the worst; that he'd crashed the truck somewhere while he was driving drunk."

"It wasn't Jerry who crashed the truck into the museum?"

"He was adamant that he'd been looking for the truck for days. I spoke with his neighbor, Helene Almquist, who said his truck hadn't been in his driveway for two days."

Floyd sipped his coffee to hide his smile. "If anyone would notice that his truck hadn't been in the driveway, it'd be Helene."

"Why's that?"

"She used to call the dispatcher at least once a month to report something amiss in the neighborhood. I swear she sits at her living room window with binoculars watching the area. She once called to report a sheep sleeping on her neighbor's front steps."

"Was there a sheep?"

"Nah, the neighbors bought a Bedlington terrier. It looked like a recently shorn sheep."

"I suppose everyone needs a retirement hobby."

Taking his cup, Floyd stood. "Which is why I'm back here."

"You didn't like retirement?" CJ asked with a smile.

"Mary says I was becoming maudlin."

"Maudlin?"

"I had to look it up in the dictionary. It means sadly sentimental."

"Were you looking at old photo albums?"

"I must've retold my cop stories too many times." Floyd stretched his legs. "I imagine she called John and asked him to find something for me to do."

"You're enjoying yourself, right?"

Pam Ryan walked in, interrupting the conversation. She stopped two steps into the room and looked at Floyd and CJ, who were both staring at her. "All right, this is spooky. Was I the topic of your conversation, or were you discussing something I shouldn't hear?"

"Floyd was becoming maudlin, so Mary kicked him out of the house."

"Maudlin? I think that was an eighth-grade spelling bee word. Who says maudlin?"

"Apparently, Mary has an expansive vocabulary," CJ replied. "What else has she called you, Floyd?"

"Tribulation may have come up. That, and she told someone I was trying. No mention of what I was trying to do, just that I was trying."

Pam and CJ broke into laughter as Floyd stood and walked away.

Sitting at the desk next to CJ, Pam leaned close. "He does seem a lot happier since he pinned on the chief deputy badge."

"You missed him."

Pam nodded. "He was my training officer, then my sergeant. We went through a lot together."

"He was your Pine City dad."

Leaning back, Pam nodded. "I was lost when I moved here from Blue Earth. Floyd was recently widowed, and the two of us leaned on each other."

"You're the daughter Floyd never had."

"I don't think he thought of me that way. He led me through the process of becoming a cop. He let me fall on my face a couple of times. My father would never have given me enough rope to do the things Floyd encouraged me to do."

The ringing of CJ's cell phone interrupted their conversation. The caller ID showed the call was from the Duluth ME's office. "We're going to do the post-mortem exam on the guy from the museum accident in about two hours. If you drove up to watch, I'd buy you supper afterward."

"You know how to sweet talk a girl, Eddie," CJ said, winking at Pam. "How could I refuse an offer to watch an autopsy followed by dinner."

There was a moment of silence. "Sorry about my social skills. After years of talking only to Tony, I sometimes forget that other people don't speak casually about dead bodies during meals."

"I'm kidding. It was a bit of gallows humor. I'd be happy to drive up for an autopsy and dinner. Let's not go to the Italian restaurant in Canal Park. I don't think I could face a platter of linguini in red sauce after watching Tony cut up a corpse."

"I suppose Mexican cuisine would seem just as gruesome."

"We can discuss dinner options later. Just be prepared to offer something else."

"Hey, there's a seafood place next to the Dairy Queen. That should be okay, right?"

Having turned on the speaker so Pam could hear the exchange, CJ replied. "Yes, eating a slab of halibut covered in white sauce would be better than Italian red sauce or a medium rare steak after watching a bloody autopsy."

"I hear laughter."

"Pam's listening in on our conversation. I doubt she and Travis have discussions like this."

Leaning close, Pam said, "No, we discuss poopy diapers and tax forfeited land, not dead bodies or autopsies."

"Hi, Pam. You could join us."

"As tempting as an autopsy and supper sounds, I have to eat with Travis. He gets cranky if I leave him home with the baby to go out and have fun."

"See, CJ," Eddie said. "Pam thinks an autopsy and dinner would be fun."

"Eddie, Pam's shaking her head and running for the door. I'll see you in a couple of hours."

*  *  *

CJ found the drive to Duluth relaxing. Passing the Highway 33 exit to Cloquet, CJ was tempted to turn into the town she's patrolled for over a decade. Reconsidering, she thought to herself, *You've moved to a better place, let the past be the past while you continue to create your new future.*

After threading her way through perpetual road construction on I-35 in Duluth, CJ parked behind the hospital in a spot reserved for police vehicles. Although she was in her personal car, she chose that spot rather than circling through the parking ramp and paying for her hour or two in the morgue. She put one of her sheriff's department business cards on the dash in case one of the hospital security guards checked the lot, then she walked into the lower level of the hospital.

CJ found Eddie working at a computer station, the screen situated so a visitor couldn't see his monitor. Seeing her in his peripheral vision, Eddie shut down the computer and stood. "It's a good thing I didn't make reservations at the Pickwick," he said, appraising her casual attire.

"You don't think jeans and a Pine County Sheriff's Department logo golf shirt would be acceptable there?"

"The Pickwick isn't one of my regular hangouts. I recall women in skirts and men wearing neckties, suits, and sport coats."

"When were you there, in 1950? I don't think anyone except undertakers and lawyers wear suits anymore."

Pushing open a nearby door, Eddie gestured for CJ to walk through. "As much as I enjoy having my memories ridiculed, Tony is awaiting your arrival."

As promised, Tony Oresek was examining the surface of the young man's body with a lighted magnifying glass. Without looking up, he said, "It appears the body was washed before it was placed in the pickup. There aren't any fibers or stray hairs anywhere on his skin. The only debris I've found on the body is consistent with the rust and wood chips in the pickup bed."

"Who would wash a body?" CJ asked, rhetorically, as she pulled on Tyvek coveralls.

The ME swung the magnifying lens aside and looked up. "Most often, it's a very canny criminal who wants to remove any evidence that would link him or her to the crime. We had a dead woman last year whose body had been washed with chlorine bleach, presumably to eliminate DNA evidence."

"Were you able to identify her killer?" CJ asked, approaching the autopsy table.

Tony's eyes sparkled, obviously proud of what he'd accomplished. "She'd eaten dinner with her killer and her stomach contents pointed us to a Two Harbors restaurant that serves venison. They had surveillance camera video of the victim and killer together. The jury only deliberated fifteen minutes before finding him guilty."

"Did you find anything on the surface of this body that points you to a cause of death?"

With a gloved finger, the ME pointed first to one upper arm, then the other. "There are contusions on the biceps, like he'd been held forcefully."

"But no bullet holes, stab wounds, needle sticks, or blunt force trauma?"

"None of the above," The ME said, as Eddie pushed a tray of stainless-steel tools to Oresek. "Let's see what the body tells us."

After opening the body cavity and taking a sample of the lung tissue, the ME stood back and studied the body. "He drowned."

CJ drew a breath, picturing the geography around the museum. "The Kettle River runs through Banning State Park near Askov. It has some class IV rapids. Do you think he fell out of a canoe or kayak?" Then rethinking her comment, she added, "Not that I've seen any naked kayakers."

Eddie had carried a water sample collected from the lungs to a microscope where he studied it. "This isn't river or lake water. There aren't any algae, diatoms, or microorganisms in it."

"So, he drowned in someone's pool?" CJ asked.

Eddie quickly mixed a sample of the water with chemical reagents and looked up. "There's no chlorine. It's not pool or city water."

"What does that leave us with?" CJ asked.

The ME stepped back, staring at the man's open abdomen. "We had a woman who drowned in a farmhouse bathtub. The well water had lots of calcium carbonate in it, but not the chlorine and fluoride we see in city water. She fell and was knocked unconscious before drowning."

"That woman had massive head trauma," Eddie said, returning to the autopsy table. "There's no evidence of a fall or blow anywhere on this guy's head."

Oresek probed the bruises on the man's upper arms. "Someone held him under water. The bruises look like they were made by fingers."

CJ shook her head. "This guy is young and fit. He would've put up a fight and there'd be broken fingernails, scrapes, defensive wounds, and other marks on his body if he'd been forcefully drowned."

"Maybe he'd been drugged," the ME suggested as he took samples of other internal organs. "We'll check his blood for drugs and alcohol."

Eddie snorted. "*We*, being *me*, will check his blood alcohol and screen for drugs."

"Ah," CJ said, "the royal *WE*."

The ME frowned. "We, being the medical examiner's office."

Eddie looked at CJ. "Like I said, I'll do the testing."

The rest of the post-mortem exam was uneventful, and CJ stripped off the Tyvek coveralls while Tony recorded his observations, and Eddie closed the body cavity with coarse stitches. Throwing the disposable coveralls into a wastebasket with the rubber gloves and mask she'd worn, CJ appeared deep in thought. "Let's eat at the Duluth Grill. I think a Walleye sammie would taste good."

Eddie wrinkled his nose.

"What?"

"Everything is so…healthy there. They use lots of herbs and fresh vegetables from the raised beds built around their parking lot."

Ignoring Eddie's description of the fresh herbs, CJ instead focused on his diet. "I can see your mind mulling over their menu. You're planning to order their pork belly grinder. It has deep fried pork belly, an egg, kimchi, and other disgusting stuff that will raise your cholesterol."

Sighing, Eddie nodded. "Maybe I'll just order a cup of soup to leave room for a slice of pie or bread pudding."

CJ held the door open for him. "Why the big sigh?"

"I'm always too full to enjoy their desserts."

"Why don't you order two desserts and nothing else?"

"Naw, the waitress looked for my tablemate the last time I did that."

After chuckling about Eddie's discomfort, CJ said. "Order two desserts. We'll pretend one is for me and I won't have room for it, so you'll have to be a gentleman and eat it for me."

* * *

The Duluth Grill parking lot was full, so CJ watched a couple who were leaving the restaurant. She drove into their parking spot as soon as they backed out. A black Honda tried to sneak in ahead of her, but she pulled in first. The other car honked at her, expressing his displeasure. As CJ exited her car, the Honda's driver, a young man wearing his baseball cap backwards, stalked toward her.

"Listen, bitch, I've been cruising this lot for ten minutes. You took my spot."

Ignoring the man's tirade, CJ walked toward the building.

"Hey! I'm talking to you! Move your car, or you'll have four flat tires when you return."

Drawing a breath, CJ took out her phone, opened the photo app, and snapped a picture of the man, then walked closer and took a picture of his license plate.

"What are you doing?"

"If anything happens to my car while I'm gone, the Duluth Police will get these photos, and they'll be knocking on your door."

Eddie pulled into a nearby parking spot as another car backed out.

The irate man held out his hand. "You can't take my picture without permission. Give me your phone."

Hearing the commotion, Eddie walked over. "What's the problem?"

The irate driver glared at Eddie as a second man got out of the Honda. "Go away, old man. This is none of your business."

CJ dialed 911 as Eddie stepped between her and the two men. "I suggest you leave before the rest of the cops show up."

The men looked around, then stared at Eddie. "There aren't any cops here, Mr. Ponytail."

Nodding at CJ, Eddie smiled. "She's a cop. I think she just called for backup."

"That's so much bullshit," the passenger said. He walked up until he was nose-to-nose with Eddie. "I think you should leave while we deal with the bitch who stole our parking spot."

"Really?" Eddie asked. "You're willing to throw a punch over a parking spot?"

"You disrespected us."

Giving CJ a disgusted look, Eddie sighed. "What are the laws about punching a smartass who's upset about being disrespected?"

With her badge in one hand and her cellphone recording video with the other, CJ stepped up to the driver. "The dispatcher said backup would be here in three minutes." She looked at her watch. "That was a minute ago. I estimate that it'll take you two minutes to get into your car and drive away. Or would you rather wait for the Duluth cops?"

"You're bluffing," the passenger said, reaching for Eddie's shirt.

"You threatened me and my car. If you touch my friend, you've committed assault. Touching his shirt gives him the right to defend himself."

Moving to insert herself between the passenger and Eddie, CJ was distracted from the driver who lunged into his car. Seeing motion in her peripheral vision, she dropped her phone and drew her weapon from behind her back as the driver opened his car's console.

"Keep your hands where I can see them and step away from the car."

The sound of crunching gravel preceded the arrival of a Duluth PD cruiser as it turned into the parking lot. Holding her badge high while keeping her pistol pointed at the Honda, CJ yelled, "Pine County sheriff's department. I called for backup." To her side, Eddie was holding his hands up, signalling non-aggression, while the Honda's passenger repeatedly pushed his chest.

The Duluth cop had his gun in hand before he was out of his cruiser. He radioed, "Officer needs assistance. Assault in progress."

Seeing a flash of shiny metal in the driver's hand as he stepped away from the Honda, CJ yelled, "Drop the gun, or I'll shoot!"

Sirens wailed nearby, and CJ heard footsteps running behind her. The Duluth cop reiterated CJ's demand, "Drop the gun!"

The driver hesitated, his hand out of sight behind the car door. He looked between CJ and the Duluth cop, apparently weighing his options while Eddie's scuffle continued behind CJ.

"Knife!" Eddie yelled just before the second Duluth cop turned.

While CJ continued to hold her gun on the driver, she heard a second Duluth cop yell, "Drop the knife, or I'll fire."

"You can't shoot me for having a knife!"

Keeping her focus on the driver, CJ ignored the showdown behind her. "Put the gun down!" she commanded.

The driver's eyes shifted from CJ to the second Duluth cop and his buddy in the knife standoff. As he straightened, a chrome-plated revolver came into CJ's view through the driver's door window.

Her focus narrowed to the driver's hand as she developed what pilot's call, "target focus." Her vision tunneled and the sounds around her were blocked out. As the driver raised the pistol, CJ's finger moved from the side of the trigger guard onto the trigger. "Do not raise your weapon! Drop it now!"

As the gun appeared over the top of the car's door, CJ pointed at the driver's center of mass. She squeezed the trigger as the shiny pistol's barrel swung toward the Duluth cop. Her first shot broke the driver's window as the revolver bucked in the driver's hand. The recoil lifted the revolver's barrel upward as CJ's second shot glanced off the doorframe, striking the driver in the chest.

Reacting to the chrome-plated revolver in the driver's hand, the Duluth cop fired at the Honda's driver.

Although he was still holding the revolver, the driver looked dazed. He looked at the second Duluth cop who was confronting the knife-wielding passenger and appeared to be preparing to swing around to fire at him. Instead, the gun slipped from his hand and clattered to the ground as he staggered back.

Regaining control of her adrenaline, CJ glanced behind her. The second Duluth cop was pushing the Honda's passenger against the side of his cruiser. Eddie kicked the knife toward the restaurant's back door as patrons started running out the front door. More sirens whined as CJ lowered the gun to her side.

Eddie's arm was over her shoulders, pulling her close. "It's over," he said as the driver sat on a low retaining wall. The driver's breath came in gasps, and his white t-shirt had a spreading bloodstain across the chest.

A Duluth PD sergeant ran onto the scene, going first to the officer who'd shot at the driver. CJ shrugged off Eddie's arm and popped the trunk of her car. Removing a first aid kit, she kicked the driver's revolver farther from the Honda and set the first aid kit on the retaining wall, next to the bleeding man. "What's your name?" she asked as she pulled on a pair of rubber gloves.

"Digger," the driver replied. Speaking was obviously a painful effort.

Ripping open a pack of gauze pads, CJ surveyed the three wounds leaking blood on the driver's shirt and another causing blood to trickle past his ear and down his neck. On closer inspection, she saw a bullet hole in the blood-soaked black cap. *Shit, this kid's*

*brains might be splattered inside the cap.*
she thought.

Digger seemed unfazed by the wound, focusing instead on the cop who was dealing with the passenger behind CJ.

"Okay, Digger, I'm going to take off your cap."

He grabbed CJ's arm with his left hand, which caused him a twinge of pain. Digger's eyes narrowed. "Don't touch my cap. It's my look."

"Your *look* is keeping me from checking the gunshot wound to your head." CJ removed Digger's hand from her arm. Lifting the cap released the accumulated blood trapped by the cap. It oozed onto Digger's dirty brown hair, then down his forehead. CJ used two fingers to spread the wound in his blood-soaked scalp.

Digger jerked his head away from CJ's touch. "Bitch, that hurts!"

Straightening up to stretch her back, CJ sighed. "Of course, it hurts. You've got a bullet wound in your scalp. I'd like to see how deep it goes."

Leaving the second cop to deal with the passenger, Eddie removed a pair of gloves from the first aid kit and eased CJ aside whispering, "I think there's a male ego issue here." Standing in front of Digger, he looked down. "I was an Army medic. I'm going to triage your wounds."

Digger's utterance was unintelligible, but he allowed Eddie to touch his head.

Taking the gauze from CJ, Eddie spread Digger's hair, exposing a gash about 40mm wide. "I'd say your thick skull protected you." Stepping aside, Eddie gestured for CJ to hold the gauze on Digger's oozing head wound.

"Hey, that makes my head hurt!"

Inspecting Digger's shoulder, Eddie replied. "You probably have a concussion, so your head's going to hurt for a while. How bad is your shoulder pain?"

"It's okay. Why?"

After unwrapping another gauze pad, Eddie held it against a hole in the driver's shirt. "Well, it's going to hurt like hell pretty soon. The bullet went in, then hit a bone, and didn't exit. You should hope the bullet didn't fragment in your shoulder socket. Either way, it's going to take a while for the surgeon to sort that out."

Obviously in shock, Digger looked up. "I don't do hospitals."

Grinning, Eddie looked up at the Duluth PD sergeant who approached them. "Do you have an ambulance on the way?"

"Yeah, it's a few minutes away." The sergeant looked at the driver's wounds, then at Eddie. "Don't I know you?"

"Sergeant Plummer, you don't recognize me in civvies?"

"Your voice is familiar too."

"I'm the ME's assistant. You've never seen my ponytail, and never seen me wearing anything but blue surgical scrubs."

"Eddie Paulson! I didn't expect you to be doing first aid. I thought your expertise was dealing with bodies who were beyond first aid."

Pressing the gauze against Digger's shoulder, Eddie smiled. "I was a medic in a previous life."

"Dammit! That hurts!" Digger said, trying to pull away from the pressure Eddie was applying to his bleeding shoulder.

"My usual patients don't complain," Eddie said, smiling at the sergeant. A siren cut out about a block away.

"What's your role in this…besides being a medic?"

"Pine County Sergeant Jensen and I were meeting for supper when this idiot showed up ranting about her stealing his parking spot."

"You witnessed the entire event?"

"I missed the parking part of the episode but arrived just as the *backwards cap idiot* got out of his car."

"His partner was shoving you when I arrived."

"Yup. His passenger didn't like my ponytail look."

The ambulance stopped on the street, because the parking lot was blocked by police cars and onlookers.

"How bad are this guy's wounds?" the sergeant asked.

"His skull took a glancing shot that didn't penetrate. A bullet entered, but didn't exit his shoulder, and it appears one of Sergeant Jensen's shots fragmented when it hit the doorframe and splattered his chest with shrapnel."

The paramedics walked across the parking lot carrying their gear. Plummer glanced at them, then looked at CJ, "Are you okay?"

"I'm just frustrated by all the stupidity. Other than that, I'm fine."

"Officer Green said your shot probably caused the suspect to jerk off a shot wildly…rather than at him."

"You know how it goes. Everything happened so fast it's hard to say exactly what caused the idiot to jerk his shot high. You may want to check the downtown Radisson Hotel to see if they've got a bullet hole in one of the upper floor windows."

Eddie gave the paramedics an assessment of Digger's wounds while CJ and Sergeant Plummer walked to his car. "Can I see your Pine County ID, please?"

"Sure," CJ said, pulling her ID case from her front pocket.

As he inspected the ID and made notes, Plummer asked, "What happened?"

"It was all because of a stupid parking spot." CJ spent several minutes explaining the chain of events leading to the discharge of her firearm. "You saw the rest of it after you arrived. I got some of the confrontation on my cell phone before things went south."

"I had one perspective," Plummer said. "Tell me about it from your viewpoint."

"That idiot was getting ready to shoot your cop over the top of the Honda. I fired when I saw the hammer of his revolver move."

"You saw the hammer move?"

"I was focused on the gun. The suspect was pulling the trigger, shooting in double-action, so the hammer was coming back as he yanked the trigger."

"I guess we should be glad he wasn't shooting an automatic," Plummer said.

"If he'd had an automatic, I'd have shot as soon as he brought the gun up to fire."

After explaining all she'd seen to Plummer, he asked for her pistol. "We'll need to test fire it and compare your bullets to the ones recovered from the suspect."

After removing the magazine and ejecting the cartridge in the chamber, CJ handed her gun to Plummer. "I understand. I'll call the sheriff and report the discharge of my firearm."

Patting her back as they walked away from Plummer, Eddie said, "It stopped being about a parking spot when you stood up to that creep. You disrespected him when you didn't back down. He couldn't let a woman win an argument."

"That's even stupider than road rage."

"I think the correct phrase is more stupid."

Looking up and rolling her eyes, CJ said, "Really? You think now's a good time to correct my grammar?"

Smiling, Eddie replied, "Yes, now is the perfect time."

# Chapter 11

Setting her cell phone aside after half an hour of reading CNN coverage of international affairs, CJ looked up to see Sergeant Plummer walking into the Duluth Police Department's conference room. During their hours spent looking at her cell phone pictures and video, then discussing the shooting, she'd decided he was a level-headed cop, probably close to retirement. He slid three sheets of paper and a pen across the table. "I got your email with the video attached. Read through this transcript of our interview, initial the top two pages, then sign and date the third page."

"Where's Eddie Paulson?" CJ asked as she read the statement.

"He and detective Ogden are drinking coffee in our break room. He finished his statement half an hour ago."

"He's not in a cramped, poorly ventilated, interview room under blistering lights?" CJ asked as she initialed pages, dated, and signed the last page of the statement.

Plummer smiled. "We don't do that to the *good guys.* We save the hot seat for recalcitrant suspects." He stood and opened the door.

Following him into the hallway, then past a room filled with cubicles, CJ asked, "Have you had an update on the shooting victim?"

"The on-call orthopedic surgeon is working on his shoulder. All his other wounds were superficial, so the ER doctor stitched them up while they waited for the surgeon."

"How is his head?"

Plummer chuckled. "Our assault suspect is more concerned about his shaved scalp than his concussion. The bullet's path was tangential to the curvature of his skull, so it didn't penetrate. But the ER surgeon shaved the right side of his head to expose the wound for cleaning and stitching."

CJ snorted. "That's perfect! The sonofabitch wouldn't let me remove his cap because it would ruin his look. He'll be mortified by the comments he's going to get in jail."

"He's got a macho problem, and when he realizes it was you who shot him, he'll go ballistic."

"I hope he doesn't know that I'm from Pine County."

Glancing at CJ, Plummer smiled. "You're probably safe. I'm not sure he's smart enough to know where Pine County is.

His turf is the West End. He might be challenged to find the university in East Duluth."

"I wonder if he got lost on his way to high school, so never went to class after eighth grade." She paused, then asked, "Where's the passenger?"

"He's being held in jail on assault charges. It'll be up to the county attorney to decide if he'll be charged with pushing Eddie around and threatening him with a knife. I assume his court appointed attorney will reach a plea agreement that will set him free with a suspended sentence."

They stopped at the break room entrance. "You've impressed me, Sergeant Plummer. I haven't heard the word tangential used since I took high school physics."

Chuckling, Plummer gestured for CJ to join Eddie and the detective at a table. "To be honest, I'm quoting the ER surgeon. Tangential is not part of my usual vocabulary."

Sliding his empty paper coffee cup aside, Eddie nodded. "Yeah, tangential and skull curvature aren't part of my lexicon, either."

Detective Ogden stood, shaking his head. "If I gave a shit, I'd look up lexicon and tangential in the dictionary." He offered his hand to CJ. "We looked at your cell phone video, and the bodycam and dashcam video provided by Sergeant Plummer and the two cops. You had a righteous shooting. The captain will convene a shooting review board, but you held your fire, and only discharged your firearm when you felt our officer's life, and the lives of the people exiting the restaurant, were in danger."

"Holy Hannah!" CJ said. "I was so focused on the driver that I didn't even notice the restaurant patrons behind your cop."

"If that scumbag had fired his Smith & Wesson before your shot hit him, chances are that some grandma trotting down the sidewalk would've been on her way to the ER."

"Or your cop would've been on his way to the ER," Eddie added.

Plummer exhaled. "Those shithead wannabe gangsters aren't known for their marksmanship. They don't know how to aim a pistol. They just spray down the area with shots and hope they hit something. I really believe they're more interested in terrorizing people than actually hitting them." He paused and gestured toward the door. "You two are free to leave."

Eddie and CJ stopped on the sidewalk outside the police station. Glancing at the nearly empty streets, CJ said, "I suppose our vehicles are still parked at the restaurant."

"I'll go back inside and ask the desk sergeant for a ride back to the restaurant."

With Eddie gone, CJ dialed the Pine County Sheriff's Department non-emergency number and left a message for the sheriff, then she dialed Floyd's home number. He picked up on the fourth ring. "Do you have any idea what time of the night it is?" he asked.

Glancing at her phone and seeing it was after midnight, she sighed. "I lost track of time. I need to report that I discharged my pistol during an incident in Duluth."

Scraping sounds followed, along with Floyd's whispered admonition to Mary, telling her to go back to sleep. "Are you okay?"

"I'm fine, but there's an idiot kid in the hospital having his shoulder repaired." She explained what led to the incident, then the details of the shooting.

"The Duluth cops said you were justified, right?"

"Yeah, the detective called it a 'righteous shooting' and said there'd be no problem when it went to their shooting review board. They have my pistol for testing. I should get it back in a couple of days."

"No civilians or cops were injured?"

"Nope. Just the dipshit driver who precipitated the incident."

"Did you try to de-escalate it?"

"I didn't even know the kid's car was there until he jumped out as I walked across the parking lot. He went ballistic when he got out of the car, and it went downhill from there. At some point, I apparently disrespected him, and that's when the gun showed up."

"What did you do that disrespected him?"

"I honestly think the problem was that I was a woman who didn't back down from him."

"I suppose that's all it takes in some guys' minds." Floyd paused. "Have you notified the sheriff?"

"I called dispatch and left a message for him. I hope that's sufficient."

Floyd blew out a breath. "I'll call his cell phone. He'll be pissed that I woke him up, but he'd be more pissed in the morning if I hadn't called him."

A police car rolled to a stop in front of CJ as Eddie stepped out of the station. "I've got to run. A cop is going to drive us back to our cars."

"Expect a call from John as soon as I get through talking to him."

Sergeant Plummer got out of the cruiser and opened the back door. "You requested an Uber?"

Ending the call with Floyd, CJ shook her head. "You can kid me now?"

"Gallows humor," Plummer said as CJ slid into the back seat. "We all use it to break the tension."

"How's your cop who shot the kid in the head?" Eddie asked as he got in on the other side of the car.

"He's putting up a good front. I suppose tomorrow he'll realize how close he came to killing that kid. It'll rattle him. If it doesn't, I know I've got a problem." Plummer paused. "Cops have to be human beings. Anyone who takes a life or comes close to it will replay the incident in their head and be disturbed by it. A cop who doesn't have empathy for the victim has a psychiatric problem. A cop without shooting remorse is some degree of sociopath and shouldn't be carrying a badge and gun."

Leaning forward, Eddie said, "Every cop has to be self-confident and prepared to draw his weapon and fire it. That doesn't make them a sociopath."

Plummer glanced in the rear-view mirror. "You're a vet, right?"

Eddie nodded. "A medic, not a soldier."

"Did anyone in your platoon ever shoot an enemy soldier?"

"Sure. We were in a couple fire fights. We had to medevac a few guys out, and we gave more than we got."

"How did the guys react?"

"Some were rattled and talked endlessly. Others…"

"I was a helicopter pilot in Iraq," Plummer said. "The sane guys did their jobs and got PTSD. Others were…natural born killers. They showed no remorse and thrived on seeing tanks blowing up and Iraqi soldiers bleeding on the ground. We all knew they were psychotic and stayed clear of them."

"Why didn't you continue flying when you got out of the Army?"

Plummer turned into the nearly empty restaurant parking lot and stopped behind CJ's car. "I couldn't hold the controls any longer. When I reflected on what I'd seen…and done, my hands shook. I have nightmares about exploding tanks and shredded vehicles with bodies hanging out of them."

They all stepped out of the idling cruiser and shook hands. Eddie put his hand on Plummer's shoulder. "I'll buy you a beer if you ever want to talk."

Nodding, Plummer stepped to CJ and put his left hand on her shoulder as they shook hands. "You probably saved a life or two today by taking the shots you did. Focus on that rather than the dipshit with a bullet in his shoulder. You stood tough when the cards were down. I'd like to think any of my cops would do the same for you."

As Plummer pulled away, Eddie blew out a breath. "I'm starving. There's a 24-hour pancake place a couple miles from here."

"You're hungry?"

"Yes! And you will be too after you rebound from the adrenaline swing. Follow me."

The cell phone rang as CJ started her car. She checked the caller ID, then answered, "Hi, John."

"What the hell, Charlene? Can't you go out for supper like a normal person and not shoot someone? Jesus, Mary, and Joseph..."

"I thought the priest scolded you for swearing."

"That was a prayer." The sheriff paused. "Floyd gave me the second-hand version. Tell me what happened."

"Having missed supper because of an idiot who instigated a road rage incident, I'm following Eddie to an all-night pancake restaurant. Can we talk about this in the morning?"

"You do remember that I'm the sheriff, your boss."

"I know that, but I really need to eat something. My blood sugar is crashing, and I need to take a deep breath. Can we talk tomorrow?" After a moment's hesitation, she added, "Sir."

After a sigh, the sheriff said, "Neither of us will be sleeping tonight. Call me when you're driving home from Duluth."

"Sure. You should probably call Sergeant Plummer of the DPD. He saw the shootout, and he can probably give you a clearer view of what happened than me."

* * *

An hour later, CJ called the sheriff as she walked to her car. "I'm sorry to have put you off, but my blood sugar was crashing, and I really needed to eat something."

Sounding wide awake, the sheriff replied, "You were probably rebounding from the adrenaline. I shouldn't have squeezed you for information at that moment."

"I'm in the car, my phone is connected to Bluetooth, and I'm on the I-35 entrance ramp. Here's what happened…" She explained how the events at the parking lot led to the shooting, her situation during the shooting, rendering first aid to the shooter, and her debriefing by the Duluth police.

"I spoke with Sergeant Plummer while you were eating supper. He said much the same thing. You, and our department, shouldn't end up being the bad guys."

"I never felt like the bad guy. I didn't even realize the dipshit in the backwards cap was angling for the parking spot I took until after I was out of the car."

"Sergeant Plummer agrees. He's going to check nearby businesses for video cameras that have a view of the parking lot."

"Is there anything else, sir?"

"I'm sorry if I came on a little strong about me being the boss. I was keyed up."

"No problem. You are the boss, and you wanted to know if the department and I would be tainted by the story before it broke on the morning news reports." CJ paused as she passed a semi going slightly under the speed limit. "I'm surprised you're concerned if you're not running for re-election."

"I haven't decided about that yet. Besides, a shooting affects the reputation of the department and the involved officers. I *do* care what happens to my people, Charlene."

"Thanks. You can get some sleep now. I'll check in tomorrow."

"Sleep in if you can. The department will get along without you for a few hours, and you'll be more useful if you've had more than three or four hours of sleep."

# Chapter 12

CJ was at her desk, re-reading her statement from the shooting, when Sandy Maki and Riley walked through the door. Riley smiled at CJ, and the momentary distraction caused him to bump into Sandy who'd stopped at the coffee machine.

"Sorry, Sandy," Riley said, backing up.

Sandy rolled his eyes as he put a pod into the coffee machine. "Would you like a cup of coffee, Riley?"

"I prefer my caffeine cold. Is there a machine with Mountain Dew around here?"

"We can stop at the gas station on the way to the highway," Sandy replied as coffee gurgled into his travel mug.

"What's your plan for today?" CJ asked.

Before Sandy could reply, Riley said, "We're serving a Domestic Abuse No-Contact order on a guy who's been beating his girlfriend."

Sandy glared at the rookie. "He's allegedly been beating his girlfriend. He's innocent until found guilty."

"If he's innocent, why did the judge issue a DANCO order?"

Rubbing his eyebrow, Sandy smiled. "I think the judge found the pictures of her bruises…compelling."

"Sandy says the guy is a hothead, and we'll have to watch ourselves."

"Would you like some backup?" CJ asked.

Riley shook his head. "Sandy's got me for backup."

Sandy pointed toward the security door. "Let's get your Mountain Dew." Pausing for a moment, Sandy mouthed, *"We'll be fine."*

After checking the clock for the fifth time in twelve minutes, CJ looked up when Floyd walked into the bullpen. "It's nearly 9:30. What time does the sheriff usually come in?"

Floyd stood, taking his empty cup to the coffee maker. "I'm not John's boss. I don't keep track of his comings and goings."

CJ looked at the clock again. "Should I continue to wait for him? The dispatcher could call me when he comes in."

Floyd popped a capsule into the coffee maker and snapped the lid shut. "Leaving now wouldn't endear you to John," he said, as coffee dribbled into his cup.

They looked at the hallway as the security door buzzed, signaling the entrance of someone. Ignoring the buzzer, CJ said, "Sandy is serving that hothead in Duquette a DANCO order. He may need backup."

With a slight shake of his head, Floyd signaled her to wait. He looked down the hallway and smiled. "Good morning, John. Would you like a cup of coffee?"

Stalking into the bullpen, the sheriff stopped at the rack of cups. He handed one to Floyd, then looked at CJ. "My office. Both of you." He turned and stalked away.

Rising from her chair, CJ glanced past Floyd and whispered, "That sounded ominous."

Slipping the sheriff's cup into the coffee maker, Floyd shrugged. "John's bark is worse than his bite."

"It looks like he didn't get any sleep."

"Yeah, I'm sure your call upset him. I assume he spoke with someone in Duluth this morning, too." The gurgling stopped, and Floyd picked up the two coffee cups and nodded toward the sheriff's office. "Into the lion's den."

Twirling an unlit cigar in his fingers, the sheriff looked up as they walked in. "Close the door." CJ closed the office door while Floyd delivered the sheriff's cup.

"What's up?" Floyd asked as they sat across from the sheriff.

"I spoke with the Duluth police chief this morning. They're convening a shooting review board in a few minutes. Since the shooting wasn't fatal and the suspect brandished, then fired his pistol, he's sure that they'll deem it a justified shooting."

"That all sounds good," Floyd said.

After sipping his coffee, the sheriff puckered his face. "I can't get that taste out of my mouth."

"What taste?" Floyd asked.

"I didn't get much sleep. I shaved, then picked up the toothpaste tube to brush my teeth. Half asleep, I didn't notice that I'd grabbed the hemorrhoid cream instead of the toothpaste."

Halfway through a sip of coffee, CJ started to cough.

"It wasn't funny," Sepanen replied. "And the taste lingers."

Grinning, Floyd leaned forward. "At least you won't have bleeding gums."

Sepanen tried to frown, but a smile twitched one corner of his mouth. "I trust that story won't be repeated outside this office."

Floyd leaned back. "I think having that story circulating around the county would humanize you. It's perfect timing before the election."

"Yeah, I'm sure people laughing about me confusing toothpaste and hemorrhoid cream would bring in a lot of votes…if I was running."

"You're still undecided?" CJ asked.

"Let's not change the subject," Sepanen said. "The DPD chief is concerned. The shooting suspect claims that you precipitated the road rage incident by cutting him off in the parking lot."

"Really?" CJ asked. "I didn't even see his car until I stepped out of my vehicle and started walking toward the restaurant."

"That's what you told their sergeant last night. There aren't any witnesses and the security camera in the back of the building only covers the rear entrance. It's your word against his."

"Put us in front of a jury," CJ responded. "No one will believe that dipshit scumbag once they look at him."

"I'm sure his public defender will put him in a suit and have his hair cut. He'll look like a fine upstanding member of the community."

Snorting, CJ rolled her eyes. "Not after they see his tattoos and hear him speak."

The sheriff stood and walked to the door. "The chief doesn't think it'll come to that. His officers are canvassing the restaurant patrons and staff. He's got a detective checking the area for security cameras. I think this will be put to bed long before it goes to court." He held the door open for CJ and Floyd.

"I sense a 'but,'" Floyd said.

Gesturing for them to walk to the bullpen, the sheriff said, "I warned Tom Bakken that someone may be filing a suit against CJ as the perpetrator of a road rage incident. He knows that it's all bullshit, but he needs to be prepared."

CJ was seething and ready to respond, but Floyd put his hand on her arm. "We've got this. The county will stand behind you. Right, John?"

"I told Tom that you were on duty, so it's not an issue of you personally being sued."

"I was out for supper with a friend..."

The sheriff stopped next to the coffee maker. "Let's be clear about this. You were discussing an autopsy with a representative of the ME's office." He set his cup on the counter and walked away.

Floyd started another cup of coffee and leaned against the counter. "I guess you're off the hook."

With one swallow, CJ finished her coffee. "I don't feel like I'm off the hook."

Down the hallway, the security door clicked, and footsteps approached. Pam stopped at the coffee machine, setting a notebook on the counter, and starting a cup of coffee. "Have you solved the murder yet?"

"Which one?" Floyd asked.

Opening her notebook, Pam flipped through the pages. "Let's talk about the naked dead body, and the hole in the Pine County Historical Museum."

Floyd grinned. "I thought Kerm solved that. Aliens were experimenting on his body and dropped it on the lawn after they completed their studies."

"Can we talk seriously about the dead kid who was found outside the museum?"

Pam asked as she sat down at her desk. "I spoke with the East Central High School Principal. Two years ago, at the beginning of seventh grade, Nick Carlton's parents notified the school they were going to home school him. They got copies of his transcripts, and the school never saw him again."

"Was there a triggering event at the school that made his parents decide to homeschool him?" CJ asked.

"Not that the principal mentioned. He said Nick's mother, Erica, showed up at school with his textbooks, announcing that she was withdrawing him from classes. The principal pointed out that state law required Nick to remain in school until he was sixteen. His mother got flustered, then said she was going to teach him at home."

Tipping his head back, Floyd stared at the ceiling. "I wonder how we can determine if Nick ever received any education after his mother took him out of school?"

After a moment of thought, Pam turned to her computer and started typing. "The State of Minnesota has stringent requirements for homeschooling. The parents have to submit an annual plan to the superintendent of their school district, including the classes to be taught, the curriculum, and a report of the student's performance on annual standardized testing." Pam looked at Floyd. "I'll call the

East Central superintendent's office to see if any of those requirements were met."

CJ finished her coffee and stood. "I'm going to check on Sandy and Riley, then take a drive around a couple of lakes."

Floyd nodded. "With gas prices as high as they are, I've been expecting reports of stolen gas cans from boats and garages."

The sheriff walked into the bullpen, catching Floyd's comments. "It's always a good idea to have our deputies drive past every house and cabin every once in a while. It keeps the bad guys guessing."

A smile crept onto CJ's lips. "Crap, I haven't driven past all the county commissioners' houses yet this week. I'll probably be fired."

The sheriff set his cup in the coffee maker and started a brew cycle. "First of all, the whole myth about driving past the commissioner's houses every shift is just that, a myth. Secondly, the county commissioners can't fire you, you're a civil servant, protected by the union." He nodded toward Floyd. "Our esteemed Chief Deputy Swenson has none of those protections. He serves at my pleasure and with the approval of the board of commissioners. He could be fired at any moment."

Brushing a piece of invisible lint from his uniform, Floyd acted nonchalant. "That's the reason I haven't wasted any time removing the sergeant's stripes from my uniforms. I could be fired at any moment." He frowned. "I would be eligible for two weeks severance pay, right?"

"You'll have to check the terms of your contract," the sheriff said as he removed his cup from the machine and walked away.

"What contract?" Floyd said to the sheriff's back.

CJ chuckled as she passed Floyd. "You have a contract?"

"Not that I know about. John called and asked if I'd fill in for a couple of weeks. I said, 'yes.' He said, 'okay.'"

"That sounds like a verbal contract to me," Pam said from her desk. "It's probably as solid as Fort Knox."

Snorting, Floyd looked at Pam. "It's not worth the paper it's written on. Oh! It's not written on paper, which makes it..."

"Worthless," Pam and CJ said in unison.

* * *

After checking on Sandy Maki and Riley, who had served the DANCO order without incident, CJ cruised the shore of Big Pine Lake. Like Kerm said when she'd first joined the department, day shift was largely an exercise in public relations.

He'd griped, "I get tired of smiling and waving to everyone I pass. Leave me on the night shift where there's actual police work to do."

CJ's moment of reflection was cut short when the dispatcher called her unit number. "A man requests assistance at fire number 41684 West Pine Lake Drive."

After acknowledging the call, CJ pulled into a driveway to reverse direction. The call was ambiguous, and given the area, she suspected a lakeshore cabin had been burglarized. Her cellphone rang as she accelerated.

"Hey, CJ," Pam said. "I asked the dispatcher to have you respond. A man called after finding a dead body in a rental cabin."

Tones sounded over the radio, dispatching the Finlayson Volunteer Fire Department and the Sandstone Ambulance. Reaching for the siren and flashing light switches, CJ sped up. "I just heard the ambulance and rescue call out. Are we talking about a possibly dead body, a definitely dead body, or a long dead body?"

Clearing her throat, as if she was checking to see if anyone was within earshot, Pam paused. "Let's say the people who discovered the body were confident they didn't need to perform CPR."

"Shit."

"They found a teenage boy in the bathtub with slit wrists."

Slowing as she passed through an intersection, CJ hesitated. "Was the kid related to the owners?"

"We didn't get that information," Pam replied. "I'll meet you there in fifteen minutes."

# Chapter 13

The fire number, also the cabin's address, was on the west side of Big Pine Lake, in an area of mostly seasonal cabins interspersed with a few year-round homes. Counting down the address numbers as she approached, CJ shut off the cruiser's siren and lights a half mile before the cabin. The area was more suburban than most people would suspect in an area full of lake cabins. Lawns, with a variety of spruce, birch, maple, and ash trees, lined the roadway providing a view of the lake beyond the structures. A couple in their mid-30s, were standing next to a Ford SUV, while three children raced around the yard playing tag.

While she announced her location to the dispatcher, CJ looked at the parents. The woman's eyes were most striking, appearing sad, stricken, and scared at the same time. *Mom's just seen something she wishes she could unsee*, CJ thought to herself as she opened the car door and stood as the children stopped their game to stare.

The woman corralled the children and led them to the dock, away from the discussion Dad was about to have with the cop. The husband, whose thinning hair blew around in the breeze, stepped up to CJ, "Um, we rented this house for a week. I wonder if we can get our deposit back?"

Judging him as irrationally rattled by the discovery, CJ dismissed the inappropriate question. "Can we start with your name, please?"

"I'm Rob McLish. My wife's name is Kate."

Glancing at the Illinois license plate, CJ made a note of the plate number. "Where's home, Mr. McLish?"

"Rockford, just south of the Wisconsin border."

"When did you arrive here?"

McLish pulled out his cell phone and looked at the screen. "About fifteen minutes ago. I'd just unlocked the door and Kate was carrying in groceries."

"Did you touch anything inside the house?"

McLish shook his head. "I mean, we touched doorknobs, but not anything inside…"

"Who discovered the body?"

"Kate carried a load of towels into the bathroom…she came right back out looking frantic."

"Did you or the children touch anything in the bathroom?"

"No, Kate shooed the kids out of the cabin while I called 911 from my cell."

Pulling on purple nitrile gloves, CJ nodded. "Please wait here while I secure the scene." A siren whined in the distance.

"Is it okay if I vape here?"

"Sure," she said, then stopped. "Just to be clear, you're vaping a tobacco product, right? Recreational marijuana isn't legal in Minnesota."

With a vaping cartridge in his hand, McLish froze. "Um, sure. No marijuana. Got it."

CJ slipped on rubber gloves as she walked to the cabin, which was the size of the three-bedroom house they'd owned before her husband's death. Opening the door, she hesitated at the threshold, sniffing the air. The metallic odor of blood mixed with the mustiness of the cabin's interior. Grocery bags covered the eat-in kitchen's table. Suitcases and duffle bags were spread around the entrance and toward a hallway. Following her nose, CJ slowly walked down the hallway, searching the floor, walls, and furnishings for signs of a struggle or blood. Seeing nothing out of place, she stopped in front of a closed door and turned the knob. Gently pushing the door open, she took in the scene. Hearing voices in the yard, she closed the door and walked outside.

A Finlayson fire truck rolled to a stop with its red and blue flashers blinking. Firemen wearing bunker gear quickly exited the truck and started pulling boxes of medical gear out of compartments on the sides of the truck. Walking past McLish, who was puffing on a vape pen with his arms crossed, CJ approached the fire chief. "You can have your crew stand down. This is a death scene."

Walt Fabin, who owned the bait shop when he wasn't the volunteer fire chief, nodded and walked to his firemen. They nodded their understanding and stowed the gear back in the slots. Returning to CJ, Fabin stared at the mother and kids who were on the lakeshore. "What do you need from us, Sergeant?"

"Try to keep the snoops away from the house while we conduct our investigation. If any news people show up, refer them to the sheriff."

Fabin chuckled. "Do you expect the sheriff?"

Composing herself and steering Fabin away from the firemen, CJ said, "You know Sheriff Sepanen. There's no way he'd pass up an opportunity to have his face on the news."

"John does love the TV cameras," Fabin said with a chuckle. Then he sobered. "Shit. I shouldn't be laughing at a death scene."

"As morbid as this sounds, cops seem to do that to break the tension." Moving away from the firemen, CJ dialed the medical examiner's office.

"CJ, are you calling to make supper plans?" Eddie Paulson asked.

"Not this time. I've got a dead guy in a bathtub. Can you and Tony come down?"

"Text me the address. I'll grab Tony and be on the road shortly." After a pause he asked, "Can you tell me anything more?"

"Yeah, I'm away from the crowd. There's a guy who appears to have slit his wrists in a tub half-full of bloody water."

"Is he the homeowner?"

"According to the people who discovered the body, they rented the lakeshore cabin for the week. I'd say it's unlikely the young man in the bathtub is the owner."

"It's a suicide?"

Closing her eyes and replaying the scene in her head, CJ paused. "Normally, I'd say, 'yes.'"

"Not in this case?"

"I don't want to influence your impression of the scene, but it doesn't feel like a suicide to me."

"You've got a guy with slit wrists in a tub half-full of bloody water, and it doesn't feel like a suicide?" Eddie asked.

"Just get down here as quickly as you can. I don't want to say anything more."

Ending her call as the ambulance arrived, CJ jogged past the fire truck and asked the ambulance crew to wait by their vehicle. The flashing lights of a second Pine County Sheriff's Department cruiser crested a hill and sped toward the scene. Pam Ryan's voice announced her arrival at the scene on CJ's radio. Behind Pam, in a third cruiser, was Floyd Swenson.

Pam edged her vehicle between the fire truck and ambulance, stopping behind CJ's cruiser. She glanced at the man smoking the vape pen, then walked to CJ, "What do we have?"

"I think someone staged a suicide scene."

Pam turned her back to the vaping man and whispered, "Staged a suicide?"

"It's not right." Gesturing toward the house, CJ said, "Put on gloves. I'll show you."

Following CJ through the cabin, Pam noted the luggage and groceries. She walked into the bathroom and immediately focused on the young man's eyes. The tip of his nose was barely out of the bathwater, but his light blue eyes were awash in the pink-tinged bath water. They were staring at the ceiling.

"What do you think?" CJ asked, distracting Pam from her focus on the victim's eyes.

Taking a moment to look around the bathroom and then refocus on the body, Pam drew a breath and exhaled. "As you said, it's not quite right. There's not enough blood." She stared at the man's t-shirt. Once white, and now tinted pink by the bloody water. "His knees are sticking out of the water, and the fabric is dry. He's been in the tub for quite a while."

"I think we can rule out the renters. There's frost on some of the groceries on the table. They haven't been here long enough to have killed him and wait for his jeans to dry before dialing 911."

"Have you interviewed the two adults?"

"I talked to the man in the driveway, the one sucking on the vape pen. His wife was keeping the kids occupied away from the cabin. The wife found the body when she carried towels into the bathroom."

Pam followed CJ out of the house, then stopped on the steps. "There's no blood anywhere except in the tub."

"But there is water on the bathroom floor."

Pam nodded. "The tub might've overflowed when he got in."

"Or a killer may have sloshed the water when he was wrestling the body into the tub."

Floyd Swenson joined the deputies on the steps. "Murder or suicide?" he asked.

Stripping off her rubber gloves, CJ shrugged. "I don't think it's a suicide."

"What do you think, Pam?" Floyd asked.

Pam shrugged and said, "I think we need to talk to the woman who found the body." Looking toward the lake where the mother and children were skipping stones, she added, "Will you interview her, CJ? I'll distract the kids."

Floyd put his hand on CJ's arm as Pam walked toward the shoreline. "Is there any point in me looking at the scene?"

After a moment's hesitation, CJ shook her head. "It's best if we minimize the traffic through the cabin until the medical examiner gets here."

Taking out his cell phone, Floyd nodded. "I'll have the sheriff request a Bureau of Criminal Apprehension forensics team. Then, I'll release the ambulance and fire department. They're just standing around, and their vehicles are blocking the narrow road."

Following Pam down the gentle slope to the lakeshore, CJ watched the children react to the sight of two uniformed officers approaching. The mother was facing the lake and didn't react until the children rushed around her like chicks running to a mother hen for protection. She looked tense, pulling the smallest child close and putting her other hand on the middle child's head. Her face softened when she saw Pam's disarming smile.

Kneeling down to be eye-level with the children, Pam reached into her pocket and took out several pieces of paper. "Who would like to be a junior deputy sheriff?" she asked as she peeled a sticker printed with a police badge and applied it to the middle child's shirt. The girl looked pleased.

The smallest child, a boy about five, raised his hand. "Can I have one?"

"Sure," Pam replied, peeling off another sticky badge. "I see a dead fish by the next dock. Do any of you think you can tell me what kind of fish it is?"

"Eww!" the girl said while her brothers ran toward the white fish belly bobbing in the gentle swells.

Pam led the girl by the hand toward the fish. "Don't worry, I won't make you touch it like my brothers did to me."

The mother watched Pam and the kids as they jogged to the nearby dock. "Kate, can you tell me what happened after you arrived at the cabin?"

The mother looked at CJ as if she'd forgotten there was a second deputy. "Um, sure. We started unloading the SUV. The kids wanted to check out the lake, but we made them carry in their bags, then they helped carry in the groceries."

CJ took out a notebook and made notes. "Was the cabin locked when you arrived?"

"Um…I don't know. The VRBO people gave us a code to use for the lock box. Rob opened the door while I unbuckled Brett."

"Did you notice anything when you walked in the first time?"

"I was a little put off because the house smelled kind of musty, like it had been closed up for a long time. I set the groceries down and opened the windows to air it out."

"At what point did you look in the bathroom?"

"Rob was putting the groceries into the refrigerator, so I opened the suitcase of towels and washcloths and carried them into the bathroom."

"Tell me what you saw?"

Kate stared at CJ, the color draining from her face. "At first, I thought someone had pulled a prank on us, dropping a mannequin and some red food coloring in the bathtub. Then I saw the guy's wrists…" Kate wrapped her arms across her chest, then turned away from CJ and gagged.

Waiting patiently for Kate to compose herself, CJ watched Pam and the children. They'd found the floating fish and were bombarding it with stones.

Kate composed herself and drew a breath. "I've never seen a dead body before. I mean, there were aunts and old neighbors who we saw in caskets, but never one…"

"It's a shock, even for cops." Pausing to shift topics, CJ took Kate's elbow and led her farther from Pam and the children. "Describe the bathroom to me."

"I suppose it was just a basic bathroom. It needed an update from the '80s tile and brass fixtures, but it seemed clean and okay."

"Did you notice if there were footprints or water on the floor?"

After closing her eyes, Kate cocked her head. "Um…I think there was some water on the floor. That's why I looked at the bathtub, because I thought maybe the drain was clogged."

"What's the first thing you noticed?"

"Jeans."

CJ stopped making notes and looked at the woman. "What do you mean?"

"I saw jeans. It took me a second to realize they were knees sticking up."

"Then what?"

"I guess I took a step closer to see why there were knees sticking out of the tub. It seemed so odd…out of context."

"Then what?" CJ asked.

"I saw his face. That's when I thought someone had pranked us by putting a mannequin in the tub. His eyes…" Kate paused, composing herself. "They reminded me of a mannequin, kind of staring. And his face was white. Then I looked at his wrists and…lost it."

CJ put her hand on the woman's arm. "I'm sorry to put you through this, but I need to know the details. They'll help us understand what happened, and the water on the floor helps with my timeline of events."

"I've never seen a suicide victim before. He seemed so…calm. Is that the way they all look when they're gone?"

The question caught CJ off guard, causing her to flash back to memories she'd suppressed. She thought to herself, I can't tell this woman how terrible death scenes are. She's a suburban soccer mom, living in a quiet community, going on Minnesota vacations with her kids. She has no idea of the drugs, criminals, or crime scenes I deal with on a daily basis.

"Sergeant Jensen?"

Snapping back from her thoughts, CJ smiled. "Sorry, I had a thought about a different case." With her notebook and pen poised, CJ asked, "What did you do then?"

"I must've stepped back and closed the door, you know, so the kids wouldn't see him. Then, I pushed Mac outside, and he dialed 911."

"Mac is your husband?"

"Yeah, that's his nickname. You know, McLish became Mac when he was a kid."

"Did either of you go back into the bathroom or touch the body?"

Kate looked shocked. "God, no!"

After noting the McLish's address and phone number, CJ thanked Kate and let her retrieve her children. Pam walked over as CJ finished making notes. "I assume she's a mess."

Closing her notebook, CJ nodded and said, "She's going to have nightmares."

"Yeah, that bathroom will be one of the things I wish I could unsee." Pam watched the McLish parents, who were trying to have a conversation while keeping the children at arm's length. "What's your take on Mrs. McLish? Should we keep them around as potential suspects?"

"They've got bags of groceries and a cooler full of frozen food. They had no idea there would be a dead guy in the cabin they rented. Look at Kate, she's barely keeping herself together, and the husband isn't much better off. I've got their contact information. I think we should let them grab their belongings so they can try to find another vacation rental."

Shaking her head, Pam said, "If that was me, I'd pack up the car and turn toward home. This is a vacation they'll remember forever…and not in a good way."

Clenching her eyes shut, CJ uttered, "Shit."

"What?" Pam asked.

"We have to preserve the crime scene. Their personal belongings are in the living room, bedrooms, and kitchen. We can't allow them inside the cabin until after the BCA evidence team processes the scene."

"The BCA won't be here for hours, and it'll take them half a day to collect and bag evidence." After a moment of thought, Pam snapped her fingers. "We have an on-scene incident commander. We don't have to make that decision."

CJ struggled to contain a laugh as the McLish family stood nearby, arguing about how to salvage the remainder of their two-week vacation. She turned toward the lake and pretended to cough. "Good thought! Go ask the chief deputy how to deal with crime scene preservation. I'm going to check the shoreline."

"Why are you checking the lake shore?"

"I don't want to have an inappropriate outburst of laughter when you dump that hot potato on Floyd."

Pam stepped in front of CJ, so their noses were nearly touching. "Okay, smartass, we're doing this together. Put on your straight face and follow me."

"I'm the smartass?"

"Yes," Pam hissed. "Your giggles are contagious, like a yawn. I can't talk to Floyd while watching you laughing by the shore. Come on."

CJ drew a breath and composed herself. "Yes, Deputy Ryan, you're absolutely right. I need to be professional and control my laughter."

"Stop that. The family is staring at me, and you're just about ready to burst out laughing…again."

"Sergeant Jensen," Mac McLish called out as he approached them. "Can we get our luggage and leave?"

Turning toward the husband, CJ shook her head. "We can't allow you back inside the cabin until the crime scene techs do their work. We were just discussing how to deal with that."

Pam nodded her agreement. "Let's speak with the chief deputy. I'm sure he'll have a solution."

The threesome approached Floyd Swenson, who was talking on his cellphone. After ending the call, he acknowledged them. "What's up?"

"We'd like to let the McLish family leave so they can make other plans for their vacation," Pam explained. "But their luggage and groceries are inside the cabin, and we have to maintain the crime scene."

Floyd nodded and addressed the husband. "I sincerely apologize for this distasteful episode. I hope this doesn't taint your view of Pine County, Minnesota. I agree that we have to protect the crime scene, so we can't let your family into the cabin. But there's no reason Sergeant Jensen and Investigator Ryan can't carry your bags and groceries out."

McLish looked at Pam and CJ, "You're willing to do that?"

Having seen some huge suitcases, CJ's mind raced, trying to devise a plan for dealing with them. She smiled and said, "It's no problem at all, Mr. McLish. I'll pack the refrigerated items in your cooler while Deputy Ryan carries out your bags."

"Thank you. I'll have the children carry them from the steps to the SUV."

Pam walked shoulder to shoulder with CJ as they approached the cabin. "Why do you get to unpack the refrigerator while I lug out all the heavy bags, Sergeant?"

"Because you're younger and stronger."

Pam held the door while CJ pulled on rubber gloves. "I'm only seven years younger than you and I had a kid less than a year ago. My abs are just past the Jell-O stage."

"Perfect! Lifting those bags will help you whip those abs into shape. Remember to lift with your legs, not your back."

"Right," Pam said, pulling the door closed. "Don't pack the freezer items too slowly. I wouldn't want you to get frostbite on your fingers."

"That won't be a problem. There's not that much in the freezer. It's going to take some time to pack all that pop and beer into the cooler. There are hundreds of cans. I'll have to go slowly so I don't drop any."

Pam glowered at CJ, "Don't overfill the cooler. I wouldn't want you to hurt your back."

"I thought we'd do a buddy lift on the cooler."

"You leave me with all the heavy stuff, then expect help with the cooler?"

CJ looked around. "Wait. No problem. They saved all the cardboard 12-pack sleeves."

# Chapter 14

The family carried the bags and cooler from the cabin steps to their vehicle. The dad loaded the last bag as the medical examiner's black SUV pulled up. Mac looked up as Tony Oresek stepped out.

"Is that your detective?" he asked CJ.

"Dr. Oresek is the medical examiner."

The oldest son perked up. "Can we watch them carry out the dead guy?"

Kate placed her hand in the center of the boy's back and pushed him toward their SUV's open rear door. "We are not hanging around while they deal with the man's body."

Mac looked at CJ, Pam, and Floyd. "I don't suppose any of you know where we could find a different two-week lake rental?"

After a moment of hesitation, Floyd said, "Have lunch at Crazy Mary's Café, in Finlayson. Ask the waitress and the other patrons. I suspect they'll know someone who's willing to rent out a lake place for a couple of weeks."

Without thanking Floyd, the husband stalked to the SUV and started the engine as the rest of the family buckled their seatbelts.

They pulled out of the driveway, spitting gravel as the SUV accelerated.

Eddie Paulson, wearing white coveralls, was pulling on rubber gloves as he approached CJ and Pam. "Was that the family who were renting this cabin?"

"Yeah," CJ said as she watched the family's SUV speed away. "They weren't pleased about the inconvenience of finding a dead body."

Eddie nodded. "It was darned inconsiderate of that guy to die in their rental."

After a grimace, CJ sighed. "That was inappropriate."

The ME overheard the conversation as he approached. "Working in the morgue with no live audience leaves us calloused, making comments inappropriate for public consumption."

"Having watched quite a few autopsies, I can see how your gallows humor seems humorous. However, those of us who live in the outside world have a different threshold for dead body humor."

Tony looked around, making eye contact with each of the others. "Huh. I don't see anyone but cops and morgue people here. Are you guys suddenly embarrassed by our comments?"

Chuckling, Floyd shook his head. "The problem is that it's easy to get caught up in your jargon, then let an inappropriate comment slip over dinner."

"What?" Oresek asked. "Your wife doesn't like an autopsy replay over spaghetti and meatballs?"

"No," Floyd replied.

Pam raised her hands. "I'm out, too. My husband saw too many battle wounds, and now there's a kid who will undoubtedly repeat any profanity or gruesome observation I utter."

Eddie laughed and looked at CJ. "Remember that couple who overheard us talking about an autopsy at the brewpub?"

Nodding, CJ said, "The woman turned green, and the guy nearly spit up his beer. They threw a couple twenties on the table, then left half a pizza. They spoke with the manager on their way out. He sat down with us and requested that we change the conversation."

Tony gestured toward the cabin, signaling the end of his tolerance for socializing. "Let's look at the body."

CJ led the group through the cabin, opening the door and stepping back so the ME and his assistant could enter the small bathroom. She and Pam looked over Eddie's shoulder as Dr. Oresek bent down and took in the scene. After a few moments, he pinched the body's upper arm, then lifted one hand before gently setting it back into the bathtub.

After a moment of contemplation, the ME looked up. Seeing CJ looking over Eddie's shoulder he asked, "What's the sheriff's department betting odds on the cause of death?"

"We don't…" CJ stammered.

Oresek waved off CJ's response. "What do you think killed the victim?"

"I…ah…defer to your expertise and experience."

Standing, the ME's lips twitched, as close as he ever came to a smile. "Eddie, get a body bag and the gurney."

After stepping aside to let Eddie pass, CJ and Pam stepped into the bathroom. "Do you have a preliminary cause of death?" CJ asked.

"Tell me what you see, Investigator Ryan?"

"A young male, maybe in his late teens. His wrists are slit, and it appears that he committed suicide."

Nodding, the ME turned to CJ. "Do you agree with that assessment?"

Feeling like a kid being called on in class, CJ cleared her throat. "I'm not convinced it's a suicide."

"Why do you say that? The victim's wrists are clearly cut."

"I feel unqualified…"

"Come on, Sergeant. How many suicides have you seen? How many autopsies have you watched? You have an opinion. Speak up."

"First of all, the knife with the body is a serrated steak knife. Having cut my finger with a sharp knife and felt a lot of pain, I think cutting my wrists with a steak knife would be incredibly painful—probably painful enough to make me rethink that approach to killing myself."

Oresek raised his eyebrows. "Impressive deduction. What else?"

"The tendons of both wrists are cut through. With cut tendons, he wouldn't have been able to grip the knife to cut the second wrist."

"Any other observations?"

CJ shook her head. "I'm out."

Pam leaned closer to the tub. "There's not enough blood in the tub. The water is pink. If he'd bled to death in the tub, there would be a layer of burgundy-colored blood settled in the bottom of the tub."

"Very good," the ME said. "I'd also expect some tentative cut marks on the wrists. Most people don't realize how deep they have to slice their arms to hit a vein, or how much it hurts. They usually make some tentative cuts before making the bigger slice that yields more than a trickle of blood. I'm convinced this scene was staged to look like a suicide by someone who hasn't watched many CSI television shows."

"What killed him?" Pam asked.

"We won't know for sure until we do the post-mortem exam."

Craning her head to see past the ME, CJ said, "He looks almost peaceful. I wonder if he died of an overdose, and his buddies staged the suicide so we'd focus our attention away from them?"

"There's a lot of opioids being distributed in the area," the ME said. "I see at least one overdose death a week. The dealers are bumping the oxycodone potency with fentanyl, making it more deadly."

Floyd, who'd been listening from the doorway, said, "Yeah, we're awash in Mexican drugs that come up I-35. We have quick killing opioids, and other people dying slowly from meth."

Pam blew out a breath. "It's nuts. These kids don't understand that they're risking their lives for an addictive high. As they're doing it, they're spending a fortune, mostly from robberies and hold ups."

Oresek, never shy about gallows humor, replied, "Yeah, Eddie and I would be playing cribbage all day if not for all of the drug and alcohol related deaths. And you cops would be bored."

Glancing at Floyd, CJ said, "I'd be happy to live with some boredom rather than racing to drug overdose calls and DUI car crashes. I've seen enough dead bodies."

The rattling of the gurney announced Eddie's arrival. The cops all stepped away from the bathroom, allowing Eddie and the ME to remove the body from the bathtub. Motioning for CJ and Pam to follow him outside, Floyd noticed the news van raising the dish mounted on its roof. "The vultures have arrived."

CJ watched as a blonde broadcaster touched up her makeup. "I'm sure happy the chief deputy is here for the interview."

Floyd glared at her. "The sheriff made it clear that he wants you to be the face of the sheriff's department. No one wants to see my grizzled old mug on the television."

CJ wrinkled her nose. "I doubt they're any more interested in seeing a woman in her 40s. Maybe Pam should take this one."

"Nope," Floyd responded. "You're it, CJ. You look professional and seasoned. Your sergeant's stripes convey responsibility, and you rarely stick your foot in your mouth."

Pam's eyes sparkled. "Yeah, you hardly ever let loose with a string of profanity or make politically incorrect comments…unlike Floyd."

Gesturing for them to keep their voices down, Floyd whispered, "I rarely curse."

"But you regularly spout off inappropriate comments about your female co-workers."

"You know I'm just kidding."

"CJ," Eddie called from inside the cabin. "Can you come in here?"

Eddie and the ME were both wet as was the floor. The victim was in the open body bag. Because of rigor mortis, the dead man's knees were still bent.

"What's up?" CJ asked.

The ME held out a cell phone in his gloved hand. "There's nothing in his pockets to identify the victim, but this phone was inside his underwear."

Accepting the phone, CJ frowned. "Not in a pocket?"

"No, it was jammed in the front of his underwear, as if he was hiding it from someone. Too bad it's been immersed in water for hours, or you might've been able to identify him."

Slipping the phone into an evidence bag, CJ said, "Maybe the BCA will be able to get something off the SIM card."

Although generally oblivious to social issues, the ME glanced into the living room while Eddie zipped the body bag. "Is the family gone? They shouldn't watch us roll out the gurney."

"The family is gone, but a news crew arrived a few minutes ago."

Oresek shrugged. "The newsrooms are usually adept at editing anything that's not appropriate for the six o'clock news."

"Better yet," Eddie said, "distract them. Drag their broadcaster to the corner of the cabin so the cameraman has a shot of the lake in the background while she interviews you."

"Um, I was hoping the sheriff would conduct the interview."

The ME pushed the gurney into the living room. "Whatever you're planning, make it quick. I need to get this body into the cooler ASAP."

CJ pushed past the gurney and trotted out the front door. Seeing only Pam and Floyd in the yard, she waved to the blonde broadcaster and pointed to the nearest corner of the cabin. Excited that she had someone to interview, the blonde moved quickly to the cabin with her cameraman close behind. He framed the picture of CJ and the broadcaster with the lake in the background as the ME and Eddie eased the gurney down the steps.

Holding the microphone aside, the blonde leaned close to CJ. "Remind me of your name and title." A moment later, she pushed a stray hair back and cleared her throat before nodding to the camera. "We're in Pine County at the scene of a tragic death. Sergeant Jensen, of the sheriff's department, was the first officer on the scene. Sergeant Jensen, what can you tell us about the tragic death?"

"Our dispatcher received a call reporting a deceased person at this location. When I arrived, I found a deceased person in the bathtub, and I contacted the Duluth Medical Examiner."

"You found the victim in the bathtub. Was it an accidental drowning?"

Looking somber and shaking her head, CJ replied, "We'll have to wait for the medical examiner to make that determination."

"Do you suspect foul play, or was it an accident?"

"I'm not qualified to make that determination. We'll await the results of the autopsy."

"Have you identified the victim?"

Taking a second to suppress a smile, CJ looked earnestly at the broadcaster, who knew the victim's identity couldn't be released. "We're withholding the victim's name pending notification of family members."

The broadcaster asked a few more inane questions that she knew CJ couldn't answer, then she turned to the camera. "Broadcasting live from Pine County, this is Callen Jardine."

"Are we done?" CJ asked.

"Come on, Sergeant. Couldn't you throw me a carrot I could use as a teaser?"

"I'm sorry Callen, but the investigation has just begun and…"

Jardine put up her hand to stop the cameraman, who was ready to walk away. "You said, 'investigation'. Does that mean there was something suspicious about the death?"

"Investigation is a generic term used to describe the process of gathering information."

"Surely you can at least tell me if the victim was male or female and make an estimate of the time of death."

"I'm sorry, but I can't divulge that information until we've notified the family. None of us want them to find out about the loss of a loved one on the evening news."

The broadcaster nodded her head, but her eyes said she'd be happy to divulge as much information as possible to "scoop" the other news outlets. She took a business card from her blazer pocket and handed it to CJ, "Please call me first when you have information."

"It's really the sheriff's role to make media notifications. I was just bringing you up to speed on the situation."

"Yeah, it's been great. I've got a nice shot of the lake with no information about the victim, the cause of death, or when he or she died. My producer will love it." Jardine hesitated while the cameraman gathered his gear and walked away with the microphone. "Off the record, was the victim male or female?"

"I can't say."

Jardine's eyes lit up. "Are you saying that the body was so badly decomposed that you couldn't tell if it was a man or a woman?"

CJ smiled. "No comment."

Floyd and Pam walked down to the cabin as the broadcaster ran to the van while punching numbers into her cell phone. Pam smiled and said, "I don't know what you just told her, but it looks like she's so excited she's about ready to pee her pants."

"She interpreted my 'no comment' statement about the victim's sex as meaning the body was too badly decomposed to identify."

Pam looked shocked, "Why didn't you correct her?"

"She knows the rules and was being a bitch by trying to get an out of bounds comment from me. I think it's only fitting that she's going to put that misinformation on the air."

Smiling, Floyd put his hand on CJ's shoulder. "You've learned your lessons well."

"Yeah, Floyd, I have."

Pam laughed. "You're going to let Floyd take credit for teaching you that?"

"He's old. He won't remember tomorrow."

The sheriff arrived as the news van lowered the dish. He walked to the group of officers as the van pulled away. "They're done?"

Floyd nodded. "CJ did an impressive job of avoiding all the questions. You'll be proud when you see her on tonight's news. I'd swear she was running for sheriff if I didn't know otherwise."

The sheriff waved his arms. "She's welcome to the job whenever she wants. It's a pain in the butt."

"Oh no," CJ said. "I am NOT running for sheriff. Don't even start that rumor."

The sheriff pulled a cigar from his pocket and unwrapped it, signaling the end of that discussion. Looking a little grayer and more haggard than he had in his early terms, he'd remained a strong candidate against anyone running against him. His deep voice played well on television, and the department's impressive arrest record made him a local celebrity.

Rolling the cigar between his fingers, he asked, "What do we have?"

Both Pam and Floyd looked at CJ for the answer. She spent the next few minutes updating the sheriff as he nodded and asked questions. "We won't know what killed the victim until the ME does the autopsy."

"It's definitely not a suicide?" the sheriff asked.

After a moment of hesitation, CJ replied, "The evidence says no."

"What's the plan?" the sheriff asked.

Pulling out a notebook, Pam said, "I've identified the cabin's owners, who live in the

Cities. There's a chance that the victim is their son or a friend, so I left a vague message asking them to call me. The BCA crime scene van is on the way with an ETA of an hour."

The sheriff looked at CJ. "How about you, Charlene?"

Bristling at being called by her first name, but knowing that correcting the sheriff, again, wouldn't change anything, CJ took a breath. "I'm waiting for a call from the ME's office. I'll attend the autopsy as soon as it's scheduled."

Turning to Floyd, the sheriff asked, "What's your plan?"

"Crowd control."

Looking up and down the row of cabins, the sheriff didn't see a single person. "What crowd?"

"You know how it goes, John. One minute there's no one around. The next minute there are people trampling the murder scene. It's a tough job, but I'm up to it."

Pam coughed to cover her laugh, and CJ turned toward the cabin and bit her lip. The sheriff drew a breath, then laughed. "I've missed your politically incorrect comments and wry wit. Welcome back, Floyd."

"I missed hanging around with the deputies."

"Not me?" the sheriff asked.

Licking his lips, Floyd composed his thoughts. "To be honest, you're a little overbearing and pompous. I can take or leave that."

The sheriff reached out and touched the sergeant's stripes on Floyd's uniform. "I told you to remove the stripes."

"And I told you that if you weren't running for re-election, I wasn't going to be in the job long enough to make it worth the effort."

"For once, would you just humor me? Remove the stripes. Better yet, buy a couple new shirts."

"There's no point in buying uniform shirts that I'm only going to wear for a few weeks."

Turning to CJ and Pam, the sheriff frowned. "If either of you ever speak to me like that, I'll have your badge."

Floyd stepped next to CJ. "You can't fire them without just cause. Me, on the other hand, can be gone if you just say the words, 'you're fired.'"

Shaking his head, the sheriff bit down on his cigar. "Get off your high horse, Mr. Chief Deputy. I'm just speaking my mind."

"Do you remember my comment about you being pompous?"

Removing the cigar from his mouth, the sheriff pointed it at Floyd. "Don't make me call Mary."

Pam's phone buzzed, ending the discussion. She stepped away and put a finger in her left ear to block out the sound of a passing dump truck as she answered the call.

"Is there something else, Sheriff?" CJ asked.

The sheriff pulled out his wallet and handed CJ a $20 bill. "Buy Floyd a cup of coffee and a doughnut when you clear the scene. That should keep him out of my hair for a couple of hours."

"Why do you say things like that?" CJ asked Floyd as they watched the sheriff walk to his car.

"I've known John a long time, and sometimes he needs to be reminded that he can't walk on water."

"Geez, Floyd. You're talking about the county sheriff."

"He puts his pants on one leg at a time, just like the rest of us. Someone needs to remind him of that. Besides, I'm bulletproof."

"Bulletproof?"

"Metaphorically speaking, I'm bulletproof. Short of firing me, there's nothing John can do to punish me. We both know he won't do that. Besides, this is what Mike Smith, the former chief deputy, did. Granted, he and John spoke behind closed doors. Mike used to tell John the things no one else in the department dared say. Sometimes, the emperor needs to hear that he's not wearing any clothes."

"You poked him in front of Pam and me. Isn't that pushing the limit?"

Taking CJ's elbow, he steered her away from Pam. "I won't be here forever, and whoever is sheriff needs to hear things like that from a senior officer. That could, or should, be you."

"ME? I'm not going to tell the sheriff off."

"Someone has to play that role." Floyd paused. "And John respects you."

"I can't even get him to call me CJ."

"That's symbolic of his respect for you. He understands that you're trying to reinvent your professional life here. But John wants you to know that he's not just one of the guys. He's someone connecting with you on a different level than the other deputies and jailers. Respect that."

CJ clenched her jaw and glared at Floyd. "Only my mother calls me Charlene."

"I think that's the message he's trying to deliver. John's trying to be your mentor."

"I don't know whether you're blowing smoke up my butt or if you're serious."

After glancing at Pam, who was having a subdued phone discussion, Floyd said, "I'm very serious. John thinks you represent the future of this department. Keep that in mind."

An approaching car slowed and eased to the side of the road. Floyd smiled. "I guess you can save the sheriff's money for later. Mary's here to take me out to lunch."

Mary's car was barely stopped when she opened the door, releasing Bailey. The basset loped across the yards, her ears flopping as if she was about to take flight.

"Oh, geez," CJ said, stepping behind Floyd. "Bailey's been cooped up too long, and she's ready to play."

Slowing as CJ hid behind Floyd, Bailey spied Pam and redirected her route. Oblivious to the approaching dog, Pam continued her phone conversation. CJ's warning came too late, giving Pam enough time to turn toward them, but not enough time to brace herself for Bailey's onslaught.

"Bailey!" she yelled, as the dog plowed into her legs like a football player throwing a block. Pam lost her balance and fell backwards, her phone flying out of her hand. Feeling nothing but joy, Bailey licked Pam's face.

While Floyd laughed, CJ rushed to Pam's aid, tugging at the dog's trailing leash. "Bailey, heel!"

Her jeans covered with white and brown dog hair; Mary approached Floyd. "I suppose I should've warned everyone before I released the dog."

Freeing herself from the slobbering show of affection, Pam pushed herself to her feet and brushed grass clippings from her pants. "Give me some warning," she said as she looked for her phone.

Circling in excitement, Bailey wrapped the leash around CJ who was hopping, trying to avoid the entanglement. "Stop it!"

After wearing herself out, Bailey sat, her tongue dripping slobber.

Mary looped her arm inside Floyd's elbow and smiled. "I should warn you, CJ. Don't bring Bailey inside the Sandstone grocery store."

"Why would I do that?" CJ asked, bending down to adjust Bailey's K-9 vest.

Mary bit her lip. "It seemed too hot to leave her in the car. And, they have a sign that says service dogs are welcome."

CJ looked up in horror. "You didn't…"

"It was going pretty well until the woman stocking lettuce bent down to pet Bailey."

"Oh no…How much damage did she do?"

"There wasn't much physical damage, but there was a lot of excitement when the potato chip display got knocked over. People ran out of the office to help, then Marchell and Craig came to remove the cardboard display that was trashed."

"Please tell me you're kidding."

Mary's pained smile answered the question.

"How much do I owe for the damage?"

"Krystee said not to worry about it. The cardboard display was supplied by the potato chip company, and they'd replace it the next time the representative came through. None of the product was actually damaged, although I'm sure some of the chips inside the bags were broken." Mary smiled at the dog. "Bailey seemed really contrite while the mess was being cleaned up."

Floyd shook his head. "Why did you bring her inside the store?"

"Bailey has that K-9 vest, and the sign says that service dogs are welcome."

Hearing her name, Bailey's tail started to wag, and she released a fart.

Tugging at his ear, Floyd grimaced. "The vest is symbolic. Wearing it doesn't transform her from holy terror into a well-behaved police dog."

Wiping the dog slobber from her face with a tissue, Pam joined the group. "The BCA mobile crime lab will be here in about fifteen minutes. I warned them about our out-of-control K-9 partner."

CJ pointed her finger at Floyd. "It's your fault. If you hadn't given me that stupid vest at the horse show…"

Floyd put up his hands. "I thought the children would be amused. I never intended for Bailey to be viewed as a real police dog."

Hiding her smile, Pam said, "Next time, buy her a seeing eye dog vest. No one would mistake Bailey for a guide dog."

"Hey!" CJ said. "I never intended for Bailey to be any variety of service dog."

Floyd wiped the tears of laughter from his eyes. "I'm glad you've lowered your expectations."

* * *

After two hours of mundane patrol, Floyd called CJ's cell phone. "Meet me for lunch at the Floppy Crappie."

CJ turned north and wound through backroads to the out-of-the-way pub overlooking Pokegama Lake. The Floppy Crappie parking lot had a few cars and two pickups. CJ backed the cruiser into the back row and stepped out just as Floyd pulled into the parking lot.

"What inspired you to pick this place?" she asked as they walked toward the lake where the entry door was located.

"It's quiet, the food is good, and I didn't want to break your budget when you bought me lunch."

"I'm buying lunch?" CJ asked, holding the door open for Floyd. "You're the one making big bucks on the chief deputy's salary."

Floyd chose a table with a view of the lake. A long bar with three patrons drinking beer was to their left, and the rest of the dining room was to their right. "It sounds odd, but the sheriff never mentioned a salary when he asked me to fill in as chief deputy."

A middle-aged waitress appeared with menus in hand. "Wouldn't you prefer a table closer to the lake?" She asked as she handed them menus.

Floyd smiled at the waitress. "We prefer the cheap seats, Carmen."

Carmen took their drink orders, and Floyd handed her his menu. "I'll have the usual."

"BLT with extra bacon," Carmen said as she wrote on an order pad. "And for you, ma'am?"

"Chef salad with Italian dressing."

"Two checks?" Carmen asked as she noted CJ's order.

"Dad's buying," CJ said.

Carmen slid her glasses to the tip of her nose and looked over the top of them at CJ, "As I recall, Floyd doesn't have any children."

"He adopted me as an adult."

When Carmen left, CJ leaned close. "You seem to know Carmen pretty well."

"I arrested her for a DWI about twenty years ago. A year later, I removed her from a domestic assault situation and got her into a women's shelter."

"You turned her life around."

"Carmen had one of the few pleasant outcomes from my career."

"Yeah," CJ replied. "Most of the people I've arrested are either in jail, or they hate me."

"Like I said, Carmen is one of the few pleasant outcomes. We need to embrace those successes."

While their lunches were delivered, Floyd asked Carmen, "Are you doing okay?"

"Yeah," Carmen replied, wiping her hands on a towel. "I'm renting a place in Stanchfield, going to AA meetings twice a week, and dating a guy who sells culverts and trailers. Life is good."

Spreading a napkin on his lap, Floyd smiled. "He's not beating you up?"

"We're both in the AA program. Somehow sobriety seems to take the edge off a lot of things that used to precipitate fights." Carmen paused. "It took me a while to realize that dating bad boys led to bad outcomes. I'm happy with a nerdy guy who works hard and treats me like a queen."

CJ nodded her agreement. "It took me a while to discover that being married to a nerd was much less stressful than making excuses for the dirtbag bad boys who treated me like crap."

"So, you're happily married?" Carmen asked.

The smile melted from CJ's face. "I'm a widow."

Carmen set their bill next to Floyd's plate. "Maybe you'll meet someone."

"I'm still in love with my husband."

Carmen's eyes sparkled, and she glanced at Floyd. "Too bad you didn't meet a nice older sergeant before he fell in love with the flower shop owner." Then she left.

Floyd swallowed a bite of sandwich and stared at CJ. "I bet you've never received relationship advice from a waitress."

"Floyd, I've been given relationship advice from everyone. The sheriff teases me about dating Eddie. Pam tried to set me up with one of her bachelor uncles. My elderly neighbor has a cute, divorced son. Hell, just about everyone but me thinks I need a man in my life."

"I've never wanted to be anything but your friend."

CJ snorted. "My friend who constantly throws out politically incorrect comments about my clothing, my life…and my dog."

"What have I ever said about that fart generator you named Bailey?"

"That's exactly it! You couldn't just let the comment die without making a snide remark about my basset hound."

Floyd lowered his voice. "Our jobs are intense. You need me to lighten things up once in a while."

Rolling her eyes, CJ took a forkful of her salad. "If you weren't a lovable old curmudgeon, I'd write you up for harassment. Be careful; there's a fine line between curmudgeon and dirty old man."

Changing the topic, Floyd asked, "What are your thoughts about the kid found dead at the museum?"

Sighing, CJ nodded. "If not for the pickup crashing into the museum, I suppose we might've found his body in the Kettle River downstream from Banning State Park in a couple of days."

Carmen picked up the cash Floyd set out to pay for their lunch. After a moment of hesitation, she leaned forward and put her hands flat on the table. "You know that saying, 'if you see something, say something?'"

"Something's bothering you?" Floyd asked.

"We had a pack of bikers in here yesterday. They brought in a couple of underage girls and tried to get the bartender to serve them beer." Carmen looked around to see if anyone was listening. "I've seen enough abused women to know those two girls weren't with the gang by choice."

"Are they staying in cabins here?" CJ asked.

"They're squatting at the Parkers' place, near the county road. They took down the for-sale sign, and the yard is full of their motorcycles and an SUV."

"Did you contact the realtor?"

"Mrs. Parker's kids tried to sell it themselves. They live on the west coast and didn't believe the realtor when he told them how little a house with swampy acreage is worth here in Pine County. I think they gave up and went with a realtor."

Floyd nodded and thanked Carmen. As they walked out of the door, he said, "Let's see if the bikers are still around."

"You don't think this has anything to do with the bodies we found, do you?"

"In my experience, bikers like to use fists and knives. A drowning would be out of character. Trying to cover up a murder seems way too complicated." Floyd stopped alongside his cruiser. "On the other hand, who knows?"

* * *

A set of tire tracks cut through the weeds growing in the Parkers' gravel driveway. Wood smoke curled into the quiet air a quarter mile away, above a barely visible roof. CJ followed Floyd's vehicle, the weeds scraping the bottom of her cruiser. As they neared the house, she announced their location to the dispatcher, stopping thirty yards from the building. She parked diagonally, blocking the driveway.

The bikers barely looked up as Floyd and CJ got out of their vehicles. A few whispers went back and forth as one of the bikers stirred the campfire with a stick. "I think they have guilty consciences," Floyd said.

"Seeing cops sucks the fun out of some parties," CJ replied.

"I think a cop showing up sucks the fun out of *all* biker parties."

"I'd love to have probable cause to search their pockets," CJ said as they approached the campfire. "I'll bet $20 they've either got an unlicensed gun or drugs."

"I wouldn't take that bet," Floyd replied.

Met with the scent of marijuana smoke, CJ sighed. "We get all these people who drive up from Minneapolis, and they think the laws don't apply once they've crossed Highway 694."

"It's not just the weekend people," Floyd replied. "We've also got all the jack pine savages who want to live off the land like it's 1800."

Floyd took the lead as they approached the campfire where five men wearing leather jackets with motorcycle club logos sewn on the back sat around on pails and pieces of wood. The men glanced among themselves, trying to appear nonchalant. An assortment of tattoos were visible on their arms and necks. The common themes seemed to be gang logos, skulls, and knives.

A biker with graying hair flicked the stub of his marijuana joint into the fire as CJ neared. "Hi, guys. Are you just up here camping, or have you done some fishing too?"

A biker resembling a stocky Willie Nelson, looked up. "What do you care?"

"We're just making sure everyone is happy and safe." Floyd looked around. "I guess you must be camping. I don't see a boat or fishing gear."

The oldest biker rolled his eyes. "We're good. You can leave."

"Are you renting the house?"

Two of the bikers chuckled, but no one answered.

"The last time I drove past, there was a FOR SALE sign next to the driveway. Did you buy the place?" Floyd asked.

One of the bikers snorted. "It's a rental. We're here for the week."

Looking toward the house, CJ asked, "Is this a boys' weekend, or did you bring your wives and girlfriends?" No one answered. A tattered drape fluttered in the living room as someone peeked out. "Do you mind if we look inside?"

"Actually, we do mind," a younger biker with greasy hair, jeans, and hands replied.

"We could get a search warrant," Floyd said.

Spying the realtor's for-sale sign in the weeds, CJ walked to it. She turned it over and punched the realtor's phone number into her cell phone while Floyd tried to strike up a conversation with the bikers. After a brief conversation with the realtor, CJ joined Floyd.

"The realtor says the house should be empty. It's not a rental, and they haven't given anyone permission to use the house."

"We contacted the owner. She probably didn't tell the realtor," The oldest biker said without looking up from the fire.

"Funny you should say that. The realtor said the owner died. Maybe you had a séance." CJ waited for the bikers to stop chuckling. "The realtor granted us permission to inspect the house for damage."

Floyd hesitated, watching the seated men as CJ walked to the wooden front steps. The weathered boards showed only a hint of white paint in the wood grain, and they creaked under CJ's feet as she climbed up to the wooden porch. She knocked once on the door. "Sheriff's Department!" she called out as she opened the door without waiting for a reply.

A middle-aged biker sat at a dusty Formica table with his arms over the shoulders of two teenage girls. His smile was more of a challenge than a greeting. The girls were dirty and dressed in long-sleeved shirts that had probably been refused by a thrift store.

"What's up?" the man asked.

"We were told you tried to buy beer for these obviously underaged girls."

"I think you were misinformed."

Walking around the end of the table, CJ stood next to the nearest young woman. "Can I see your ID please?"

The man next to her smiled, revealing several missing teeth. "We all left our wallets in Minneapolis. Tell the nice officer that you're over twenty-one, Lila."

The girl turned toward CJ but didn't meet her eyes. "I'm twenty-one."

"What year were you born?" CJ asked.

The girl hesitated, obviously trying to do math in her head.

CJ looked at the other girl. "What year were you born?"

The biker turned to her and attempted to kiss her. When she turned her head aside, he whispered something as Floyd walked into the kitchen, where he stood with the door open so he could watch the men sitting at the campfire and provide cover for CJ.

The girl, who'd resisted the biker's kiss, fidgeted. "1999."

"You don't look twenty-four," Floyd said.

The girl looked at her fingers while trying to count backward. After failing to come up with a different answer, she looked at the biker. "What year was I born?"

CJ took a step forward and put her hand on the nearest girl's arm. "Please come with me."

Recoiling from CJ's touch, the girl asked, "Am I under arrest?"

CJ looked at the girl's stringy blonde hair, her dirty hands, and broken fingernails. "I'm taking you into custody. We'll have your parents pick you up at the jail."

The other girl, taking advantage of the distraction, jumped up from her chair, barely escaping the grasp of the biker. She took three steps, so a chair separated her from the table.

Half the size of the biker, and probably twice his age, Floyd smiled and walked behind him, forcing the man to turn in his chair to keep watching him. "Your friends threw you under the bus. They claim that you're the one who's been taking advantage of the girls."

The biker continued to smile as CJ led the blonde girl out of the kitchen into the living room.

"Nah, they wouldn't throw me under the bus, and the girls are here by choice. No one is keeping them here against their will."

Sobbing sounds in the living room caught the biker's attention. CJ returned with the blonde girl. "Lila says you bought her from a La Crosse pimp. She's fifteen."

The biker was unruffled. "That's quite a story. I've never been to La Crosse, and Lila told me she was twenty-one."

CJ walked behind the biker and looked into an open drawer in the cabinet. "I don't suppose any of these syringes have your fingerprints on them."

"I've never seen them before."

Floyd walked toward the brunette girl, keeping the biker distracted from CJ who was guiding the blonde toward the door. He said, "When we confirm that these girls are under sixteen, you'll all go to jail for rape and the sale of drugs."

The biker stood, expecting Floyd to back away. "I think you'd better get back into your clown car and drive off."

Floyd sighed like he was tired of the discussion. "You know that's not happening. I can't leave the girls with you. I suspect that one or more of you and your buddies are carrying illegal guns or drugs. Maybe we should check with the guys around the campfire."

"Maybe you should be more concerned about your health," the biker said, smiling as he clenched and unclenched his fists.

Floyd slipped his pistol from its holster. "You *do* understand that you're not locals, and there are no witnesses in this house. Being city bikers, there's not a jury of farmers in this county who'd do anything but pat me on the back if I shot you. They'd thank me for thinning the herd."

The black-haired girl made a chirping noise to Floyd's left. "Husky has a switchblade in his pocket, there are guns in the SUV, and Max has brass knuckles."

Floyd gestured for the biker to walk outside. As the biker moved toward the door, Floyd whispered to the girl, "Are you okay?"

She grabbed his arm and broke into tears. "Get me away from here."

As CJ jogged to her car with the two girls, Floyd faced the circle of bikers. "Because of the girls' statements, I now have probable cause to search you. Not knowing which of you are Husky and Max, who have the knife and brass knuckles, I'll have to search all of you."

The biggest biker stood, clenched his fists, and took a step toward Floyd. "Go ahead, search me."

With the girls in her car, CJ pumped her shotgun, chambering a round. The sound froze the men who had gathered shoulder to shoulder in front of Floyd. CJ jogged to his side. "Okay, boys, put your hands behind your heads and face away from us," she said, aiming the shotgun at the big man who had taken a step toward Floyd.

"You can't shoot us," the man said.

"You're about to assault the chief deputy. I *can* shoot you. And this shotgun has no choke, so I'll probably hit three, or maybe four of you. Hands behind your heads. NOW!"

The man who'd tried to kiss the girl jammed his right hand into his pocket. Floyd raised his pistol and aimed it at the biker's chest. "Unless you want a hole in that nice leather jacket, you'll ease your empty hand out of that pocket slowly. Otherwise, I have to assume that you're pulling a gun."

The biker hesitated, looking at his buddies. The biggest biker sighed. "We're all going to walk away. No harm. No foul. You two county yokels can do whatever you want with the girls. We'll get our gear and leave."

"They kidnapped Chloe from Brooklyn Center and raped her," CJ said. "They offered her a motorcycle ride, then drove straight here. She told me she's been passed around to the whole gang for three days."

A siren whined nearby, and the bikers glanced among themselves, like they were planning an escape. Then, they turned toward CJ as if preparing to rush her.

Spreading her feet to improve her balance, CJ pointed the shotgun's muzzle at the nearest biker. "I can put six shots into a silhouette in five seconds. Who's first?"

Floyd took a step back while keeping his gun raised. "I'll back away to avoid the blood splatter," a comment that riveted the biker's attention.

As if on cue, a cloud of dust and a whining siren preceded Deputy Sandy Maki's arrival. Jogging to the campfire, he drew his pistol while calling for additional backup on his radio.

Floyd pointed at a beefy biker. "Okay, Husky. Empty your pockets on the bucket beside you." Drawing his taser, Floyd held it next to his leg.

"Are you talking to me?" the biker asked, pointing to his chest.

"Yep. I figure that you're Husky, and you have a knife in one of your pockets. Set it on the bucket."

The biker crossed his arms. "Fuck you."

Floyd aimed the taser at the biker's torso. "Have you ever been tased? I hear it's extremely unpleasant." When the biker didn't respond, Floyd shrugged. "Three, two, one."

With a pop, two darts flew from the taser. One struck the biker's upper arm. The other hit his chest above the leather jacket. He collapsed instantly and laid on the ground twitching with his eyes rolled back in his head while gagging. The other bikers backed up until they were against the campfire.

After pulling on rubber gloves, Floyd ran his hands over the twitching biker's jeans. Feeling the knife, Floyd put his hand into the man's front pocket. He withdrew the knife and pressed a button which caused the knife blade to snap open. "Well look at that, CJ. It's an illegal spring-activated switchblade." Reinserting his fingers into the man's pocket, he pulled out a small plastic bag. "And this looks like it might be an illegal substance."

Moving closer to Floyd, CJ kept the shotgun pointed at the remaining bikers. "Max, put the brass knuckles on the bucket closest to you."

When none of the bikers responded, CJ nodded to the second biker. "You should wear looser pants if you don't want people to see the outline of the brass knuckles in your pocket. Or is that the point? You want people to see the brass knuckles."

The biker made a face like he'd bitten a rotten apple. Using two fingers, he removed a set of brass knuckles from his front pocket. He held them out to CJ.

"Set them on the bucket. And, if any of the rest of you have a weapon, drugs, or a needle, set them on the bucket, too."

Floyd snapped his handcuffs on the tasered biker, then stood. "Listen, boys. All of you empty your pockets and hand over IDs. We're going to call in for wants and open warrants, then we'll process you through the jail."

The biker with missing teeth smiled. "Lawyer."

Sandy Maki stepped forward. "You'll be able to make a call from jail."

"You can't arrest us," the biker said.

"We can arrest at least two of you for having illegal weapons. The rest of you have been accused of rape and are refusing to identify yourselves. We can hold you until you either provide identification, or until we determine your identity from your fingerprints. I hope you ate lunch, because your next meal will probably be the jail breakfast."

"Our lawyer will have us out of your backwater jail before we hang up the phone."

Floyd smiled. "I suspect your Minneapolis lawyer couldn't find Pine County on a state map. Hell, he might end up in Fergus Falls or Bemidji. It might be a week before he even finds the courthouse to attend a bail hearing."

"Yokels," the smallest biker said, holding out his wrists. "If you want to know what's in my pockets, have that woman cop run her hands over me."

CJ shook her head. "I'll pass."

Pam Ryan's cruiser pulled into the driveway. She jogged up to the group as Sandy Maki put plastic handcuffs on the men. "Husky Redmond, I just saw a warrant for you. The judge wasn't pleased when you didn't show up for your drug sentencing."

"Shit. We're in that county?"

Pam smiled. "It's a state-wide arrest warrant. Judge Peale in Kanabec County revoked your bail, so you'll be a guest of our county until you're shipped to Mora for sentencing. I imagine there'll be additional charges because you skipped bail."

* * *

Floyd followed CJ into the bullpen where they both made cups of coffee. CJ blew out a breath as she sat in her desk chair. "I hate dealing with bikers."

"They push boundaries," Floyd replied, sitting in CJ's guest chair.

"Boundaries? I don't think that bunch knows any boundaries."

Pam joined them, collapsing into her desk chair. "I delivered the two girls to the Sandstone hospital. The female physician's assistant in the ER took a quick look at them, then summoned Dr. Mlankoch. They shooed me out of the exam room, but Doc Mlankoch briefed me after his exam. "They're both strung out on something, probably heroin, and both had… 'experienced multiple sex partners.' He sent them to North Memorial. He hoped they'd be able to locate a teen residential treatment facility because they're both experiencing withdrawal."

CJ tipped her head back and whispered something.

"Are you praying?" Floyd asked.

"If there's a loving God, how can he allow things like this to happen to kids?"

Floyd stared into his coffee cup, weighing his words. "It's hard to see adults who've made poor life choices, but when the victims are kids…"

Pam nodded. "Those girls are really messed up, both physically and mentally. They can go through rehab, but they'll never have a 'normal' life."

Floyd grimaced and nodded. "Most of our citizens don't realize that there are evil people out there preying on innocent teens."

Pam nodded. "My criminal justice professor put it really well when he said that 95% of people are sheep, unaware of the evil wolves waiting to prey on them. Then, there are the 4% who've been abused, robbed, beaten, raped, and more. They're the ones who shy away from the wolves. The rest of the folks just go about their lives oblivious to the wolves until they walk into a situation where they become the victims."

Floyd cocked his head. "That only adds up to ninety-nine percent."

"We're the other one percent," Pam replied. "We're the cops who try to keep the sheep from becoming victims."

CJ nodded. "I see young people walking around Minneapolis laughing and oblivious to the predators around them. It makes me want to scream."

Pam slid her coffee cup around her desktop, making circles. "Those girls won't ever testify against the bikers. They're strung out and terrorized. They couldn't take the witness stand. A good defense lawyer would shred them."

Floyd looked resigned. "I'll talk to Tom Bakken, the county attorney. He might be able to use the threat of the rape kit evidence and the testimony of the treating doctors to get a plea bargain, so the girls won't have to testify."

CJ looked at Pam. "I hope your children will be smarter than those girls."

Rolling her eyes, Pam replied, "I'm going to keep them locked in their rooms until they're thirty."

"They?" Floyd asked. "You're planning on having more than one?"

"I hate talking around you, Floyd. One slip of the tongue and you pounce on it like a lion on raw meat."

CJ leaned on her knees. "I'm not surprised that you're considering having more than one child. I wish…" She stopped talking and her eyes teared up. "Never mind."

"It's not too late to adopt kids," Pam said, sliding her chair close to CJ.

"I'm not raising kids alone while working rotating shifts, and I don't see any marriage prospects on the horizon."

Floyd raised his eyebrows. "Eddie."

Shaking her head, CJ drew a breath. "He's a friend, and that's really what I need him to be. We're both a little too seasoned to be changing diapers."

Floyd smiled. "Friendship is a good starting point for a great relationship. We've all discovered that as we've matured. Raging hormones and flaming romances make great movies. The reality is that the best thing you can do is marry your best friend."

Draining her coffee cup and standing, CJ said, "I value Eddie's friendship too much to mess it up with romance." She checked the clock. "I've got another hour before my shift ends. I'll see you two tomorrow."

After buying a frozen dinner from the gas station, CJ retrieved Bailey from doggy daycare. After dinner and a walk, they curled up on the couch and watched the first episode of *Longmire*, a television series based on the character created by Craig Johnson, a Wyoming mystery writer.

# Chapter 15

CJ's phone rang while she was having coffee with a group of local businessmen at Crazy Mary's Café. Excusing herself, she answered as she walked to the front door. "Hi Eddie, what's up?"

"Does the name Bob Olsen mean anything to you?"

Glancing around to make sure no one could hear her, CJ said, "He's the county assessor who's hospitalized with food poisoning. Why would *you* ask?"

"His body was just delivered for an autopsy."

"He died?"

Chuckling, Eddie replied, "We don't usually do autopsies on live patients."

"Jeez, I sometimes wish you would tone down the gallows humor."

"Sorry. I thought…anyway, his body is here. Tony's going to cut this afternoon."

"Did the attending physician give a cause of death?"

"The paperwork says, 'cardiac arrest after multiple organ failure.' The cause of death was listed as undetermined."

"The doctors assume he suffered some type of poisoning. They haven't been able to identify the toxin."

"I've been reading the hospital notes. They tested for every common food poisoning toxin and most common poisons without identifying the chemical."

"He's been hospitalized for days. What are the chances that you'll be able to find a toxin after this length of time?"

"It depends on the chemical. Some flush out of the patient's system quickly. Others, like heavy metals, are stored in the brain, liver, and muscle tissue. I'll test his liver, kidneys, and brain tissue for residual toxins, but the doctors have ruled out all the easy chemicals."

"There was that spy who was poisoned in England..."

"I seriously doubt that the Pine County tax assessor was poisoned by the KGB with a designer chemical from a Russian lab. There was also a former Russian spy who was dosed with polonium and died of radiation poisoning. I think it's safe to rule that out, too."

CJ blew out a breath. "Yeah, I doubt the Russians are interested in Pine County property tax issues."

"You're assuming this has something to do with his job as the tax assessor. Maybe there was something going on in his personal life that got him killed. Have you checked to see if he was into drugs, deeply in debt, or had a gambling problem?”

“You’re right. We may have narrowed our focus too much.” Pausing, CJ watched a couple get out of an older Buick and walk into the restaurant. “I’ve been more focused on the guy who was found in the bathtub, assuming Bob was going to eventually recover.”

“About that…as you expected, the guy didn’t die from slit wrists. He drowned.”

“He drowned in the lake, then someone dragged his body into the cabin and slit his wrists to cover up the drowning?”

“The water in his lungs was well water, not lake water.”

“Okay, so he drowned in the bathtub and…”

“I’m testing the water. I’ll know more tomorrow.”

“Tomorrow?”

“Meet me for supper at the Mexican restaurant in Cloquet.”

“Will you have the water testing results?”

“No, but I’ll buy you a margarita that’ll make you more patient.”

* * *

CJ patrolled the west central portion of the county while mulling Eddie’s comments about the drowned body found in the summer cabin. Pulling into the empty parking lot of the rural Dell Grove Lutheran Church where her mother had grown up, CJ punched in Floyd's cell phone number.

"How's the new K-9 recruit working out?"

With a heavy sigh, she replied, "Bailey's just fine, but her role as the sheriff's department K-9 is…inappropriate."

"Think of her as the goodwill ambassador."

"She can do that as long as we don't bring her inside any stores and restrict her contact to people who don't mind slobber and farts. By the way, Eddie is buying me supper in Cloquet, and I plan to be off duty unless rioting breaks out in Pine City."

"Try not to get into a road rage incident over a parking spot."

"You're extremely helpful, Captain Obvious. I can't tell you how much I appreciate your words of direction and encouragement."

"No problem, Sergeant Smartass."

Smiling, CJ drove away from the church parking lot and thought, *I can't tell you how much I had missed your banter while you were retired, Floyd.*

* * *

After walking and feeding Bailey, CJ had an earnest discussion with the dog. "I'm going out for supper, and I won't be back for a couple of hours. You've been entertained today, so I want you to behave yourself. No chewing up anything and no surprise puddles or piles. Do you understand?"

Bailey, who was pleased with the focused attention, stared up with sad eyes while wagging her tail. Sensing that her conversation was as effective as speaking to a piece of furniture, CJ tied on her running shoes and walked to the door. Hearing Bailey's tail thumping, she looked back and realized that the dog was staring at the leash hanging on a hook near the door.

"We've already walked. I'm going out for supper." Closing and locking the door, CJ looked heavenward. "Please let her behave tonight."

Startled by a chuckle behind her, CJ turned. Her gray-haired neighbor, Blanche Venberg, was shaking her head. "You know that dog is going to do whatever dogs do."

"I know," CJ conceded. "I always hope that she'll grow out of this puppy stage and wait patiently for my return."

"Good luck with that."

Aware of the relatively thin walls between the apartments, CJ grimaced. "I hope Bailey doesn't howl or bark after I leave her alone."

Touching her ear, Blanche said, "She only makes noise for a few minutes. I turn down my hearing aids."

Using the mindless drive up the interstate as an opportunity to think, CJ mulled the three recent deaths. Reflecting on conversations they'd had before her husband's death CJ thought, *Bobby always said there were no coincidences in law enforcement. I don't see how these three deaths are connected, but I shouldn't discount the possibility that there's a connection I haven't seen.*

Eddie was standing outside the restaurant when CJ parked. "How long have you been waiting?"

Shrugging, Eddie held the door. "A few minutes."

"I would've been here earlier, but Bailey and I had an earnest talk about not chewing up anything while I was gone."

"Does that usually work for you?"

They followed the hostess to a table. "Not really, but I feel like I've given it my best effort."

A harried waitress rushed to their table. "Has anyone taken your drink orders?"

"I'd like a light margarita," CJ said.

"Um…light? I don't think we make a low-calorie margarita."

Eddie leaned forward. "Light as in a half shot of tequila. I'll have a Corona."

Noting their order, the waitress said, "That's a first. Most people order doubles, not half the booze."

"I don't have a designated driver," CJ replied before the waitress scurried away.

Surveying the other diners, Eddie commented, "I don't think many of these people have designated drivers, either."

"I bet the waitress or bartender cuts them off before they're unable to drive."

Raising his eyebrows, Eddie looked at the booth next to them where four noisy women were pouring from their second pitcher of margaritas, the first pitcher sitting empty next to the wall. "I'd take that bet."

"I'm off duty, and Cloquet is outside of my jurisdiction. Let's talk about something else."

Eddie smiled. "We've already talked about your discussion with Bailey. What else have you got?"

Their discussion stopped when the waitress delivered their beverages and took their dinner order. Staring at CJ, she said, "The bartender made a light margarita. He hopes it tastes okay because he's never mixed one with half the tequila."

Taking a sip, CJ nodded. "Tell him it's good."

Their dinners arrived on hot plates. Smoke rose from Eddie's fajitas as the meat sizzled in the cast iron pan. "Do you need drink refills?" the waitress asked.

"Thanks, I think we're fine," Eddie replied.

After unrolling the napkin wrapped around her silverware and making sure the neighboring tables had returned to their discussions, CJ leaned forward and whispered, "What else should I know?"

"I sent Bob Olsen's liver tissue samples to the FDA for analysis. I'm convinced he was poisoned, and they're better equipped to test for obscure toxins." Spearing a piece of meat, he waited a moment while it cooled. "Have you considered the possibility that your three deaths are connected?"

Nodding, CJ said, "I'm struggling to see how two drowning victims found fifty miles apart are connected. I can't envision how a tax assessor's poisoning is related to the drownings."

Eddie smiled while he chewed. "I suppose I'm accustomed to seeing the worst in people. My job makes me cynical and suspicious. That happens when you're a witness to the dark underbelly of life."

CJ waved off his comment. "I'm a cynical cop."

"You are, but my cynicism has risen to a far higher level. I've seen the worst of what one person will do to another. I distrust everyone and everything."

"You trust me..."

"Granted, I trust you and Tony, but everyone else is a suspect until proven otherwise."

Lifting her margarita glass in a toast, CJ said, "To cops and other cynics."

The waitress saw the gesture and came to their table. "Are we celebrating something tonight?"

Eddie nodded. "Absent friends."

Not recognizing the traditional military toast to friends killed in action, the waitress frowned. "You should've invited them along."

After glancing at Eddie, CJ nodded and said, "They weren't available."

"Bring them along next time. Maybe one of them would be the designated driver so you could have a full-strength margarita," the waitress said before leaving.

"Yeah," Eddie said, lifting his beer. "Bring Pam along as the designated driver next time so you can drink a pitcher of margaritas."

The women at the neighboring table split the last of the margarita pitcher between their four glasses and gestured for the waitress to bring another.

CJ shook her head. "I saw a logo on a girl's t-shirt. 'Tequila. Helping people wake up in strangers' beds since 1521.'"

The smile melted from Eddie's face as he watched the waitress retrieve the empty pitcher. "I hope I don't see any of their faces in the morgue tomorrow."

The waitress appeared with the manager, who politely explained that the restaurant wouldn't refill their pitcher, instead offering a pitcher of soda pop. The women booed and asked for their check.

"I'd be happy to call an Uber to take you home," the smiling manager said.

Giving Eddie a pained look, CJ removed the badge in her pocket and showed it to the women. "Take him up on his offer of an Uber, or I'll arrest the first one of you who puts her keys in their car's ignition."

The manager winked at CJ, then he led the unhappy women toward the lobby.

"I thought you were off duty and out of your jurisdiction?" Eddie asked.

"They were too drunk to notice that my badge wasn't local."

As they finished their meals, the manager appeared with a flan that he set between them. "Thank you."

"We didn't..." CJ protested.

"The ladies are in an Uber, safely on their way home. Thanks to you, there wasn't much argument or fuss. Enjoy the flan." The manager was about to turn away, then stopped, and rolled up his sleeve, revealing a Marine Corps logo tattoo. "Absent friends," the manager said, repeating the traditional military toast to fallen comrades.

"Iraq?" Eddie asked as he scooped up a spoonful of the custard.

"Iraq. Kosovo. Back in Iraq. I got around."

As the manager stepped back, CJ said, "I expect to pay for the flan."

The manager studied CJ's face for a moment. "Weren't you a Cloquet cop?" He snapped his fingers. "Charlene Johnson…or Carlson?"

"I was Charlene Holm in a previous life."

"Yes. You were a year ahead of me in high school, then you became a Cloquet cop." The manager's smile melted. "I was sorry to hear about your husband. Absent friends." The manager stepped away as the waitress delivered their bill.

Eddie took the bill from the waitress and handed her a charge card. He leaned across the table and whispered, "The flan wasn't on the bill."

"You'd better tip our waitress well. I doubt the drunk women left a tip after the manager refused to refill their margaritas."

Grinning as the waitress returned with the charge slip, Eddie picked up the pen and signed the receipt. "Gee, Mom, that hadn't occurred to me." He wrote in an amount equal to food and beverage total on the tip line, then totaled the amounts. "Ready to go?" he asked as he stood.

Eddie walked CJ to her car. Instead of unlocking it, she leaned on the passenger's door. "Sometimes I hate being a cop. Anyone else would've let the women drink another round."

"What's wrong with saving someone's life?"

"We don't know…"

"That's the nature of prevention. You don't know what might've happened if you hadn't stepped in. Worst case scenario was that all four would've been killed when their car hit a tree."

"No, the worst case would've been them hitting a family minivan and killing a couple kids." Pulling her car remote from her pocket, CJ clicked the lock release. "I suppose I should go home and see what havoc Bailey wreaked on my apartment while I was away."

"Thanks for a nice dinner. You're much better company than frozen pizza and stupid reality shows on TV."

Grimacing, CJ said, "Please tell me you're not watching some sappy show about people locked in a house together."

"I don't watch much broadcast TV. I prefer the History and Discovery Channels."

"Wow. Watching fake gold miners is so much better than seeing who's being voted off the island."

Eddie pointed his finger at her. "How do you know about those things if you're not watching them yourself? Hmm?"

CJ laughed as she got in the car. *I've been busted.*

# Chapter 16

CJ walked into the bullpen and picked up the coffee cup on her desk. "We're working on Bob Olsen's murder today."

Pam looked away from her computer. "I thought he died of food poisoning."

"The autopsy was inconclusive beyond his multi-organ failure. Tony Oresek thinks he was poisoned. Eddie's having his tissues tested for foreign substances."

"He was hospitalized for a couple of days," Pam said, "Wouldn't any poison have passed out of his system or metabolized in that period of time?"

"Apparently our livers filter out toxins until they're metabolized. Eddie's hopeful there will be at least traces of the poison left there."

Pam shuddered. "That makes me feel so good about the beef liver my mom made us eat after we butchered cattle."

"I like fried liver and onions," Floyd replied.

"Eww!" CJ said, grimacing. CJ slid her cup in the coffee maker after Floyd removed his. "The Duluth hospital ruled out all the common food poisoning agents as soon as he arrived at the ER. They moved through the list of less common bacteria and chemicals quickly, leaving an unknown, more obscure poison as the probable culprit."

"Well, crap. It'd be so much easier to track down a bowl of tuna salad that had been left out of the refrigerator, than to find a poisoner who's smart enough to use something other than rat poison or Drano." After the end of the brew cycle, Floyd walked to CJ's guest chair and sat down.

Following him, she sat, looking perplexed. "Why are we sitting here, in the bullpen, when you have an office?"

"Force of habit," he replied. "This feels comfortable, and the office feels claustrophobic."

CJ lifted Floyd's cup and slid a coaster under it. "Did you have something specific you wanted to discuss?"

"Without the cooperation of the two girls, Tom Bakken says he's unwilling to file charges against the bikers, so they'll be released. Their lawyer is threatening to sue the county for harassment."

"Bullshit. They'd broken into the house and were trespassing. One had an illegal switchblade, another had brass knuckles. There were four guns without serial numbers in their van. I bet they're stolen and have been used in crimes."

Pam leaned toward them. "Don't forget the drugs we found in their pockets and the drug paraphernalia in the house."

"Tom's plate is full with the recent drug busts at the motel and rest area. He's not interested in prosecuting the bikers."

"But the girls…" CJ pleaded.

"The girls are in no condition to be cross-examined. They'd crumple…if they were even willing to testify."

"Shit," CJ said. "We can testify about their ages, appearance, and the needle tracks on their arms. The hospital took rape kits so there's DNA evidence."

Floyd stared into his coffee. "I pointed out those things to Bakken, but he's unconvinced that's enough to get a conviction."

Pushing her coffee cup aside, CJ stood. "I've got to get out of here. It may take a while for me to get my head around this."

Deep in thought, Pam stared at her computer. "We watched an episode of a British mystery series last night. A man ate poisoned mushrooms, and he died days later. Maybe someone fed Bob poisoned mushrooms."

"I thought poisoned mushrooms killed almost instantly," Floyd replied. "People who eat magic mushrooms have immediate hallucinogenic symptoms."

"The mushrooms in the television show were called destroying angels. They apparently kill your kidneys and liver slowly and painfully."

"I assume that show is fictional," Floyd replied. "They can make up whatever fits the plot."

Pam typed a search into her computer. "Here they are. Destroying angel mushrooms are in the genus amanita. Wikipedia says, 'Symptoms do not appear for 5 to 24 hours, by which time the toxins may already be absorbed, and the destruction of liver and kidney tissues is irreversible. As little as half a mushroom cap can be fatal. The symptoms include vomiting, cramps, delirium, convulsions, and diarrhea.' It also says they're easily confused with button mushrooms and other edible species."

CJ tipped her head back. "I just deleted mushroom hunting from my bucket list."

"Ask Eddie if they looked for mushroom amatoxin."

Taking out her cell phone, CJ punched in a text. "I assume that's already been checked, but I asked the question."

"Maybe Bob was a mushroom hunter," Floyd suggested.

Feeding on the conversation Pam said, "Or, maybe Bob's wife was a mushroom hunter, and she fed him a deadly mushroom."

"Pam, those are great questions you can pose to his wife when you ask about Bob's life insurance and financial situation."

"I thought CJ was…"

Floyd glanced at CJ. "Sergeant Jensen is the patrol sergeant. You are the investigator. She's going to patrol while you investigate."

"Floyd, I'm swamped with the two drownings. I don't have time to investigate Bob Olsen's death."

CJ cocked her head. "Eddie suggested that the drownings might be linked to Bob Olsen's death."

Shaking her head Pam said, "Wait. Wait. Wait. Bob was poisoned and the two young men were drowned. I don't see any connection between those deaths at all."

After a moment's contemplation, Floyd said, "Eddie had an interesting point. It's coincidental that all three men died in Pine County within the span of a few days. My experience is that there are no coincidences in law enforcement."

"Fine," Pam said as she made notes. "I'm on this. The two of you need to leave so I can concentrate."

* * *

Alissa Preston read the last of Bob Olsen's report on the commune. Leaning back, she contemplated the commune, its tax status as a religious property, and Bob's report that "something fishy is going on out there." She'd seen the commune members shopping in town, wearing old-fashioned clothing. The women were always accompanied by a man, and the teenage girls were usually accompanied by someone older. *That's odd, because every other teenager I see is in a group with people their own age*, she thought.

Picking up Pam's business card, Alissa considered driving to the commune, then realized there was nothing visible there. She dialed Pam's cell phone, which rolled over to voicemail. "Hi, Pam. This is Alissa. I want to talk to you about the commune."

Alissa had just picked up a note from her boss when her phone rang. "County Attorney's office."

"Liss, you left me a message."

"I barely hung up."

"I was on the office phone. What's up?"

"Have you ever seen a teenage boy with the commune people?"

"I don't understand your question."

Alissa opened the commune file. "I've been reading Bob Olsen's complaint about the commune. Beyond his view that there's something 'not right' about the commune's finances, there's an anomaly. Have you ever seen a teenage boy with a group of people from the commune? He's seen young women, but they're always accompanied by older men."

"I haven't paid any attention..." Pam paused while pieces of the puzzle started coming together.

After a few moments of silence Alissa asked, "Did I lose you?"

"Sonofabitch," Pam uttered. "I think you just uncovered the motive for murdering the two young men we found this week."

"What?"

"The commune doesn't need young men. They have older men who need wives."

"You've lost me, Pam."

"Imagine that you're running a commune, and you have unmarried older men, either bachelors or widowers. How do you find brides for them?"

"Using a matchmaker?" Alissa guessed.

"No. You remove the young men from the commune, making the young women available to marry the older men."

"They're a religious group, Pam. They wouldn't kill off teen boys."

Pam chuckled. "You're not cynical enough yet, Liss. Tell your boss what we just discussed."

Alissa knocked on Tom Bakken's doorframe, distracting him from a document he was studying. "What's up?"

"I just had the strangest conversation with Pam Ryan. She thinks the two young men who were found dead this week were killed by the commune so the teen girls could marry older bachelors and widowers."

Bakken leaned back, holding a pen in both hands. "Bob Olsen said something was strange, but he couldn't figure out what seemed wrong. Maybe the commune leaders thought Bob knew more than he did, so they had to kill him."

Alissa was shaking her head. "I can't buy into that theory. People don't go around killing off others because they need brides."

"Alissa, welcome to the world of sociopaths."

"Sociopaths?"

"Some people will do anything, even kill another person, to get what they want."

"There aren't really people like that out there."

"Sadly, there are quite a few of them. Finding and prosecuting them is our job."

Alissa shivered. "I'm not sure I'll be able to sleep tonight."

"Go down to the sheriff's office and talk to Pam Ryan or Floyd Swenson. Tell them we're with them one hundred percent, and we need to strategize how to put together a prosecution of the commune leaders."

"But I don't know what we're strategizing about..."

"We're going to help them solve two murders." Bakken paused. "And you were right, you're not going to sleep tonight because you'll be in the office scouring records, strategizing, and drafting search warrants."

Emotionally steaming, CJ drove out of the law enforcement center parking lot and onto Highway 61. Turning north, she drove through the town of Beroun, staying on what had been the main highway between St. Paul and Duluth before the construction of I-35.

*Maybe I should get a different job, one where I don't get shot at, spit on, and sworn at.*

Abandoning that thought, she focused on the two young men whose bodies had been recovered in Askov and Finlayson. *How can those two deaths be any more different, yet tied together by the water in their lungs? And are they related to the tax assessor's death?* A thought flew into her head as she drove through the town of Rutledge, now nearly a ghost town after it was bypassed when I-35 was built in the '60s. She pulled into the parking lot of a closed gas station and tipped her head back. Flashing back to a criminology class, she recalled the professor's lesson. "There are very few types of crime that aren't usually repeated by an offender. Rape, burglary, robbery, and car theft are often repetitive crimes that occur in geographic clusters. The criminals are often high school dropouts who are rearrested for the same crime within four years of their release. On the other hand, murders are usually one-time crimes. They're often committed by more educated criminals who have carefully planned their crime, making it more difficult to identify, arrest, and convict them. The one factor in favor of the investigator is that murderers are usually known to their victims."

CJ blew out a breath and contemplated the murders of the two young men. *Murderers are usually known to their victims. Crimes occur in clusters. Criminals are often high school dropouts.*

Startled by a knock on her window, her head snapped around. A middle-aged man with a well-worn shirt and blue jeans was staring at her, looking concerned. She rolled down her window. "Can I help you?"

"Are you okay?" he asked. "I mean, you kinda looked like you were passed out."

CJ glanced at the pickup covered with ladders, idling behind the man. The logo on the door advertised a construction company operated by two brothers in a nearby town. "I'm fine. I was just thinking."

The man straightened up like his back hurt. "That's good. I just wanted to make sure…" the man paused. "We're all a little creeped out by the dead teenagers. I wanted to make sure you weren't hurt."

Smiling, CJ nodded. "You just reminded me that there are genuinely nice people around here who have my back. I appreciate that."

"We like seeing a sheriff's car drive through once in a while. If I ever see one of you cops in trouble, I'll help."

"Thank you." CJ nodded to the truck and asked, "How is business?"

"I quit accepting requests to bid on new jobs. My brother and I are booked up with houses and garages through next year. My wife would kill me if I took on another project right now." The man froze. "Um, she wouldn't really *kill* me. She'd just be upset."

"It's okay. I sometimes tell people my dog will kill me if I don't get her out for a walk before supper."

"Is it true that the tax assessor died from food poisoning after eating at Rolf Erickson's funeral? I heard he got some bad tuna salad."

"I can unequivocally state that he *did not* die from anything eaten at the Erickson funeral."

"That's good. My brother told me that story. I figured it was something started by the anti-church bunch."

"There's an anti-church group?"

"Nothing formal but there are a number of people who prefer the Christian Brothers brandy to the communion wine at the Lutheran church." The man removed a business card from his wallet and handed it to CJ. "I'm Jim. If you ever need a house or garage, give me a call."

"I thought you were overbooked?"

"My wife would forgive me if I told her we were working for a deputy sheriff. Especially if I told her we were working for a female deputy.  She likes to see women in careers that are considered men's jobs."

CJ held up the card. "Thanks. I'll give you a call if I ever decide to start a building project."

"We do decks, too."

"Good to know. Thanks."

As the builder's truck pulled away, CJ pondered the down-to-earth people who really appreciated the law enforcement community.

She was surprised when the pickup stopped, then backed up next to her cruiser. The passenger window rolled down, and the builder leaned across the seat. "Sergeant, there's something off about that commune down by Finlayson."

"What do you mean?"

"They had us remodel a barn so they could use it as a church sanctuary. We dealt with their minister exclusively, and everyone else seemed to shy away whenever we tried to ask a question or strike up a conversation."

"I guess they're reserved."

"I think they were afraid to talk to us. I've met lots of shy people, and I get that. But the women seemed afraid of us." He paused, then added, "I mean, they were nice enough. One of the men brought us sandwiches on homemade bread and some strange tea, so they were thoughtful. But they were strange."

"You made a barn into a church sanctuary?"

"It was a good project, and they paid us in cash. What really freaked me out was when they asked us to put hasps on the inside of the doors. I understand locking a building to keep people from breaking in and stealing stuff. Who locks a church to keep people out when they're worshipping inside?"

* * *

With her cell phone ringing, CJ pulled to the side of the road, hoping to catch the call before it rolled over to voicemail. "I thought you were planning to drive up for the faked suicide victim's autopsy."

"I got caught up in some stupid drama with a bunch of bikers and totally forgot."

"It wasn't that exciting. As you predicted, the slit wrists were a red herring. Your victim drowned," Eddie said.

"We talked about that. He drowned in the bathtub at the cabin."

"The minerals in the water we found in his lungs were different from the water samples I took from the bathtub. He drowned somewhere else, and his body was moved to the cabin. The water in the cabin is softened, with a high sodium content from the water softening process. There was hard water in the victim's lungs. The water from his lungs contained traces of fuel oil, the same as the victim from Askov."

"Both had traces of fuel oil?"

"Yes."

"Does that help you pinpoint the location?" CJ asked.

"Not really. It only tells me the well was shallow, not down into the deep aquifers that hold more pristine water. The well that pumped this water is near a leaking fuel oil tank or somewhere there's been a spill. Have there been any train derailments that spilled fuel oil?"

"Not that I recall."

"This isn't necessarily a recent spill. It could've happened decades ago and has slowly leached into the groundwater."

"I wouldn't know where to start that search."

"Ask Floyd. He's a human trivia encyclopedia."

"I hadn't thought of Floyd in those terms, but you're right, he might remember a train derailment or leaking semi from before I was born."

"On the other hand, it may just be from a leaking farm bulk tank of fuel next to the well."

"Gee, Eddie. You sure know how to lift a girl's expectations."

"I'm just trying…"

CJ cut him off. "Yes, sometimes you're very trying."

After sighing, Eddie said, "Let me make it up to you by taking you out to supper."

"Let's eat somewhere closer to Pine City."

"Hey, you're the one who said you didn't want to eat anywhere you might run into someone you've arrested. That puts us in Duluth unless you want to meet somewhere in Carlton County."

"Let's go to the Mexican restaurant in Cloquet again."

"Six o'clock tonight?"

"I'll have to rush through a shower and walk Bailey, but I should be able to be in Cloquet by six."

By the way, I paid last. Remember the big tip I left to make up for you chasing off the drunk women. It's your turn to buy supper."

CJ called Floyd as she walked to her car. "I need to tell you a tidbit from my discussion with Eddie. The water in both drowning victim's lungs contained traces of fuel oil."

"That certainly ties those two murders to each other. Did he say how the fuel oil got there?"

"Eddie speculated that both men drowned on a farm where there's been a nearby diesel fuel spill. Maybe Pam can track that information down."

Floyd chuckled. "She's been making calls already. I'm sure she has nothing else to do."

* * *

Floyd found Pam staring at the computer on her desk. "Eddie Paulson analyzed the water from the two drowning victims' lungs. He said there was a trace of fuel oil in both water samples. That gives you a new line of inquiry."

Frowning, Pam asked, "Do you remember any fuel oil spills?"

"None come to mind," he replied before walking away.

Pam wrote FUEL OIL SPILL on a Post-it note. She took her coffee cup to the machine and thought while it gurgled and hissed.

Returning to her desk, she dialed her parents' number. "Pam?" her mother said. "What's wrong?"

"Hi, Mom. It's nice to talk to you, too."

"You never call in the middle of the day."

After exchanging news about her husband and son, Pam asked, "Is Dad around? I have a farm question."

"I'll have to pry the newspaper out of his hand, but he's sitting right here."

Her father's voice sounded happy. "I thought you'd outgrown calling me once you graduated from college and didn't need my money anymore."

"I appreciated your loans…"

"Especially the ones you didn't have to repay!"

"I need to pick your brain, Dad. I'm trying to locate a well tainted with diesel fuel. There aren't any reported spills in the area, and I've got no idea who might know if there has been a farm leak."

"That's easy. Call the co-op that delivers farm diesel fuel. If someone's bulk tank was leaking, the supplier probably pumped out their old tank and helped them get a new one installed."

"Do you think it would've leaked a long time before the farmer noticed it?"

Laughing, her father said, "You're dealing with two conflicting farmer issues: Farmers are cheap and losing fuel to a leak is like having money running out of their wallet. That's in opposition to a farmer's hatred of recordkeeping. I'd guess the farm either noticed the smell around the tank, or they eventually realized they were refilling their tank more often than they used to."

"Thanks, Dad."

Pam was about to hang up the phone when she heard her father say something. "When are you bringing Noah down to ride the tractor with his grandpa?"

"He's crawling, Dad. I don't think he'd appriciate the intricacies of a tractor or combine."

"You crawled into a wet cowpie when you were about six months old. It's never too soon to learning those lessons."

"I'll talk to Travis. Maybe we can get away when I have a weekend off."

The regional farm cooperative, the co-op to most people, had stations in most towns, but was headquartered in Mora, west of Finlayson. Pam found the phone number for their bulk delivery business and called.

"Consolidated Co-op, how may I direct your call?"

"I need to talk to someone who'd know about recent bulk tank replacements."

"I'm sorry, we don't install bulk tanks. We just deliver fuel."

"This is Pam Ryan, from the Pine County Sheriff's Office. We need to know who has replaced a leaking bulk tank in the past few years. I assume someone in your office was involved in the replacement process."

"Maybe Leo would know about that. He oversees the bulk fuel delivery service and schedules the drivers. Hang on."

After vaguely describing her interest in finding a leaking tank, Leo opened a squeaky file drawer. "There were three leakers replaced in the past few years. One was replaced in 2020. That was outside Quamba, which is in Kanabec County. Here's one from 2008 in McGregor, in Aitkin County. Here's an older one, but it probably doesn't interest you. It was replaced in 2001."

"Where was that tank?"

"Well, it's gone now. It was on Gerry Caswell's farm in Royalton Township. The mailing address is Finlayson."

"Why did you think that wouldn't interest me?"

"The farm was sold, and the bulk tank was removed and not replaced."

"Do you know who bought the farm?"

"I think some religious group bought it for a camp of some kind."

Pam smiled. "I appreciate your help."

"Is someone suing because of the spilled fuel?"

"No. We just got a water sample from a nearby well with a hint of fuel oil in it. I don't think it'll be a big deal."

Rushing to Floyd's office, Pam knocked on the doorframe. Floyd looked up. "Is it lunchtime already?"

"I might've found the well with the tainted water." Pam sat in Floyd's guest chair. "The co-op helped replace a leaking bulk tank on a Royalton Township farm in 2001. The farm was later sold to a religious group."

"Wow! The question now becomes whether that is the contaminated well."

"Let's assume it's the well. Who drowned the boys in their well water, and why?" Pam stood. "Let's talk to the county attorney about a search warrant."

"Whoa. Let's brainstorm a bit before we run up to Tom's office."

Pam sat down. "You just complicated this mess."

"On the contrary, I may have found the link between all three deaths."

"Why would the commune people want to kill Bob Olsen?"

"As I recall, Bob fought them over their request for a religious property tax exemption for their compound. They may believe that old adage, 'Revenge is a dish best served cold.'" Floyd stood. "You were going to talk to Bob's wife."

"That's when we thought he might've had a gambling problem. If his death is related to something at the commune, his gambling situation is irrelevant."

"Like most people, Bob might've complained to his wife about the tax situation with the commune. She might give you a better view of how heated their arguments had been. Besides, maybe she collects mushrooms."

Pam stood. "Remember how I used to value your wise advice?"

"I thought it irritated you."

"Yup. Your advice used to piss me off. I'd drive around fuming after you'd sent me on what seemed like a wild goose chase."

"And now you see the wisdom in my words."

Pam walked toward the security door. "Nope. I still need to drive around to cool off."

Floyd chuckled.

"I heard that, Floyd. It wasn't meant to be funny."

As Pam left the bullpen, the sheriff emerged from his office. "What were you two yammering about?"

"Pam thinks I sent her on a wild goose chase."

Gesturing for Floyd to join him, the sheriff said, "I've got a few minutes. Tell me about the murder investigations. I might have some input."

"Jeez, John. I thought my job here was symbolic. I never enjoyed briefing you on our investigations when I was a sergeant, and your suggestions often have us chasing wild hares."

Ignoring Floyd's response, the sheriff said, "We've got three dead bodies and you think they're somehow connected?"

Resigning himself to the certainty of an extended discussion, Floyd replied, "The murders may be related." The men spent the next half hour discussing the evidence, the suppositions, and the plan Pam and CJ were pursuing. As expected, the sheriff had several suggestions that Floyd deflected.

The sheriff stood, signaling the end of discussion. "If there's anything else I can do, just let me know."

Pausing with his hand on the doorknob, Floyd thought for a second. "Please don't call your contact at channel seven until we nail down a few more details."

"Building bridges with our media friends keeps them from second guessing what we've done and why we've done it."

"In this case, it might blow up in your face if our intuition is wrong. Give Pam a day to nail down some details. I'm hoping we'll have enough to get a search warrant by tomorrow."

Without further comment, the sheriff nodded, then closed the door behind Floyd.

* * *

CJ's shift was about over when her cell phone rang. She eased onto the road shoulder and answered without looking at the caller ID. "CJ."

"How soon can you be in Cloquet?"

The excitement in Eddie's voice was electric. "I've been thinking. We ate out last night and Bailey might retaliate if I leave her alone again."

"You *have* *to* meet me. I have information I can't relay over the phone."

"Can you give me a hint?"

"I just heard back from the FDA lab."

"The people testing Bob…"

"Not over the phone. Meet me in Cloquet."

"I have to find someone to watch Bailey."

"Trust me, it'll be worth your while."

# Chapter 17

The Mexican restaurant was only half full. The waiter, who obviously spoke English as a second language, was doting over them after seeing a flash of CJ's badge when she showed her driver's license to prove she was legal drinking age.

Smiling, Eddie watched the waiter hustle away. "I think it's hilarious they feel the need to verify that we're over twenty-one. We both have gray in our hair and a few worry lines on our faces. It should be apparent that they're not going to lose their liquor license because they served us a margarita."

"It's easier to card everyone than to have the waiters guess who is or isn't legal to drink."

"The waiter's eyes went wide when he saw your badge."

"I'm not sure if he's an ex-con, or if he's just got a guilty conscience."

Chuckling, Eddie leaned back as the waiter delivered their drinks in salt-rimmed glasses. After the waiter left, Eddie leaned close. "It's like people slowing down when they see a speed trap on the interstate.

They're not sure if they were speeding or not, so they slow down and check their speedometer."

Sipping her margarita, CJ nodded. "It's so stupid, because by the time they see the cop car with the radar, we've already got their speed locked in."

"The drivers don't know that."

"Don't tell anyone, but we sometimes park an empty cruiser on an interstate bridge just to keep the speeders under control."

"That's devious."

"No, what's devious is putting a speed trap a mile down the road from the unoccupied cruiser. For some reason, people think that there isn't going to be a second cop car a mile away from the other one, so they throw caution to the wind. I issued a citation to a guy going over a hundred miles-an-hour a few days ago."

"Did you arrest him for careless driving?"

"His record was clean, so I only put 99 mph on the citation. A lot of paperwork and time is involved in arresting and booking someone for careless driving." CJ dipped a chip in salsa and ate it, then took another sip of her margarita. She looked around for the waiter. "These chips are great, but I need some real food in my stomach before I drink any more of this margarita."

"Don't worry about it. If you're intoxicated after supper, I'll drive you home."

"That's sweet, Eddie, but it means I'd have to drive back here to pick up my car tomorrow after I'm off."

"I could sleep on your couch and drive you back in the morning."

Reaching across the table, CJ touched Eddie's hand. "I appreciate your offer, but I'd rather not get drunk and impose on your friendship."

Shrugging, Eddie said, "It's not an imposition. I like your company and spending the night on your couch is no big deal. Bailey loves to see me."

Their dinners arrived and after a bite of her enchilada in salsa verde, CJ checked to make sure they wouldn't be overheard. "Tell me about the toxicology from the tax assessor's autopsy."

"As you know, he died of multi-organ failure. The likely cause was poisoning, but the poison was probably administered days before he actually died, so there's nothing in the basic toxicology tests I ran indicating which poison was involved. I spoke with his doctor, and she sent me the results of all the blood tests she'd run." Eddie paused and ate a bite of enchilada while composing his thoughts.

"The doctor in Sandstone thought it might've been food poisoning."

"His blood was screened for microbes, parasites, and viral agents. I also spoke with the department of health, and they've had no reports of any similar incident in northern Minnesota. I can say with ninety-nine percent certainty that this wasn't a food poisoning incident."

CJ rolled her hand, urging Eddie to move on. "We know, it was an unusual toxin."

"An extremely unusual toxin. The hospital checked for heavy metals, botulinum…" Eddie gestured with his hands. "They looked for virtually everything."

"There was a Russian spy who was poisoned with a tiny hollow bead."

"That was polonium, a highly toxic radioactive substance. Your tax assessor wasn't killed with anything radioactive. The symptoms are different."

Seeing that Eddie was excited by the mystery, but frustrated by his the slow revelation of his information, CJ sighed. "You've ruled out hundreds of things. What's left?"

"It's not from a blow fish, Amazon frog, or jellyfish."

"Wow, you've looked at nearly everything. How was the poison administered?"

"I suspect he ingested the poison, based on his early nausea and intestinal distress."

"Intestinal distress? Is that a polite way of saying diarrhea?"

"Diarrhea is a symptom of the bowel irritation he experienced." Eddie paused. "Based on anecdotes from the medical staff,

I'd say his guts were trying mightily to expel whatever he'd eaten."

"I brought a bag of food remnants from the horse show. Did you find anything in them?"

Eddie drew a breath. "I can't thank you enough for delivering a bagful of garbage that had been sitting in the sun for a day. Digging through it and swabbing each piece was…delightful. I wish you'd been there to help."

Smiling at Eddie's sarcasm, CJ said, "That couldn't have been worse than many of the corpses you examine."

"Let's say it was near the top ten of miserable experiences. I could deal with the smell of rotten food, but the sheer volume of a weekend's fair garbage was overwhelming. I could've used some help."

"I was put off by the maggots."

"Actually, the maggots may hold the key to solving this."

CJ cocked her head. "How so?"

"There were live maggots everywhere. But I found a bowl with dead maggots in it."

"And…"

"Maggots are hardy. They thrive on rotten stuff and fecal material. They can tolerate food that's filled with microorganisms that would kill a human, but they prosper. I was intrigued to find the dead maggots, maggots that had eaten something so toxic it killed them."

"What had they eaten?"

Eddie's eyes sparkled. "Chili."

Shuddering, CJ asked, "The horse show chili killed maggots?"

"One bowl of chili killed maggots. The maggots eating from the other bowls were fine."

"But there's no way to know if that one bowl of chili was the one our tax assessor ate."

"There are three questions: Did he eat from that bowl of chili? And the answer is yes—his fingerprints are on the bowl."

"The other questions are?"

"Was the chili intended for him, or did he eat a bowl intended for someone else? And what was special about that one bowl of chili?"

"The chili was served by a church commune. They probably served a hundred bowls of chili." CJ paused. "Someone poisoned one bowl."

"It looks like it," Eddie replied. "Otherwise, there'd be dozens of people in the morgue."

"What was special about that one bowl?" CJ froze. "I was in line behind the tax assessor. They made a big deal about serving him a less spicy bowl of chili that was seasoned with brown sugar. Was there something in the brown sugar?"

"Not in the brown sugar. The poison was phytohemagglutinin."

"What?"

"It's poisonous and contained in raw and undercooked kidney beans."

"You're kidding me. Kidney beans aren't poisonous."

"Cooked ones are harmless. Raw or undercooked kidney beans contain phytohemagglutinin. It causes red blood cells to coagulate, leading to a bunch of unpleasant, irreversible symptoms that lead to death." Eddie paused. "The FDA said all Bob's symptoms point to phytohemagglutinin as the poison, but it had apparently been metabolized by the time he died."

Recognition swept over CJ, and she tipped her head back. "When Bob ate the chili at the horse show, he commented to me that the kidney beans were crunchy. Those sonsofbitches at the commune killed him."

"Whoa," Eddie said, putting up his hands. "What I've told you is speculative. I found traces of the poison in the dead maggots. Jumping from there to arresting someone for poisoning is a leap."

CJ leaned forward. "How do I make a case against the commune?"

"You can't."

"Of course, I can. How do I make the connections?"

"I can't supply you with anything but suppositions. I think your only hope of an arrest and conviction is finding someone who'll admit to feeding the tax assessor raw kidney beans."

"Come on, Eddie. There has to be more."

"There's nothing in the tissues of the deceased to point to a specific poison. There's circumstantial evidence that the chili was the source of the poison. You said the commune fed him a separate bowl of chili, but without the contents of the cooking vessel, there's no way to connect them to the poisoning."

"Debbie Downer."

"What?" Eddie asked.

"You're being a Debbie Downer, shooting down all my ideas."

Eddie wiped his mouth and signaled the waiter for their check. "My job is to provide evidence that will stand up in court. I don't have anything but theories and a bunch of dead maggots. I won't get into a witness stand with only that."

CJ put on her best pout.

"Hey! The only reason I've said this much is because we're friends. If any other cop had called asking for the autopsy results, I would have told them it was inconclusive. The cause of death was multiple organ failure due to unknown causes."

When the waiter approached their table, CJ pulled a credit card from her back pocket. "It's my turn to pay."

Eddie struggled to get his wallet out of his pocket. During his attempt, CJ pushed the waiter away. "We can split the bill," he said, holding out a twenty-dollar bill.

"You can leave the tip," CJ said as the waiter returned with her credit card and the slip for her to sign."

Walking to CJ's car, Eddie put his hand on her shoulder. "You've only had one margarita. You feel unimpaired, right?"

"Yeah, I'm fine. A second drink would've put me under the table, but I didn't even finish the entire first margarita." CJ paused. "If another guy had asked that question, I'd assume he was fishing for an invitation for a nightcap or more. I can't tell you how much I appreciate your friendship and concern. More than that, knowing that it comes unconditionally means even more."

Eddie smiled, accentuating the crow's feet at the corners of his eyes in the harsh streetlights. "Yup, Bailey and me; your two sources of unconditional love."

CJ hugged him. "You forgot to include my mother."

"No, your mom has conditions. She wants a weekly phone call, and she expects you to show up for dinner at least once a month."

"You're my big brother. The one who looks out for me."

Eddie laughed. "Your adopted big brother. I like that. It's easier to explain than my platonic female friend. No one believes me when I say that."

"Yeah, my mom expects me to show up with an engagement ring from you one of these days. I keep telling her that's not the friendship we have. I guess people of her generation don't have friends of the opposite sex."

CJ clicked the car remote and walked to the driver's door while Eddie watched from the curb. She paused and said, "Send me a text with the name of that poison."

"You'll have it before you reach the interstate."

CJ stopped at the weigh station south of Cloquet to read Eddie's text. She forwarded it to Pam and Floyd with a brief explanation.

# Chapter 18

Bailey was in need of a potty break when CJ got home. Dancing by the apartment door, the dog whined and whimpered while CJ attached the leash to her harness. "Really, Bailey. I haven't been gone that long."

They walked nearly a block before Bailey found a patch of grass worthy of her attention, then she turned away from CJ as if she was being polite. Or, perhaps as a signal of her disdain, considering CJ's view. Once done, Bailey was ready to continue the walk, so they went another block while she sniffed every signpost, fire hydrant, fence post, and tall stalk of grass.

Needing to verbalize her thoughts, CJ talked to Bailey as they walked. "It's like this. I'm about ninety-nine percent sure the people at the commune poisoned Bob Olsen, but short of someone confessing to the poisoning, there's not much I can do."

Bailey stopped abruptly and looked back as if unhappy with CJ's point of view.

"Don't give me that look. I'm bound by the law, and without probable cause, I can't get a search warrant, and I certainly can't arrest anyone."

As if offering a reply, Bailey farted, turned away, and started walking down the sidewalk.

"I know! I feel just as frustrated by the situation. But my hands are legally tied."

A black dog appeared out of the darkness. CJ's first instinct was to assume he was attacking, so she yanked on the leash to stop Bailey, who was initially oblivious to the other dog, then wagged her tail happily as if a friend had appeared.

"Easy, boy," CJ said, noting the black dog's collar with license and vaccination tags. "You've been cared for. Where is your owner?"

"I'm right behind you."

Startled by the male voice, CJ turned to face the person who'd walked up behind her as she was talking to herself. "I didn't hear you," she said, squaring herself, tensing her muscles, and shifting her weight to the balls of her feet where she was better prepared to deal with an attack or to run.

"I didn't want to interrupt your conversation," the red-haired man said. "For a while, I thought your phone was on Bluetooth mode and you were talking to someone other than the dog."

Placed somewhat at ease by the man's youth, polite demeanor, and empty hands except for a retractable leash, CJ nodded. "I was trying to sort out my thoughts. I probably should've done it in my mind instead of out loud."

"Sampson, come here," the young man said. The black dog was much more interested in Bailey than the man's commands. The dog's owner looked at CJ sheepishly. "A hundred bucks and four weeks of obedience school, and he still ignores me."

"Yeah, my irregular hours with the sheriff's department make my attempts at dog obedience ineffective."

"Ah, you're the person who parks the sheriff's department cruiser in front of the apartment building." The man put out his hand. "I'm Russell Hayden. Everyone calls me Rusty."

"CJ Jensen."

Hayden smiled. "Is it CJ because I'm a stranger, or because you hate the name your mother gave you?"

"Some of each. I don't advertise or use my name."

Hayden took a step ahead and clipped the leash on Sampson's collar. "I've seen you walking Bailey a few times. We've never been on the same schedule or route before."

"Yeah, Bailey led me off our usual path while my mind was wandering. We should go back home. It's nice to meet you."

Hayden hesitated, reading CJ's body language. "I'm not a serial killer or a rapist. If you don't mind the company, I'll walk back with you."

"You know, every serial killer or rapist I've ever met has used that line on me before offering to walk me home."

"Listen, if I'm making you uncomfortable, I'll loop around the block and leave you alone."

Smiling, CJ nodded back down the street. "You've convinced me that your intentions are genuine. A serial killer or rapist would've come up with some reason why he needed to walk with me. Let's walk back. Do you work locally?"

"I'm the assistant manager at Walmart. Long hours. Poor pay. But okay benefits and career potential if I stick with it and am willing to relocate."

"Where's home?"

"I grew up near Omaha, then went to school in Eau Claire, Wisconsin."

"What kind of a degree qualifies you to be a Walmart assistant manager?"

Hayden chuckled nervously. "Um, art history. As it turns out, there really aren't many art history positions that open up unless you've got a Ph.D."

"I always wondered what art history and music majors did for a living if they didn't teach."

"One of my classmates is an actress at the Chanhassen Dinner Theater. Another is selling real estate. He's probably making more than most of the other art history grads." After a few steps, Hayden asked, "How did you get into law enforcement?"

"I took a criminal justice class and found it interesting. It became my major, and I got hired by my hometown police department."

"Not the sheriff's department?"

"Not initially. I spent a few years working for the Cloquet police first."

"It sounded like you were talking about problems with a case."

Tensing, and wondering how much Hayden had overheard or understood, CJ said, "I was just tossing ideas around. Talking to the dog sometimes helps me sort the thoughts in my head."

"You've got a problem with the commune?"

"I really can't comment."

"I was kinda hoping you were investigating them."

"Why?"

Hayden stopped, considering his comments. "I can't really file a police report, or anything, but when the commune members shop, it's strange."

"Strange how? Are they shoplifting?"

Hayden sighed. "There are macho guys who browbeat their girlfriends and wives, but this is different. I mean, it's like the women are…like beaten dogs. Do you understand what I'm saying? They're afraid of the men from the commune. They cringe when the men speak to them, like a dog who thinks it's going to be struck."

Reflecting on her observations of the younger woman who was working in the commune's food venue at the horse show, CJ remembered how the woman had almost slunk away when Brother Palmquist stepped forward to wait on the tax assessor. Suddenly, bells and whistles went off in CJ's brain as she remembered Brother Palmquist scooping up a special bowl of chili for the tax assessor from a separate crock pot.

"CJ, are you okay?"

Hayden's voice jarred her back to the conversation. "Your comment had me thinking back to the times when I've seen the commune women interacting with the men."

"Have you noticed it too? I mean, did the women seem like they were afraid of the men?"

"I think their religion requires women to be deferential to the men. I don't think that means they're being beaten."

"Maybe I'm way off base. It's so different from Ophelia and me. We're partners, and she'd be gone in a heartbeat if I ever raised a hand to her."

"Ophelia's your wife?" CJ asked, thinking that the name was very old-fashioned.

"We're life partners. I met her in a Renaissance art class and knew I was in love with her. It took her a while. She thought

I was fifteen, you know, because of my freckles and light skin. But I wore her down.”

“Ophelia is an art history major too?”

“She was until she figured out there was no way to make a living knowing the difference between a Klimt and a Picasso.”

“What does she do?” CJ asked.

“She’s an on-air personality. You may have heard her show on KPPX radio.”

“Ophelia! Sure, I’ve heard her call-in lovelorn shows. Women calling in for advice on how to deal with their clueless or abusive boyfriends. Doesn’t she have a psychology degree?”

“No, she switched to women’s studies. Being an empowered Black woman with a resonant voice, she’s a natural for radio.”

“Do radio personalities make more than art history majors?” CJ asked, thinking that she knew the answer.

“Not until they break into a major market. She figures that after a year at KPPX, she’ll be recruited by one of the bigger Twin Cities or Duluth stations. For now, she’s happy to work for minimum wage until she gets her breakout job.”

“How’s that going to work with your relocation plans?”

Rusty became silent for a few steps. “We’re rolling with the punches. With any luck, I’ll get transferred to a store near where she lands a job.”

CJ nodded but thought, *You're one job relocation away from a breakup and heartbreak.*

They stopped in front of CJ's apartment building with Bailey straining at the leash to go up the steps. Sampson sat obediently at Rusty's side. "Are you going to check on the women at the commune?"

"I'll see if there are any reports of abuse. Without something concrete, I can't do much more than talk to the women. If they won't make a complaint, there's nothing I can do." Ready to climb the steps, CJ paused, thinking about the Walmart bags and prescription in the Henriette house. "Do you know Colleen Brady?"

Rusty hesitated. "Why?"

"That's an odd question, Rusty."

Even in the darkness, CJ could see the man's face blush. "I mean, why would I know them?"

"Them? How did you know I was thinking about two people? Spill it. What do you know about Colleen and Molly Brady?"

"I…um…really don't know anything about them. Who are they?"

"Don't give up your Walmart job to join the professional poker tour. You are possibly the worst liar I've ever interviewed."

"What about them?"

"Molly stopped showing up at school and their house is empty."

"I suppose they moved."

"Rusty, they did move. Right now, we think they're in hiding after some kind of confrontation at their rental house. Do you know where they are?"

"Why would I know where they are?"

"You're lying, Rusty."

"What?"

"Your face is bright red, and you're sweating like you've been baling hay. You're lying through your teeth. Tell me what you know."

"I promised…"

"Dammit, Rusty, I've been searching for them for days, afraid that they've been kidnapped or killed. If you know where they are, and if they're safe or not, you'd better spit it out, or I'm going to arrest you on the spot for withholding evidence in an investigation."

"Um, they're safe. Okay?"

Awareness dawned on CJ. "Ophelia took a call from Colleen. Off air, your girlfriend helped Colleen and Molly get to a safe place."

"Please don't tell Ophelia I let that slip."

"Ophelia is the least of your problems if you don't tell me where they are right now."

"I don't actually know exactly where they are."

CJ pulled on the leash. "Then we're going to talk to Ophelia right now."

"No, no, no. Ophelia is sleeping and…she gets really cranky if I wake her up."

"That's not a problem for me. I'll wake her up. Pull out your keys."

Rusty stopped. "Um, no. The house is a mess."

Gesturing for Rusty to lead the way, CJ followed. Bailey seemed happy to walk alongside Sampson, who ignored her. Rusty stopped at the front door of a small house next door to the apartment building. There were two tired, rusty cars parked in the driveway, and the concrete steps were pitted from the salt used to de-ice them. Rusty unlocked the door, and CJ stepped inside to the odor of cooked food and barbeque sauce. As Rusty had warned, the living room was littered with clothing, dirty dishes, and take out containers. The dishes and food containers had been licked clean by Sampson. Clearly, neither Rusty nor Ophelia was into cleaning up after themselves. "Hello!" CJ shouted, hoping to roust Ophelia from bed without physically shaking her.

Rustling sounds came from a room down the hallway. Rusty released Sampson, who romped down the hall and through the open door.

"Get away from me, you filthy beast!"

Smiling at Rusty, CJ said, "Ophelia doesn't like Sampson?"

"I think there's a bonding period."

"Stop licking me!" Ophelia complained. "Rusty, call off your damn dog."

After a yelp, Sampson ran from the bedroom with his tail between his legs. CJ felt bad that Sampson took the brunt of her intrusion. "Ophelia, can you come out here, please?"

"Who in hell are you?"

"I'm a Pine County Sheriff's Department sergeant with a few questions."

Ophelia appeared in the hallway, wrapped in a comforter. Her hair was flattened from the pillow, and she had bloodshot eyes that seemed overly bright against her dark skin. "What in hell do you want?" she asked, glaring at Rusty.

"We're investigating the disappearance of Colleen and Molly Brady."

Stepping into the living room with a comforter dragging behind her, Ophelia looked more annoyed than afraid. "You don't look like a cop."

Rusty cleared his throat. "CJ lives in the apartment building next door. It's her police car that's parked in the lot."

"CJ? Didn't your momma give you a proper name, just initials?"

Ignoring the question, CJ asked, "Do you know where Colleen Brady is staying?"

"What makes you think I'd know anything about some Irish girl?"

CJ felt bad about *outing* Rusty but looked at him. "I heard you'd spoken to Colleen after she called in. Where did you tell her to go?"

Gripping her comforter more firmly, Ophelia glared at Rusty, but spoke to CJ, "She's somewhere safe."

"Where? I need to speak with her."

Ophelia froze. "She's…a confidential source. I can't be forced to divulge her location."

"That's not how it works," CJ explained. "You can't be compelled to divulge the name of a confidential source. Besides, you host a call-in radio show, you're not an investigative journalist, and I already know her name is Colleen Brady."

"Her real name isn't Colleen Brady. She assumed that name…" Ophelia stopped. "You're trying to trick me. Are you really a cop, or are you one of the people from the commune?"

CJ looked down at her jeans. "Have you ever seen a woman from the commune in pants?"

"You could be undercover."

Digging a badge holder from her front pocket, CJ held up her credentials.

"I can't see them from across the room," Ophelia complained.

"Then walk over here."

"I'm not wearing anything under this comforter. If you handcuff me, I'll be naked."

"Listen, Ophelia, this is not a television reality show. I'm not going to cuff you. All I want is Colleen and Molly Brady's location."

Propping up her comforter, Ophelia walked closer to inspect CJ's badge. "Cops are always harassing Black people."

"Trust me, this is not harassment, and I don't care if you're Black or White. I'm concerned about Colleen and Molly's safety. Their location is my only interest."

"They're safe."

"Where are they? I won't accept anyone's word on their safety. I have to talk to Colleen."

"Give me a minute," Ophelia said, turning and walking to the bedroom.

*Oh shit,* CJ thought. *I hope she's not going for a gun.* She stepped close to Rusty, using him as a shield and dropping the leash to free her hand if she needed to draw her pistol. "You have no knowledge of their location, Rusty?"

"This is Ophelia's thing. I just know she's been talking about the Bradys."

Ophelia returned wearing a white t-shirt and denim shorts, holding a cell phone to her ear. "Yeah, I've got a female cop here who wants to know you're safe." After a moment, Ophelia held her phone out to CJ. "It's Colleen."

CJ glanced at the number Ophelia had dialed and committed it to memory. "Colleen?"

"Who am I speaking with?"

"I'm Sergeant CJ Jensen, from the Pine County Sheriff's Department. We've been trying to locate you since Molly failed to show up for school. Technically, she's truant."

"I'm homeschooling her."

"Colleen, where are you?"

"We're safely out of Brother Palmquist's reach."

"Was he threatening you?"

"He'd sent his minions to retrieve us. We weren't safe in Henriette anymore."

Deciding to change tactics, CJ asked, "There was blood on the floor of your kitchen. Are you or Molly injured?"

"Elder Thompson grabbed Molly to bring her back for the baptism ceremony. I stuck him in the arm to make him let go."

"Where are you staying?" CJ asked, ignoring the assault Colleen had admitted.

"We're out of the commune's reach. That's all you need to know."

"Legally, that's *not* all I need to know. I have to talk to you, face to face. I need to assess your physical and mental condition. I need to know that Molly is safe, taking classes, and keeping up her schoolwork. Those are legal requirements, Colleen."

"No."

"Colleen..."

"I don't trust you. The commune will steal Molly, marry her off, and cast me aside like chattel."

"I won't let that happen." CJ paused. "What's your real name?"

The silence lingered. "I..."

"Why did you assume the names Colleen and Molly?"

"I thought we'd be safe from the commune."

"The house you rented is owned by the father of a commune member. There were cameras in all the rooms so the commune could watch you."

Colleen sobbed. "They're everywhere. Brother Palmquist said we'd committed our wealth and lives to the Church. We had to be obedient to his orders and the orders of the elders. I didn't want Molly marry some smelly old farmer so she could give him a dozen children while living as his slave."

Images of the commune women and children popped into CJ's head. "Help me put an end to Palmquist's hell, Colleen."

"I told you. His people are everywhere. They see and know all. For all I know, you're one of them, too."

"Ophelia's seen my credentials. I'm a sergeant in the sheriff's department. I have nothing to do with the commune, but I'd be happy to see them shut down and sent away. Help me."

"They're devious. For all I know, there are sheriff's deputies who are commune members."

"Have you ever seen a cop at the commune?"

"Not in uniform, but Brother Palmquist claims his members are far and wide."

"The sheriff is Catholic. I'm Lutheran, as is the chief deputy. Brother Palmquist holds no sway over us. I promise, all I want to do is ensure your safety and make sure Molly is getting an education. Can I do that?"

"No! We're safe here, and I won't jeopardize that by telling you where we are."

"Do you have a pen and a piece of paper?"

"Hang on," Colleen said. In a moment she was back. "I've got a pen."

CJ recited her personal cell phone number. "Call me any time if you feel threatened. You can also call the sheriff's department non-emergency number. You can leave a message or have them call me."

"Okay. What now?" Colleen asked.

"Meet me somewhere you'll feel safe, somewhere away from your residence. Make sure you're not being followed and have your cell phone in your hand, ready to dial 911 if any commune people show up."

"It needs to be somewhere outside of Pine County."

"I think that's a good idea, Colleen. Give me a time and location, and I'll be there."

"How about ten tomorrow morning, at the Sportsman's Café in Mora."

"Is that far enough from where you're staying?"

"I think so."

"Will Molly be safe alone, or are you bringing her along?"

"She won't leave my side," Colleen replied. She paused then added, "There's one more thing. You need to stop the baptisms."

"What baptisms?"

"Brother Palmquist is baptizing the girls. You need to stop him."

"When are they going to take place?"

"Tomorrow."

"Why do I need to stop them?"

"Because it's the beginning of the end for those three girls."

"The beginning of the end?"

"They have to be virgins to be baptized. They won't be virgins when they fall asleep tomorrow night."

CJ froze, staring at Ophelia and Rusty, who couldn't hear the conversation. "Will I have time to step in after we meet?"

"I think so," Colleen replied. "But you'll have to hurry."

"Can we meet tonight, rather than in the morning?" CJ asked.

"Ten tomorrow is as soon as I can be in Mora."

"Then, let's meet somewhere else."

CJ realized that the line was dead. She tried redialing the number, but the message said the phone was out of service.

Ophelia glared at CJ. "Did she hang up, or did someone grab her?"

Holding out the phone, CJ replied, "She hung up."

Ophelia snatched the phone from her. "Then, why did you redial? You didn't get an answer the second time, did you?"

"Her battery went dead," CJ replied, hoping what she said was the truth.

"Satisfied?"

"I'd be happier if I knew where they were staying so I could provide security for them. This will have to do, for now."

Ophelia's gaze shifted to Rusty. "What the hell were you thinking, bringing a cop into the house?"

Rusty's face turned crimson again. "She…was persuasive."

"Maybe she can persuade someone else to put up with your sorry ass."

"I'm sorry! We got talking and…"

CJ stepped between the roommates as Ophelia's temper flared. "Listen, what I'm doing is required by law. You can't lay this on Rusty. You are shielding a missing woman and her truant daughter."

Ophelia pulled at the hem of her shorts. "I'm keeping them safe."

"For how long? Until you run out of rent money for them? Until you get bored? Until you move to a new radio station?"

The last comment rattled Ophelia. "Colleen said they'd be okay in a few days."

"Where are they?"

Ophelia clenched her mouth shut.

"Listen, if something happens to them before we can get an order for protection and in contact with social services, it's on you. You! You're not a cop or Wonder Woman. You're just a do-gooder who's in over her head."

Rusty was about to say something when Ophelia cut him off. "Leave it be, Rusty. This isn't your fight."

"I thought you two were partners," CJ said, softening her tone. "I was married, and we didn't do things behind each other's backs or hide things from each other."

Ophelia snorted. "Until your divorce?"

"Until he died in a car accident," CJ said softly.

Ophelia tried to measure the truth in CJ's words, then saw the sadness in her eyes. "Sorry."

"Please. I'm trying to save them, Ophelia. I have more resources than you do." Seeing that she was making little progress in breaking the woman's resilient front, CJ said, "They may be in real danger, as long as the commune is in existence. Let me get them long term help, okay?"

"They're staying with my college roommate and her husband near St. Cloud. I won't say any more. If you can convince Colleen of your ability to protect them, then she can provide their location. I won't."

CJ bent down and clucked her tongue, hoping Bailey would behave and walk to her. When that didn't work, she took up the leash's slack and gently pulled. Bailey, who'd been laying next to Sampson, didn't respond to the gentle tug. Instead, she looked up at Rusty with her sad basset hound eyes, hoping he would intercede. "Come on, Bailey, we're leaving."

Groaning and pushing herself onto her feet, Bailey stretched, then farted. Ophelia coughed, then squinted. "My god, what do you feed her?"

"Just dog food," CJ said, gently pulling on the leash, hoping to escape without further explanation.

"Are you sure she isn't dying from the inside out? Maybe she has cancer."

"Bailey's healthy, just flatulent."

As CJ left, she heard Ophelia say, "If Sampson ever starts farting like that, either he or I will be gone."

Rusty's response was lost behind the closed door.

"Well, Bailey, I should do something tonight. I'm not sure what, but I need to call…Floyd!"

CJ touched Floyd's name on the screen, and his cell phone rang. She was surprised when Floyd's wife, Mary, answered, "Hi CJ, can you hang on for a moment? Floyd's getting dog food from the garage."

"No problem. How are you, Mary?"

"Between you and me, I'm a much happier wife now that Floyd's back at work. He was moping around here driving me crazy. Now he complains about John's re-election indecision, Pam's inexperience, and how embarrassingly good you're doing his old job. He's as happy as a clam."

"You're kidding. He can't think I'm doing an adequate job of filling in for him."

Mary's voice got soft and sounded like she was covering the phone. "He says you're so good, he should've hired you twenty years ago and retired back then."

"Now I know you're kidding."

Mary's voice got louder. "He's right here, CJ."

"What prompts a call from you this time of night?" Floyd asked.

"Actually, there are a couple things I want to bounce off of you."

"Can't they wait until tomorrow?" Floyd asked.

Chuckling, CJ said, "I didn't want to be the only one losing sleep over them tonight."

"Call Pam. She needs to step up as your sounding board."

"Nope. These are right up your alley."

Sighing, Floyd said, "I'm listening."

After recapping her discussion with Eddie about the commune's chili being the likely, but unprovable source of the poison that killed the tax assessor, CJ was ready to move on.

"Eddie actually said that the maggots died?"

"Only the ones that had eaten out of one bowl."

"What are we supposed to do with information like that?" Floyd asked.

"Eddie said there was nothing we could do except hope that someone admitted to putting raw kidney beans into the tax assessor's bowl."

"That's just wonderful. Now, I'll be up all night trying to find a way to leverage that information. You *could've* saved that until morning. What's your other issue?"

"I spoke with Colleen Brady tonight."

"How did you find her?"

After a lengthy discussion that went on as CJ ended her dog walk and unlocked her apartment, she explained the link to Ophelia's radio show. "Colleen Brady isn't her real name, and the reason she ran away with her daughter Molly is because she was about to be baptized, then married to one of the older men in the commune."

"Again, we could've discussed that tomorrow."

"Actually, tomorrow morning might've been too late. According to Colleen, the commune is baptizing three other girls tomorrow."

"Kids are baptized every Sunday. What's the rush to step in?"

"The virgin girls are turned over to their new husbands after they're baptized, and their marriages are…consummated before sunset."

"Their new husbands? You said they're just teenage girls. Who are they marrying?"

CJ sighed and looked at her shoes. "According to Colleen, Brother Palmquist arranges for older bachelors to buy their way into grace. By transferring their worldly assets to the church, they achieve a higher level of…church membership. These men have deeded their farms to the church. In return, they're entitled to sit in the front row of the church and more."

Floyd smacked his lips as if he'd bitten into a bad apple. "And more, includes getting a virgin bride."

"Apparently," CJ replied. "We need to stop the weddings."

"Aw shit." Floyd growled. "I suppose we need a court order or something."

"Floyd, I've been a cop long enough to know that a judge won't issue a court order to stop a church baptism based on a discussion with a disenfranchised former member."

After a moment's pause, Floyd sighed. "I wish I'd been as realistic and smart as you are when I was your age."

After a snort, CJ said, "Quit trying to butter me up and help me develop a plan."

"I'm not buttering you up. If nothing else, you were smart enough to call me, so the monkey is on my back now."

"I really don't mean to dump this on you, but I'm struggling to find a solution."

"Meet Colleen and get her story in person. I'll talk to the county prosecutor. I think your judgment is right on. Perhaps, we'll have something to go on before nightfall."

"Or?"

Sighing again, Floyd said, "I suppose we'll have to kidnap some underaged newlyweds."

"WE? I have years before I retire," CJ kidded.

"If you weren't close to acting alone on this, you wouldn't have called me. Yes, *we* will have to figure out how to deal with this information. Go to breakfast with Colleen. I'll call my contact in Kanabec County and have one of their deputies meet you there. Call me before you act on what Colleen tells you. Okay?"

"Floyd," she said, softly.

"Is there something else on your mind?"

"Don't ever retire."

"Are you kidding? Mary almost killed me when I told John I'd come back for a few weeks after Mike Smith retired."

CJ hung up the phone and looked at Bailey. "Men are so clueless. Floyd thinks Mary was mad because he went back to work."

# Chapter 19

CJ started her morning patrol by calling dispatch from her cruiser as she drove away from the apartment building. Driving back roads northward, she saw a few deer grazing on the edges of pastures. Seeing a flock of turkeys picking gravel on the shoulder of a back road, she slowed and moved to the far side of the pavement to avoid spooking them. Having been called to numerous turkey/car collisions, she knew a grown turkey could cave in a windshield when hit at highway speeds. The turkeys ignored her as she passed, and she sped up once they were behind her.

Approaching Highway 23 from the south, she crossed over the interstate, then took back roads to the Pine/Kanabec County line. She pulled over and called Floyd's cell phone. "Who's going to meet me in Mora?" she asked.

"I spoke with their dispatcher. There's a big accident west of Ogilvie and all their deputies are there. Our liaison is going to call the Mora PD and have one of their officers meet you at the Sportsmen's Café."

"Mora has city cops?" CJ asked.

Floyd chuckled. "It's a small department. But, yes, Mora has city cops."

* * *

CJ was sipping coffee in the farthest corner of the café, half an hour early for her ten o'clock meeting with Colleen Brady. As most cops do, she scanned the crowd, assessing the patrons. Most were polite, upright citizens. In private moments, cops sometimes referred to them as sheep. Like most people, these folks went through the day unaware of the wolves around them. They'd never been preyed upon by a ruthless criminal. None had been burglarized, had their identity stolen, or been assaulted. While she was on probation with the sheriff's department, CJ heard Floyd refer to them as the salt of the earth. The businesspeople, mothers, and workers who made the non-criminal world a nice place to live.

A woman, sitting alone at the counter, was what cops call a victim. She was alone. Eating in quick bites, she scanned the room as she chewed. Like CJ, she was assessing the other patrons, hoping none of them would approach or threaten her. When the woman's eyes met CJ's she smiled, then quickly looked away.

Two young men in the corner were what CJ thought of as *wannabe bad guys.* They wore their caps backwards and had tattoos on their arms. In contrast to the upstanding citizens who tipped their head in acknowledgement of people they knew, these two raised their chins to acquaintances. The heavyset middle-aged waitress reluctantly served them, probably aware that they would leave a meager tip regardless of the service. Or, they'd said something offensive or provocative to her when they arrived, and she had no inclination to offer herself up for their comments or taunting.

That waitress walked over and topped off CJ's coffee, smiling. "What brings a Pine County sergeant to Mora? Just passing through?"

"I'm meeting some friends," CJ replied. "The guys in the corner look like real jerks."

Setting the coffee pot on the table, the waitress leaned close, as if she was straightening her apron. "They're assholes. You know the type; guys who'll steal a tool from a workman's truck when they walk past it in the parking lot. I think they've got a half dozen DUIs between them. Duke drives, because Larry's license was suspended."

"Where do they work?"

The waitress, whose name tag indicated she was Susie, snorted. "They don't work at anything but making trouble. If I don't watch closely, they'll walk off without paying their bill. They tried sneaking out the back door last week by pretending they were going to the bathroom. The manager caught them halfway across the parking lot. Duke threw a ten-dollar bill at him, then jumped into his pickup and sprayed the parked cars with gravel as he sped off."

"Why do you put up with them?"

Susie sighed. "If it was up to me, they'd be out the door. The manager doesn't like confrontation. He says it's bad for business."

A freckled redhead accompanied by a blonde teenager entered the café. Both wore jeans and western cut long-sleeved shirts. Their long hair was styled in French braids. They looked like two deer sneaking out of the woods, checking the open field for a wolf. CJ waved, noticing the two guys in the corner sizing up the new arrivals. *I'll walk them to their car after we talk,* CJ thought to herself as she glared at the two jerks.

Standing up and sliding a chair away from the table for Colleen, CJ smiled. "Thanks for meeting with me."

Molly, who seemed less paranoid than her mother, sat at the table and smiled at CJ.

Colleen glanced at the two guys who were sizing her up, like a lamb in an auction ring. She leaned over the table, speaking furtively as if afraid someone would overhear her. "I'm doing this against my better judgment."

"I understand. I'm obligated to make sure you're safe and to offer you protection."

"Ophelia's friends are taking care of us. They bought us clothes and fed us."

Smiling, CJ nodded. "That's a great short-term option, but you need to find a permanent secure place for you to move on with your lives."

"How can you help us with that?" Colleen asked.

Realizing that Molly was smiling at the two jerks in the corner booth, CJ put her hand on top of Molly's. "They're predators, Molly."

Briefly breaking eye contact with the men, Molly said, "They smiled at me."

"Trust me. They're the kind of men who'll tell you anything they think you want to hear, then they'll take advantage of you."

Molly met CJ's eyes. "They're cute, not scary."

"I've been a cop for twenty years, Molly. It's the cute ones who are the most dangerous. Ted Bundy, the serial killer, was cute and charming. That's how he met all the victims he abused, killed, and dismembered."

Molly wrinkled her nose in obvious disbelief.

Colleen glanced at the men, then quickly looked away. "We've been living in the commune for five years. Molly is unprepared for life in the outside world."

"Mom, I'm an adult!"

Collen leaned across the table. "In the eyes of the Church of the Holy Sepulchre, Molly became an adult when she turned fourteen. That's when Brother Palmquist baptizes the girls. After that, he marries them to men he's chosen for them."

CJ was about to say something, when Colleen's words struck home. "What about the boys?"

"Brother Palmquist says they're too immature to marry until they're twenty-one. Most of them leave the commune in their teens. They're unclean during puberty, and they have to work off their penance."

"They have to go to confession, like Catholics?" CJ asked.

Molly spoke quickly, before Colleen could respond. "Brother Palmquist knows their minds and gives them penance for their lustful thoughts."

"That's harsh," CJ said. "It's more like handing out penance because of the lustful thoughts Brother Palmquist had when *he* was that age."

"The boys are separated from their parents and moved into a separate dormitory when they turn twelve," Colleen explained. "Brother Palmquist gives them a lot of one-on-one counseling, you know, to help them through that period of transition. Most of them run away before they turn twenty-one. The Brother says it's for the best, since there are more adult men who need wives."

"You've not bought into that?" CJ asked.

Colleen looked around nervously. "I know what happens when the girls marry after their baptism."

CJ waited for more explanation, but when it became obvious that Colleen had spoken her piece, CJ leaned forward. "I've spoken with social services. They can place the two of you in a secure location with other women and children from abusive relationships. The only requirement is that you not contact anyone who will divulge the location where you're staying."

Colleen quickly shook her head.

Molly shrugged. "Mom says we should just stay with the Hickmans in St. Joseph."

The color drained from Colleen's face, and her head snapped to face Molly. "She doesn't need to know where we're staying."

"Mom, she's a cop."

A young Mora police officer entered the café and looked around. Seeing CJ's uniform, he walked to the table and took the chair next to her. "I'm Cody Bergquist. The chief said you were here on a courtesy call about the commune."

Colleen stood and grabbed Molly's hand. "We're leaving!"

CJ glared at the cop, then stood, putting her hand on Colleen's arm. "It's okay."

Molly smiled at the cute cop, making Colleen even more nervous. "Come on, we've got to leave."

"Mom, we're safe with two cops."

Colleen looked at CJ. "You lied to us. You said we could talk to you in confidence and safety. He knows we're from the commune."

Cody looked confused. "What's the big deal? Everyone knows about the commune. They shop in town and sell food at the Vasaloppet cross-country ski race and summer festivals. I think Brother Palmquist is cool."

Colleen tugged at Molly's arm. "We need to leave."

"Please," CJ pleaded. "I can assure your safety."

Cody looked between them. "What's the problem?"

"They're trying to escape from the commune, Officer Bergquist. I'm trying to get them into a safe house."

Cody stood. "Aren't they safe at the commune? I mean, there's no crime there at all."

"How clueless are you, Cody?" CJ asked, trying to stop Colleen from dragging Molly away. "They're marrying off fourteen-year-old girls to older men."

"So what?" Cody replied, standing.

"If you've read the Minnesota statutes, you'd know that's statutory rape of an underaged teen."

"But they're married!" Cody argued.

CJ shuffled along behind Colleen, pleading, "Please wait. We'll sort this out."

Halfway to the door, Colleen froze, then spun around. "You told them we were going to be here. They're here to take Molly back for the baptism."

Cody was on CJ's heels when two men appeared at the café's door. "They just want to reason with you! It's all good. They assured me that they'd respect Colleen's decision. They just want to talk to Molly."

Colleen turned and bumped into CJ. "Is there a back door?"

Turning to the waitress, CJ leaned close. "Get them out of here." Getting a nod, she slipped past Colleen and stood toe to toe with the men in the narrow aisle between tables and people seated at the counter. Both men wore white shirts with dark pants. Their black hats were out of place in the café filled with people in jeans, shorts, and baseball caps.

The taller man, probably ten years younger and fifty pounds heavier than the other, tried to shoulder CJ aside. "It isn't your place to interfere in this."

Continuing to block the narrow walkway between the patrons sitting on stools along the counter and the booths behind them, CJ put her hand on the man's chest. "They're not leaving with you."

The other man, close to fifty years old, with white mutton-chop sideburns and a bushy moustache, tried to see past CJ. "That's my fiancé. Molly and I are betrothed."

When he tried to push past CJ by pressing his ample belly against the backs of the people eating at the counter, a restaurant patron protested and elbowed the intruder. "Give it a rest, Clarence. You can do what you want on your reservation, but you've got to act like the rest of us when you're in town."

After retreating a step and extending her hands to block the two men, CJ noticed a red stain on Clarence's shirt. "You're bleeding. What happened to your shirt?"

"It's nothing."

Connecting the dots with the man and the blood in the rental house, CJ stared into Clarence's eyes. "That knife Colleen used to stab you was probably contaminated. You should have a doctor look at your cut, Elder Thompson. He might want to start you on antibiotics after putting in a few stitches."

"The Lord takes care of us. There's no need to see a doctor."

"Does the Lord cure gangrene and tetanus?" CJ asked as she was jostled between the men and the diners.

Having been bumped repeatedly, a large well-muscled man over six-feet tall, wearing a red Mack Truck cap stood up, blocking the aisle. "The lady cop told you two to knock it off. She may be too polite to punch you for spilling food all over my shirt and pants, but I'm not. Let's take this outside."

"I apologize," the younger man said, sizing up the trucker, then retreating. "We're totally non-violent. There's no need to take this outside. I'll pay for your lunch."

Obviously driven by the sight of his fiancé, Elder Thompson continued to push CJ's shoulder, trying to get past her. Bumping bellies with the trucker, he tried to shove him aside, too. "I'm getting married this afternoon and my fiancé just went out the back door. Go get her, Terry!"

CJ pulled a pair of cuffs from her duty belt and grabbed Clarence's wrist. "That's enough. You've just assaulted an officer. Give me your wrists."

Although he appeared fat, Clarence easily ripped his hand free of CJ's grip, while shoving her into the lap of a man seated in a booth. Pushing herself upright, CJ was ready to take on Clarence with renewed vigor when he unexpectedly doubled over. Placing both hands on Clarence's shoulders, the trucker shoved, causing Clarence to backpedal, flailing his arms while trying to remain upright.

A cook and dishwasher appeared from the kitchen, and together, they turned Clarence toward the door and escorted him to the parking lot with CJ at their heels. Thinking the incident was over, CJ was ready to follow the men to their beat-up car when Cody stepped around the corner of the building with Colleen and Molly.

"Cody, get them out of here!" CJ said, inserting herself between the two groups.

"Molly is going with them," Cody said.

Customers started filing out of the restaurant to watch the event unfold. One of the tattooed guys used his cell phone to capture video while the other joined the two men from the commune. In a stage whisper, he spoke to Clarence, "You take the girl. We'll take her mom, the red-haired cougar. I'm into freckles."

Activating her mic, CJ announced, "Officer needs assistance." She was jostled from behind before she could announce her location.

"No one needs assistance," Cody said, raising his hands. "The show's over. Everyone, go back inside."

"What in hell are you doing?" CJ asked.

"I'm de-escalating the situation. You're out of control. The girl is going to the commune, and you can do whatever you want with her mother."

"Like hell she is," CJ replied. "The girl is leaving with her mother, and we're all meeting with Pine County Social Services."

"Nope. You have no jurisdiction here. It's my call, and the girl is leaving with her fiancé."

Clarence brushed past CJ with his hand extended to Molly. After a second of hesitation, Molly sized up Clarence, then stepped behind her mother. "No, I'm not going with him. He smells of sweat and…farm poop!"

A siren started to wail a few blocks away, and Cody responded to a radio transmission from his dispatcher. He sighed and stepped in front of Colleen. "The chief is on his way. We're not doing anything until he says so."

Dragging Molly by the arm, Colleen jogged to a car near CJ's cruiser, pushing the remote to unlock the doors, with Cody and Clarence close behind.

CJ nodded to the trucker. "Keep the two dipshits and the other commune guy out of this."

"You got it!" he said as CJ raced after the women.

When Molly pulled away from her mother to get into the passenger seat, Cody grabbed her arm. "You're going to a baptism."

To CJ's amazement, Molly kicked the cop in the shin, then pulled open the car door, knocking him on his butt. Clarence stepped in front of the car with his hands raised as the engine cranked, then sputtered and died. CJ was at Colleen's window as she ground the starter, which quickly became a clicking noise as the car's battery ran out of juice.

Gesturing toward her cruiser, CJ said, "Quick! My car is right here. Get in the back seat and we'll be out of here."

With Cody running behind her car, CJ turned on her flasher and siren, splitting the crowd in the parking lot, and going out the side entrance as a Mora police car pulled in on the other side. Announcing her location, CJ raced east on Highway 23. Convinced they weren't being followed by the men from the commune, CJ dialed Floyd's number on her cell phone.

"I've got the Brady mother and daughter in my car. I'm eastbound from Mora. Tell me where to meet the social services person."

"I'm awaiting her return call." He paused, then said, "You sound rattled."

"It was a flipping zoo, Floyd. Molly, Colleen, and I were having a chat when a Mora rookie cop showed up with two of the men from the commune. He was helping them!"

"Helping them, how?"

"He delivered the women to the commune people, then interfered when I tried to get them out of the restaurant."

"The Kanabec County Attorney attends our church. I'll give him a call and ask him to file a complaint against the Mora cop. You can talk to the sheriff later to fill in the details."

Colleen and Molly were so quiet, CJ had to look in her rear-view mirror to make sure they were still there. "Where are we going?" Colleen asked.

"I'm delivering you to a Pine County social worker who will find you a safe place to live."

"Will the commune find us?"

Chuckling, CJ said, "Hell, I won't even know where you are. There's no way the commune will find you."

"You're sure? I mean, we're betting our futures on your word."

Suddenly feeling the weight of the responsibility on her shoulders, CJ looked into Colleen's eyes in the rear-view mirror. "I swear." After a moment of hesitation, CJ asked, "What are your real names?"

"I'm Connie Bailey. My daughter's name is Megan."

"I suppose it's convenient to keep the same initials and Irish names."

"It was a quick decision. When we showed up at the high school to register Megan for school, I realized I couldn't use our real names. I threw out the first names that came to mind. They're my mother's and grandmother's names."

CJ's vibrating phone nearly slid off her lap before she grabbed it. "Yeah."

"I explained that the commune people might be watching the courthouse, so the social worker agreed to meet you at The Floppy Crappie Pub."

"I'm bringing two women I've rescued from a religious commune to a bar?"

Colleen's voice came from the back. "I could use a beer."

Shaking her head, CJ accepted the meeting at the bar. After she disconnected, Colleen asked, "What about the other girls? They're going to be baptized and married this afternoon."

CJ looked at the clock on her dashboard. "What time is the ceremony?"

"The baptism is usually at four, followed by the weddings. We eat a feast, then the newlyweds retire to the husband's quarters to…"

"I'll be at the commune before the feast."

* * *

Although petite, Polly Foss projected professionalism and authority. Dressed in a golf shirt and khaki slacks, she looked far younger than her fifty years. She stepped out of her county-issued Camry and met CJ and the Brady/Baileys in the parking lot. After introductions, Polly gestured toward the car.

"Actually, Colleen would like a beer if that's possible."

Polly checked her watch, then looked at the anxious mother and daughter. "We need

342

to fill out some paperwork somewhere. I suppose this is as good a place as any."

CJ stopped Polly before she walked away. Clasping the social worker's arm, she said, "I promised them they'd be safe. Please don't let them down."

Smiling, Polly shook CJ's hand. "We haven't worked together before but let me assure you that I am extremely good at my job. Their biggest threat of exposure is through their own phone calls and social media posts. I'll make that very clear to them. Your integrity is not at risk, Sergeant Jensen. Their safety is in their own hands."

"You make it sound like the internet is their biggest risk."

"Believe me, convincing a fourteen-year-old girl not to contact her friends is akin to herding squirrels. It's not impossible, but it is challenging."

I don't think they had access to cell phones or the internet in the commune," CJ said. "They should be safe."

"They'll be in a group home with other abused mothers and children. Don't kid yourself. Molly will have access to a phone. Hopefully, she'll be receptive to coaching on phone and internet safety."

"Thank you, Polly."

"Just doing my job. It's rather like yours, only I've never been shot at."

"I hope that never happens again."

Polly took a step toward the door, then paused. "What's going to happen with the commune? You said Colleen is trying to escape from them."

"Two of their members are in the Kanabec County jail facing assault charges, including the man who claims he's Molly's fiancé. Colleen says there are three more girls who'll be baptized and married to older men this afternoon. My next stop is the interruption of the commune's baptism ceremony."

"Can you stop the baptisms?"

"The baptisms may be protected by the members' rights to practice their religion. However, we can stop the weddings of underage girls to older men."

Polly grimaced. "They're marrying off girls of Molly's age to older men?"

"That's what Colleen claims."

"But they're just kids. They can't…" Polly stared at the door that Colleen and Molly had used. "Even with a parent's consent, that's statutory rape."

CJ nodded. "I have to leave."

# Chapter 20

The commune appeared unnaturally quiet to CJ when she opened the steel gate across the driveway. A padlock dangled from a chain, but it wasn't locked. Thinking back on her previous visit, she didn't recall the lock or chain.

*Maybe I'm more paranoid now, than when I was last here,* she thought to herself as she drove up the quarter mile gravel driveway.

Muted music drifted across the parking area as she stepped out of the car. Most of the vehicles were older models with the rusting fenders common to vehicles exposed to Minnesota's salted winter roads. The exceptions were a full-sized white van and a black Cadillac SUV. A patina of dust lay on the shiny black SUV. It was stark against the shiny black paint. CJ dragged her finger through the dust. *I wonder if this is a day, a week, or a month's accumulation of dust. It's hard to tell on a black vehicle.*

A small white cross was nailed above the door of the steel-sided barn where the music originated. Tempted to walk over there first, CJ hesitated, turning instead to the white building that had once been a farmhouse, now having undergone numerous additions. The smell of baking bread emanated from an open doorway. Knocking on the screen door, CJ didn't expect an answer.

"Hello, is anyone around?"

Getting no immediate response, she turned and looked at the cattle grazing in the pasture behind the barn. There were black angus beef cattle mixed with black and white Holstein dairy cows, once common in what was *dairy country* a century ago. With stricter USDA rules on milk handling and relatively low milk prices, most farmers had shut down their dairy operations and switched to beef cattle.

"Can I help you?"

The woman's voice behind the door startled CJ. "I was admiring your dairy herd. I can't think of more than a handful of Pine County farms who still raise dairy cattle."

The woman behind the screen stood in the darkened entryway, silhouetted by the kitchen light. "The youngsters drink milk. What they don't drink, we make into cheese or cook with."

"The aroma of your bread reminds me of my mother baking when I was a child."

"Is there something special you wanted?" the woman asked impatiently.

Hoping for an invitation into the house, CJ asked, "Can I ask you a few questions?"

"I'm busy baking and washing clothes. Everyone else is at the prayer service."

The singing stopped, and a male voice emanated from the barn. His words weren't discernable, but CJ sensed the intensity of his sermon, bringing back memories of the fire and brimstone sermons of her youth. "I'll walk over and sit in on the service."

The screen door opened and an older woman wearing an apron over a blue dress appeared. Her hair was salt and pepper, braided and tied back. "You can't interrupt the service."

"I'll just sit in the back. No one will notice."

"No," the older woman said, putting her hand on CJ's arm. "The door is locked."

"You lock people out of your services?"

The woman froze. "Brother Palmquist doesn't like his sermons interrupted. Why don't you come into the house? I'll pour you a glass of iced tea."

Reading the woman's tense reaction, CJ stepped away from her. "I'll just catch the last of the service."

Stepping after her, the woman grabbed CJ's shoulder. "You really can't do that."

Turning and lifting the woman's hand off her shoulder, CJ stared into her eyes. "What's going on in there that you don't want me to see?"

"Eugene's baptizing the eighth graders. It's a sacrament that's restricted to our membership."

"I think it's time for an exception," CJ said, spinning around and stepping toward the barn. She switched on her mic and said, "Officer needs assistance at the commune."

Grabbing CJ's sleeve, the woman said, "You can't go in!"

Turning to confront the woman, CJ saw the fear in the woman's eyes. "What's going on?"

"It's a baptism. Just leave." The woman hesitated. "You're trespassing. Leave."

A wailing came from the barn, causing CJ's neck hair to bristle. She pushed the woman back and ran across the yard to the barn. As she'd been warned, the door was locked. She trotted around the corner with the persistent woman at her heels, tugging at her sleeve. The only window was covered with dust and CJ wiped it with the edge of her hand as the woman tugged at her other arm.

Inside, voices called, "Hallelujah." Shielding her eyes from the sun, CJ pressed her face against the window. A second later, she felt a pain in her shoulder. She pulled her pistol as she spun around to face the woman who held a vegetable peeler dripping blood in her hand.

"You have to leave!"

"Do you have a church key?" CJ asked, pointing her pistol at the woman's feet.

"No. The doors are locked from the inside. Only Brother Palmquist and Elder Thompson have keys."

"Get me a crowbar or an ax!"

"You don't understand. It's a baptism!"

Pushing past the woman and rolling the shoulder where she'd been stabbed, CJ spoke into her radio. "Officer injured, needs assistance!" CJ requested an ETA on backup. Retrieving the shotgun from her cruiser, CJ pumped a shell into the chamber. She walked to the locked door and fired at the upper door hinge. A second shot shattered the lower hinge, and she kicked the door, causing it to collapse into the barn. A cruiser with flashing lights and wailing siren turned into the driveway as CJ stepped inside.

Giving Sandy Maki's unit number, the dispatcher replied, "Your backup is on site. A second car is less than five minutes away."

The scene in the barn was chaotic. A naked teenage girl, coughing and spitting, struggled to stand while shivering in a water-filled stock tank. A man with salt and pepper hair stood behind the tank. An older man helped the girl to her feet, then pulled off his shirt and wrapped it around her shoulders. Recoiling from his touch, the girl wrapped her arms over her bare breasts, looking scared.

The minister, his white shirt and dark pants streaming water, stepped out of the tank apparently being used as a baptismal.

Two teenage girls standing next to the stock tank, were paired up with older men. One girl's hair was wet and plastered to her head. She was coughing and shivering, her arms covered with goosebumps. Standing behind her, a bald middle-aged man covered her with a white bedsheet. The other naked girl, probably next in line for the stock tank, had a bedsheet quickly thrown over her head by the barrel-chested, gray-bearded man standing behind her. Women in long denim skirts rushed forward to help their girls, while angry men who'd been sitting on rough-cut wooden benches, charged toward CJ. She leveled her shotgun at the onrushing men, freezing them.

Struggling to maintain her composure while the men at the stock tank covered the naked teen girls CJ said, "You're under arrest. All of you."

To her left, CJ saw motion and turned. "Leave the camera right now!" she shouted to a young woman who stood frozen with her hand on a video camera tripod. "That's evidence. DO. NOT. TOUCH. IT," CJ ordered.

Recovering his composure, Brother Palmquist pushed past the men who were facing CJ. "We're practicing our religion. You *can not* interrupt our service."

"I'm not aware of the tenets of your supposed religion, but a minister nearly drowning naked teenage girls in a stock tank is not going to look good to a jury." CJ nodded toward the video camera. "Luckily, it's not my word against your congregation. You were kind enough to provide video coverage of the scene."

"Your lack of understanding does not preclude us from practicing our religion!" Brother Palmquist yelled as he stalked down the aisle, water streaming from his pants and fingers. "We're having an immersion baptism ceremony."

"It looked a lot like a near drowning," CJ countered. "What's with the old men standing by the girls? Are they their fathers or husbands?"

A woman in a long dress with her hair covered by a white kerchief, sobbed. "They're going to be the husbands. My daughter is only thirteen. The deacons decided that she has to marry the bald man with hairy arms after the baptism."

Running footsteps approached behind CJ as another siren wailed nearby. "Everyone, step back from Sergeant Jensen," Sandy Maki shouted.

CJ nodded to Sandy. Riley Sanders, the department's rookie, motioned for the crowd of worshipers to back away.

The sobbing woman from the house, still clasping the bloody vegetable peeler in her hand, pushed through the crowd. "I told that cop she was trespassing. She had no right to interrupt our sacraments."

A flicker of a smile crossed Brother Palmquist's lips. "You're trespassing and you were told to leave. Your evidence is inadmissible."

"There's a term called 'exigent circumstances,'" CJ said. "If I believe there's a crime in progress, or if I think someone is in danger, I have the authority to stop the crime. I think a judge would agree that stopping the assault and forced marriage of underage girls fits those circumstances."

"We have a good lawyer," Palmquist replied.

Sandy pushed himself between CJ and Palmquist. "Take a step back, sir."

Another siren stopped in the driveway and tires skidded on the gravel. CJ sneered and said, "Even if you get this thrown out of court, you're done. You'll be tried in the court of public opinion. People will know what you're up to. You'll be persona non grata anywhere you go."

"Fine. We'll relocate to Mexico. They're much more open-minded than you back-country hicks."

Floyd rushed in, unaware of anything but the crowd of people around the deputies. CJ spotted him and pointed to the video equipment. "Seize that camera and anything attached to it."

The camera operator raised her hands and nervously stepped back.

CJ removed a pair of handcuffs from her duty belt. "Eugene Palmquist, if that's your real name, you are under arrest for the attempted rape of a minor and child pornography." CJ paused as she opened the handcuffs, "I'm sure there's more, but that'll do for now. You have the right to remain silent…"

"You can't arrest Brother Palmquist!" the woman with the potato peeler yelled.

Floyd, dealing with the video equipment, saw the threat posed by the advancing woman and yelled, "Riley, cuff her!"

The woman backed away from the deputies, holding the potato peeler high above her head. "Leave me alone. I haven't done anything."

From behind Brother Palmquist, CJ yelled, "She stabbed me with that damned peeler. Arrest her, Riley."

Riley, six inches shorter and fifty pounds lighter than the woman, walked toward her with his hand out. "Give me the peeler."

Sandy, with CJ's shotgun in one hand, shook his head. "Just pull her arm behind her back and cuff her, Riley."

The woman continued to point the peeler at Riley. "She's not cooperating."

Sensing Riley's reluctance, the woman poked the peeler at Riley, menacingly. "Stay back or I'll…stick you in the eye."

Riley paused and reached for his pistol.

"Geez, Riley," Sandy said. "You can't shoot her because she's threatening you with a potato peeler. Just take it away from her!"

Backing away from the woman, Riley shouted, "She threatened to poke my eye out. What should I do?"

"Ask her to give you the peeler," one of the women said, chuckling. "Wanda's a sweetheart. She wouldn't hurt a fly."

Another woman chuckled. "Try saying please."

Nodding, Riley put out his hand. "Please hand me the peeler before this gets ugly."

"You step back," Wanda said. "I'm not above sticking you with this peeler."

Riley kept his eyes on the woman but spoke to Sandy. "They told us we should de-escalate situations like this."

"Good idea," Sandy said, switching his focus from the now docile commune members to his rookie.

"How?" Riley asked.

Frustrated, CJ shoved Brother Palmquist toward the main doorway. "Riley, de-escalation techniques aren't effective if you tell the aggressor what you're going to do. Figure it out!"

Riley nodded and looked earnestly at the woman. "You look a lot like my mother. She wouldn't stab anyone."

Wanda's eyes narrowed. "I'm not your mother. You know nothing about me."

"You're not in much trouble now, but if you put my eye out, we'll arrest you for assault."

Fed up with the situation, Floyd walked past Riley and grabbed Wanda's hand. The peeler clattered to the ground. He held out Wanda's wrist to Riley. "Cuff Wanda and put her in the back seat of your car."

Riley clipped a cuff on Wanda's right wrist, but as soon as Floyd let go, she danced away. "I'm not going to the police station!"

Hanging onto the other cuff, Riley wrapped his arm around Wanda's waist and tried to reach her other wrist. Stumbling, Wanda fell, pulling Riley to the ground with her. The crowd from the barn gathered outside to watch the rookie wrestle with the gray-haired woman. Finally getting on top of Wanda, Riley pulled her left arm down, but struggled to hold it still enough to cuff as more sirens approached.

# Chapter 21

A girl's scream distracted everyone who'd been focused on the wrestling match. CJ pushed Brother Palmquist toward Floyd as the hairy, fat man ran toward the parked vehicles, a girl wrapped in a white sheet clamped under his arm. With Sandy on her heels, CJ yelled, "There must be another door behind the stock tank."

Kicking, the girl yelled, "Help me!"

Twenty yards behind the man and girl, CJ and Sandy sprinted to catch up. Opening the passenger side door of a rusty pickup, the man threw the girl onto the front seat and slammed the door. CJ was barely past the truck's tailgate, reaching for the door's handle when the engine roared. A step behind her, the bumper, then fender, hit Sandy, who was thrown aside by the impact as the pickup backed up.

With the tires spitting gravel, the pickup backed onto the driveway, then shifted from reverse to drive with CJ running alongside the truck, pounding on the fender. "Stop! Stop!" She clicked on her radio mic. "Kidnap suspect in a rusty red pickup, departing our location. Officer down. Send an ambulance!"

Floyd raced to Sandy, who was covered in dust and writhing in pain. "Hold still. Are you okay?"

Sitting up, Sandy wiped dust from his eyes. "That sonofabitch tried to kill me."

Kneeling, Floyd put his arm around Sandy's shoulders. "Are you okay?"

"Yeah. I'll be bruised tomorrow, but I'll be fine."

Seeing Sandy sit up, CJ ran to her cruiser and sped after the fleeing pickup. She was barely turned around when an unmarked Pine County cruiser blocked the driveway ahead of the fleeing pickup. Locking the pickup's brakes to avoid a collision, the driver skidded off the gravel and into the pasture, pulling down a section of fence where the pickup stopped, its tires tangled in barbed wire.

Pam Ryan leaped out of the unmarked cruiser with her pistol drawn. Leaning across the trunk, she yelled at the driver. "Get out with your hands up!"

Commotion erupted inside the pickup where the driver wrestled with someone in white. A girl screamed, and Pam rushed toward the pickup until a gun appeared outside the pickup's window. She darted behind her cruiser as a shot flew in her general direction.

CJ braked to a stop, blocking the pickup's escape route toward the house and barn. She jumped out of her cruiser and took refuge behind the car door and heard Floyd announce that shots had been fired. Within seconds, a state patrol officer and a Chisago County deputy responded that they were enroute.

"Pam, are you okay?" CJ yelled.

"He missed by a mile," Pam yelled from behind her car.

The girl screamed again, and the man yelled, "Get outta my way, or I'll shoot the girl."

"She's your fiancé. You won't shoot her," CJ yelled.

"I'll shoot myself. Stay back." The gun appeared from the pickup and two shots shattered the windows of Pam's car, the bullets striking far away from Pam's location.

Sensing the man's reluctance to actually hurt anyone, Pam yelled, "Stop that! You're going to hurt one of us."

"I just want to leave with my fiancé," the man sobbed. "Just let us go."

CJ peeked around the front of her cruiser and yelled. "Your fiancé is only thirteen."

"Bring Brother Palmquist here. I'll put the gun down after he marries us."

"Nooooo!" the girl wailed. "Let me go."

Sirens whined in the distance as a white news van appeared on the road. Seeing the van with its satellite dish on top, Pam groaned. "CJ, we've got company."

"Aw shit," CJ replied as Floyd's cruiser pulled behind her car.

Floyd ran to CJ's side as the van stopped. The satellite dish tipped up and started to rise on a mast as they watched. "Whatever happens is going to be recorded for posterity," Floyd said.

"Where's the sheriff?" CJ asked. "He's good at distracting the media and putting a spin on the situation."

Floyd patted CJ's shoulder. "Stall. I'm going to bring Brother Palmquist up."

"Why?"

"We're going to have a wedding ceremony."

"What's wrong with you?" CJ asked. "The girl is only thirteen and she's begging to be released."

"The wedding will be invalid. There's no marriage license. And, like you said, the girl is only thirteen." Seeing that CJ was unconvinced, Floyd added, "It's a way to defuse the situation without anyone being hurt."

Floyd trotted back to his car, and the man in the pickup yelled, "What's going on?"

"We're going to bring Brother Palmquist up to perform your marriage."

"Really?" the man asked.

"Chief Deputy Swenson just drove back to the commune to get him." CJ paused.

"You'll let the girl go after the marriage, right?"

There was a long pause. A siren got closer as the highway patrolman announced his imminent arrival.

"Why do I have to let her go? We'll be married."

CJ leaned back and stared at the sky. *Lord, give me a plan.* A moment later, CJ leaned around her car. "She'll need clothes for your honeymoon. She can't go on a honeymoon in a bedsheet."

The girl wailed, but the man nodded. "I guess that's so."

A blonde woman jumped out of the news van with microphone in hand. A long-haired cameraman appeared behind her and within seconds, they were filming.

Watching in horror, because they were easily within range of the driver's pistol, CJ yelled to Pam, "Can you get them out of here without exposing yourself?"

The pickup driver yelled back, "Leave them be. They can record our wedding."

The state trooper's car came into view followed by an unmarked patrol car. They pulled in front of the news van. The highway patrolman drew his pistol and took cover behind his vehicle. The sheriff got out of the other car and casually walked over to the news team. The blonde immediately held the microphone in front of him, and they conducted an interview within thirty yards of the pickup with the kidnapper and his would-be bride.

CJ watched, shaking her head and thinking to herself. *Sheriff, you may not live until the next election if that guy starts shooting.*

Floyd's car stopped behind CJ. A moment later, he was kneeling beside her. "Brother Palmquist is scared. He won't come down here."

"Are you shitting me?" CJ asked, in disbelief.

"Brother Palmquist said someone could get hurt. I think the *someone* he's concerned about is himself."

"What's plan B?" CJ asked.

"Sit tight. I think the sheriff is going to conduct a wedding."

"You are insane! Sheriffs can't preside at weddings."

"The only person who has to believe it's possible is sitting in that pickup."

Before CJ could argue further, Floyd jogged to Pam, then on to the news van. CJ watched Floyd explain the plan, and to her horror, the sheriff smiled. Floyd jogged back as the sheriff spoke to the news crew. Floyd stopped to speak with Pam, then jogged to CJ.

"The sheriff is going to approach the pickup. When he's got the driver out of the truck, Pam's going to create a diversion. You and I are going to sneak up behind the driver. I'll grab him. You grab the girl."

Shaking her head, CJ said, "I don't like this plan. Someone's going to get killed."

Floyd smiled. "It'll be fine."

"No, it won't. The guy is like a hundred pounds heavier than you, he's got a gun, and there are a million things that could go wrong."

Floyd put his hand on CJ's arm. "Don't worry about the other parts. Get the girl out of there. Okay?"

"It's not okay. You guys are my colleagues and friends. I don't want any of you hurt. This plan sucks. Come up with something else."

Floyd pointed to the news van, where the sheriff stepped down into the ditch, moving toward the pickup. "The highway patrolman is a sniper, and he's getting set up on the trunk of his car. If this goes south, he'll shoot the driver."

"Oh, great! The sheriff is between the sniper and the driver, and you're going to tackle him. Gee, that seems to violate about five of the rules we learn on the firing range."

Floyd's earnest stare scared CJ. "Our priority is getting the girl away from that man unharmed. That is your *only* concern. Understood?"

"That sounds like an order."

Floyd drew a breath. "It is."

The sheriff climbed between the strands of the barbed wire fence and stopped a few yards in front of the pickup. "I'm going to perform the marriage."

"Where's Brother Palmquist?"

"He's…indisposed. Under my authority as Pine County Sheriff, I'm going to conduct your wedding."

"Can you do that?"

The sheriff beamed. "It's one of my many responsibilities."

CJ noted the tiny TV microphone attached to the sheriff's collar. Whatever happened, would be recorded and broadcast.

The pickup door opened, and the groom stepped out. He kept the gun in his left hand while dragging the sobbing teenage bride in his right hand. As the sheriff stepped toward them, Floyd crept forward with CJ behind. They paused at the pickup's tailgate. The planned diversion began when Pam's siren shrieked. With the groom distracted by the siren, Floyd ran forward and threw himself against the man's back, knocking him off balance. CJ ripped the girl from the man's grasp and put herself between the struggle behind her and the girl. With the girl in her embrace and protected by CJ's bulletproof vest, they dove behind the pickup's tailgate as a gunshot cracked. It was followed by four or five more pistol shots and the single sharp crack of the trooper's rifle.

Racing to her car with the girl still shielded by the bulletproof vest, CJ saw the confrontation unfold. With the girl safely in the backseat of her cruiser, CJ ran back toward the pickup. Over the tailgate she saw Pam, with her pistol still in her hand, staring down at something out of sight. The trooper, with his rifle slung over his shoulder, jogged across the field. As she rounded the tailgate, CJ spotted the sheriff sitting against the pickup's fender with a splotch of red spreading across the shoulder of his white uniform shirt. They were all focused on Floyd, who was doing chest compressions on the groom. The victim's torso oozed blood from multiple chest wounds as he stared at the sky with unseeing eyes.

CJ walked next to Pam and whispered, "What happened?"

"Shh. We're on live TV."

The ambulance which had been called earlier to treat Sandy's injuries from the pickup impact, arrived moments later. The paramedics checked the would-be groom. The lead medic stopped Floyd's chest compressions with a shake of his head. After throwing a sheet over the unresponsive driver, they checked the sheriff's injury.

Floyd sidled up to CJ and whispered, "They bandaged the sheriff's upper arm. The bullet broke the skin but didn't penetrate any muscles. He'll be back at the office tomorrow."

Making sure the news cameras weren't on them, CJ whispered, "With the sheriff out of action, requesting a Bureau of Criminal Apprehension shooting investigation team is up to the chief deputy."

Looking sheepish, Floyd replied, "Yeah. Being retired for a couple of months turned my brain to Jell-O. Calling the BCA never even crossed my mind."

* * *

While Brother Palmquist and the woman who assaulted CJ with the potato peeler were arrested and taken to jail, the kidnap victim, still wrapped in a sheet, and her mother were led away by Polly Foss from social services. The video equipment was tagged as evidence and put into the trunk of Pam's cruiser. The two remaining girls involved in the baptism ceremony were interviewed by Child Protective Services. The commune's men and women were separated to be interviewed individually by the BCA team.

After segregating the commune members to limit their ability to shape their narratives, CJ conferred with Pam about how they would conduct the interviews. Riley walked over to them. "Wow! We were in the barn when we heard all the fireworks. I'm really pissed that I missed all the excitement."

In a motherly move, CJ reached out and straightened Riley's collar. She smiled and leaned close. "Listen you cut-off little shit. Shootings are serious and no one, NO ONE, feels good about the outcome. There is no glory in taking another person's life. If you think otherwise, find a different job because you're not suited for this one."

Riley's eyes went wide. "But…"

"You should keep your mouth shut until you're experienced enough to make an intelligent comment. Are we clear on that?"

"Sure, CJ."

"I'm Sergeant Jensen until you're off probation."

"Yes, Sergeant."

CJ rolled her head and reached up to rub a sore muscle in her shoulder.

"What's the matter?" Pam asked.

"I've got a muscle spasm."

Seeing blood on CJ's fingers when she finished massaging her neck, Pam took a step behind her. "You're bleeding. Did you get hit with a ricochet?"

"Shit. It's where the crazy woman stabbed me with the potato peeler."

"There's a hole in your shirt over the top of your vest. You need to have a doctor look at it."

"It's just a nick."

Pam peeled back the neck of CJ's shirt and examined the wound. "It's a crescent shaped puncture wound. At a minimum, you need a tetanus shot."

"I had one a couple years ago. I'll be fine."

"What year did you last have a tetanus shot?"

"I don't know exactly. I was still with the Cloquet police."

After pulling up CJ's collar, Pam gestured toward their cars. "Am I driving you to the ER, or are you driving yourself?"

"It's just a scratch, Pam."

"Good point. I think the regulations say an injured officer can't drive herself to the hospital. Get in my car."

* * *

The Sandstone hospital ER waiting room was empty. Seeing Pam and CJ's uniforms and the blood on CJ's fingers, a nurse immediately escorted her to an exam room. After making a cursory examination, the nurse said, "Take off your bulletproof vest and shirt, then put on this hospital gown with the opening in the back."

Accepting that argument was futile, CJ undressed and put on the gown. While waiting for the doctor, she probed the wound with her fingers. It ached, but the pain wasn't intense. Her fingertips were covered with blood when she finished her exploration.

Bert Mlankoch MD, the on-duty doctor, knocked on the exam room door, then entered without waiting for an invitation. "Kristen says you've got a puncture wound in your shoulder."

"It's a scratch."

Mlankoch walked behind her and untied the gown. "Are you in a lot of pain?"

"Not really."

"When was your last tetanus shot?"

"I can't remember."

The doctor sighed. "Puncture wounds usually heal better if they're not stitched. I'm going to tape a piece of gauze over the hole to absorb any bleeding. You can remove it tomorrow when you shower, but you'll want to keep a dressing on it for a few days, until it stops oozing. Kristen will be back in a minute to give you a tetanus booster." The doctor pulled on rubber gloves and opened a sterile gauze package. "What caused that interesting crescent wound?"

"I was attacked with a potato peeler."

The doctor snorted. "That's a first for me."

Completing the bandaging, the doctor pulled off the gloves and put them into a biohazard garbage can. "Do you need something for the pain?"

"I'll take Tylenol."

"It'll hurt worse tomorrow."

"I'll be fine. Can I get dressed now?"

"Sure. Kristen will be back with that tetanus booster in a minute."

CJ had her shirt on with the bullet-proof vest laying behind her on the exam table when the nurse returned. "Left arm, or right?"

"If it's going to make my arm ache, use the left."

"The sheriff was in the next room," Kristen said as she administered the injection.

"How is he?" CJ asked.

"HIPAA rules prevent me from answering…but he'll be going home before you." Kristen put a band aid over the injection site and pulled down CJ's shirt sleeve. "Did you hear that there are reporters in the hospital lobby?"

Rolling her eyes, CJ asked, "Is there a back door out of here?"

Kristen chuckled. "You can sneak through the ambulance entrance."

There was a knock on the exam room door. Expecting Pam, CJ said, "Come in."

The sheriff stuck his head in the room. "I'd like you beside me while I address the news people."

Uninterested in facing the press, CJ reached out and steadied herself on Kristen's shoulder. "I feel queasy. It's probably better if you spoke to them alone rather than having me throw up during an interview."

"Um…sure. Take it easy."

When the sheriff closed the door, Kristen looked at CJ. "Do you need something for nausea?"

"Hell no," CJ said, hopping off the exam table. "Show me how to get out of here before the sheriff comes back from his press conference to check on me."

* * *

The bullpen was empty when CJ walked in. Backtracking to the dispatcher's cube, she asked, "Where is everyone, Jodi?"

"Pam and the assistant county attorney are interviewing the women from the commune. Everyone else is on patrol."

Bypassing the bullpen, CJ followed the sound of voices down a hallway past the interview rooms. Seeing her, Pam stepped away from her conversation with Alissa Preston. "You were in the ER."

"And now I'm not. What's going on?"

Alissa nodded toward the first interview room. "Erica Carlton is speaking with her public defender."

"What's she charged with?" CJ asked.

"Nothing," Pam replied. "I asked her what had happened to her son, and she asked for a lawyer."

Connecting the Carlton name with the naked body found outside the Askov museum, CJ frowned. "You don't think she had anything to do with her son's death, do you?"

"We don't know what to think," Alissa replied.

"Maybe the BCA pulled something off the phone we found in the bathtub at the cabin."

"We had a call from the BCA. The phone had been in the water too long. The data was unrecoverable."

A knock on the interview room door interrupted their discussion. A young, baby-faced lawyer stuck his head out of the door. "Mrs. Carlton would like to speak with Sergeant Jensen."

CJ pointed at herself. "Me? I've never met Mrs. Carlton."

"You impressed her at the commune, and she feels like you are honest."

Alissa nodded. "Go ahead. We'll watch you on closed-circuit TV."

Erica Carlton had been crying and was twisting a tissue in her hands. "Tell me what happened to my son, Nicky."

CJ sat across from the woman and composed her thoughts. "His body was found outside the Pine County Historical Museum."

Erica stared at the tissue and twisted it with vigor. "Was he really naked when you found him?"

"Is that significant?"

Erica looked at her lawyer, who nodded his approval. "Brother Palmquist was going to re-baptize him."

"Re-baptize?" CJ asked.

"The first baptism was ineffective. Nick continued to have impure thoughts. Eugene said he needed to be immersed longer."

"Were you present for the second baptism?"

Erica shook her head. "Eugene said it might be…unpleasant to see the evil being cast from Nick's body."

"You never saw Nick again?"

Erica shook her head.

"What did Brother Palmquist tell you after…?"

"Eugene said the evil was too deeply embedded, and that Nick had to leave the commune. I couldn't see him again."

"But you suspected Nick was dead?"

"I was told he was no longer my son. Eugene said he was dead to me. I didn't immediately suspect what that meant."

"When did you catch on?"

"I think I knew Nick was dead before Eugene told me. I felt it."

"Have any of the other teen boys disappeared?"

Erica drew a deep breath. "There are two or three a year who decide that the commune life isn't for them. They pack up and leave."

"Have others needed re-baptism?" CJ asked.

Erica looked at her lawyer, who nodded. "There have been a few."

CJ's pulse quickened as she asked, "Has there been a rebaptism since Nick's?"

"Ethan McElvry was rebaptized a few days after Nick."

"Were his parents told he was dead to them?"

Erica nodded.

"I need you to say yes or no, Mrs. Carlton."

"Yes, his parents were told he was dead to them and was gone."

"Describe Ethan to me."

Erica's description of Ethan exactly fit the teen whose body was found in the cabin bathtub. "Do you think he's actually dead too, Sergeant Jensen?"

There was a knock on the interview room door before CJ could respond. Alissa Preston stepped into the small room. "Were Ethan's parents at the girl's baptism ceremony?"

Erica shook her head. "No, McElvrys left the commune when they got the news. Ethan's father planned to look for him."

"Did Brother Palmquist try to stop them?"

Erica shook her head. "Eugene told us that they'd had a crisis of faith and were no longer members in good standing."

"Did that happen often?" Alissa asked.

"Not often. I think the last one was Connie Bailey. Someone said she changed her name to Colleen Brady after she and her daughter left."

The assistant county attorney looked at CJ, "Is there anything else you'd like to ask Mrs. Carlton?"

"I think we've got all we need, Alissa."

As CJ and Pam walked to the bullpen, CJ commented, "Alissa seems to be growing into this job. I hope she stays around for a while."

"I talked to her about small town life. She's struggling with the social aspects of living in Pine County. She's used to the social scene in the Twin Cities, where she went to law school."

"I had culture shock moving from Cloquet to Pine City," CJ said as she put a k-cup into the coffee machine. "Moving here from Minneapolis would turn your world upside down."

"Alissa is young and would like to be attending concerts and dating. Most of the guys she's met locally aren't boyfriend material, in her eyes. I think she'd like to meet someone who's got a career instead of just a job."

Taking her cup from the coffee maker, CJ paused. "That's an issue. I think a lot of young people find dates on websites. You could suggest that to her."

"Keep your eyes open," Pam replied.

CJ snorted. "Right. Like I meet so many young eligible bachelors."

* * *

After reciting the day's events to the BCA investigators, CJ picked up Bailey from doggy daycare and returned to her apartment. Although Bailey had peed before getting into the car, she strained at the leash as soon as she jumped down from the car until CJ relented and let her sniff around the narrow strip of grass between the sidewalk and street.

"You do realize that my shoulder is injured, and it hurts when you tug on the leash."

Ignoring CJ, Bailey sniffed around a signpost, then peed next to it. The dog hesitated for a second, then ran for the apartment, dragging CJ along behind her.

CJ stripped off her uniform and sprayed stain remover on the bloodstain. "Why in hell are you bothering to do that?" she said to herself. "There's a hole in the shirt. It's ruined." After throwing her uniform into the hamper, she put on fresh panties, a t-shirt, and jogging shorts. She had the television remote in her hand when she noticed the dog staring at her. Bailey lumbered over to the door, the effort seemingly almost too much for the Basset. She stopped, let out a fart, and sat unceremoniously, her sad eyes drooping with dismay.

"Don't you dare give me that look. I'm a good dog mom." CJ wagged her finger at her dog. "Just because you don't get to destroy my cruiser with your drool and clear the bullpen with your gas everyday, doesn't mean you're mistreated. I pay good money so you can eat and sleep at doggy daycare all day. I will not allow you to manipulate me into dragging you to the sheriff's department every damn day!"

Bailey lay down, groaning with the effort.

Seeing the special K9 vest Floyd had purchased for Bailey, CJ stopped mid-rant, grabbed it off of its hook, and stuffed her plus sized, drooling companion into it before pulling a Pine City Dragons sweatshirt over her head. "Come on. Let's go. I guess we need to be good PR people for the Sheriff's Department." She tugged on the leash.

The Basset felt no inclination to hoist herself up until the fifth, "LET'S GO." Bailey lifted her hind end from the floor. It took CJ five more pleas as she stood in the apartment hallway before she coaxed the dog into leaving and heading down the stairs.

CJ's neighbor overheard the end of her conversation with Bailey as he stepped out of his apartment. His hearty laughter followed them down the stairs and out the door.

"You're lucky I love you, Basset. My neighbors are going to think I need a 72-hour psychiatric hold the way I converse with my damn dog!"

# Chapter 22

CJ was asleep when her cell phone rang at ten the next morning. "Yeah," she said, answering the call without looking at the caller ID.

"Be at the courthouse in ten minutes," Floyd said.

Expecting more information, she listened, but heard only dead air followed by the dial tone. The basset hound opened her eyes without getting up, wondering what her master was up to. "Crap, Bailey, I wonder what this is all about?"

Dashing into the bathroom to brush her teeth and pull on her uniform, CJ rushed around her apartment, gathering her gear and cap. Hesitating while holding the door open, she stared at the dog who seemed uninterested in whatever was happening. "Stand up. You're coming along."

Rising slowly, the basset stretched, then passed gas before lumbering to the door. "You could hurry," CJ said, attaching a leash to the dog's harness. "I've only got about two minutes before I'm supposed to present myself."

A male laugh stopped CJ as she inserted her key into the deadbolt. "Does the dog ever answer you?" The neighbor, dressed in hospital scrubs, was standing at the top of the stairs.

Feeling color rise from her neck to her face, CJ locked the apartment door and forced a smile. "Of course not. I just talk to her as a way of…" The correct phrase failed to come to mind.

"A way of processing your thoughts?" The young, dark-haired man offered his hand. "I'm Paul Martin, the new x-ray tech at the Sandstone hospital."

"You probably know that I'm CJ from my name on the mailbox. This is Bailey."

Hearing her name, the basset's tail wagged. Bailey passed gas to punctuate her excitement.

"I've seen the police cruiser in the parking lot. Being new to the building, I hadn't connected you with the sheriff's department car."

Having had enough of the conversation, Bailey started down the short set of steps to the landing inside the front entrance. CJ lunged after her to keep from being yanked down the stairs.

"It's nice meeting you," CJ said over her shoulder as she pushed the door open.

The x-ray tech jogged to keep up. "If you ever need someone besides the dog to talk to, I'm still trying to establish some social connections and would like to get some hints on where to meet people.”

CJ unlocked the cruiser and tried to urge Bailey into the backseat. Martin rushed to her side and helped lift Bailey’s hind quarters onto the seat. “To be honest, I’m not the best resource for social contacts. I usually crash on the couch when I have some time to myself.”

“What restaurants are good?” Martin asked as CJ got into the driver’s seat. “I’m tired of eating at the A&W and Dairy Queen.”

“Try Maxwell’s barbecue and The Garage,” CJ replied as she closed the door.

As they drove away, CJ looked at Bailey in the mirror and said, “If I were ten years younger... Wait, Alissa is ten years younger and looking for male companionship.”

Bailey flopped down on the seat and farted.

“Don’t criticize my ideas. I’m going to set up a blind date with Paul and Liss.”

* * *


The bullpen was filled with deputies when CJ and Bailey arrived. Noticing Pam, her sometimes dog-sitter, Bailey rushed across the room, yanking the leash out of CJ’s hand. Sandy Maki shook his head. “Oh good, CJ and the fart machine are here so we can get started.”

Ignoring the dig, CJ popped a k-cup into the machine and started a cup of coffee. Feeling a hand on her arm, she looked behind her at Riley, the rookie. "Um, Sergeant Jensen, I was out of line yesterday. I understand that now."

CJ nodded as the sheriff entered, his arm in a sling. Having seen the sheriff's rather minor wound, her immediate thought was that he was milking the injury. Nodding to Floyd, his appointed chief deputy, the sheriff stood next to CJ. "I've left the decision about running for another sheriff's term dangle while soul searching and talking to my family. I've got to admit that yesterday's events have prompted me to move ahead with that decision." He drew a breath, like a game show host letting the anticipation grow. "I've filed the papers to run for re-election this morning."

With most everyone in the department convinced that Sepanen was going to retire, the room was silent. Glancing around, Pam started clapping, which prompted the others to join in, although not all the faces looked happy.

"My near-death experience reminded me of how precious life is, and how all of you are in danger every day. Because of that, I've decided to become more *hands-on,* assisting with decisions about operations, and responding to calls."

Sandy groaned, garnering a glare from the sheriff. Floyd jumped in, "It was the dog, John. That basset groans and farts all the time."

Satisfied with that answer, the sheriff nodded. "I think my greatest contribution can be made by assisting with Pam's investigations, so she and I will be working more closely together."

Pam's eyes flew to Floyd, who made a gesture with his hand, indicating she shouldn't comment.

"Since I assume my administration will continue, I'm formally asking Floyd to stay on as the chief deputy. The rest of this team is working well, and I don't plan to change a thing."

As soon as the sheriff departed for his office, the room was filled with conversations, most involving concern about the meaning of the sheriff taking a more active role in operations. Pam pulled Floyd over to CJ. "Floyd, I can't work with the sheriff looking over my shoulder. He drives me crazy as it is. You're all out on the road, and he comes in here, interrupting whatever I'm doing, offering suggestions and asking questions."

Floyd's sly smile seemed to make Pam even more agitated. "John's attention span is shorter than CJ's dog. All you have to do is get into the case details, he'll yawn, make a cup of coffee, then tell you to keep up the good work."

"And if that doesn't work?" Pam asked.

"I've known John for twenty years. He loves the limelight and hates details. Trust me on this, okay?"

After threading her way through all the legs, Bailey walked over and sat on Pam's foot, then immediately passed gas. "Geez, CJ, have you ever thought that Bailey might have some kind of illness?" Pam asked. "We had dogs on the farm and none of them farted as much as Bailey."

"I took her to the vet. He said I should try changing her diet. I tried the food he suggested, but it gave her diarrhea, which was NOT an improvement. I also tried feeding her an anti-gas supplement. If anything, her farting got worse. I'm out of ideas."

Riley walked over and bent down to pat Bailey's head. Her tail started slapping Pam's calf. "Stop petting her, Riley! She's bruising my leg."

CJ picked up the leash that Bailey had dragged across the room and held it out to the rookie. "Here, Riley. I didn't have time to walk her. Will you take her across the parking lot so she can pee?"

"Really? That's not in my job description. As a matter of fact, it might be seen as hazing."

CJ's withering glare shut him down, and he accepted the leash, leading Bailey away.

Pam watched, shaking her head. "You can't really expect him to be your dog-sitter just because he's a rookie."

Rolling her eyes, CJ said, "Walking Bailey may be the most useful thing he can do."

Floyd chuckled. "Yeah, his wrestling match with the woman wielding the potato peeler was pathetic."

"He wrestled with someone?" Pam asked.

Floyd leaned close to Pam. "It's too noisy in here. Let's grab a cup of coffee."

"What about Bailey?" CJ asked.

Floyd's eyes sparkled. "Maybe Riley won't notice that we're gone. Meet me at Nicholls Café."

* * *

Before going to meet Floyd, CJ ran up the stairs to the county attorney's offices. Her sudden appearance in the door startled Alissa. "What's up, CJ?"

"If you're free for lunch tomorrow, I can update you on yesterday's shooting."

Alissa glanced at the files on her desk. "I know about the plea deals."

"But you didn't hear about the shootout at the commune. Meet me at Amy's Café at noon."

"That's in Sandstone, right? It's a long drive for lunch."

"You need to get out of the office and see more of the county than Pine City."

"I suppose I could use a break."

While walking to her cruiser, CJ called the Sandstone hospital and asked for the radiology department. "Is Paul Martin available?"

CJ listened to the canned music as she unlocked her cruiser and started the engine. "This is Paul."

"Hi, this is CJ, your neighbor with the basset hound. I'm having lunch with a colleague at Amy's café in downtown Sandstone tomorrow. Can you meet us there at noon?"

"Lunch somewhere other than the cafeteria would be nice. Where is Amy's?"

"It's downtown Sandstone, past the hardware store. I'll see you tomorrow at noon."

* * *

Sitting at a corner table with Pam, Floyd signalled for coffee. "CJ doesn't know what happened this morning. Three of the women from the commune have offered to testify against Eugene Palmquist about a variety of crimes at the commune. In addition to their testimony, the BCA searched the compound and located cameras in virtually every private space, all of them feeding to the office computer. Palmquist had recorded the private moments of every woman's life. His computer had financial records documenting the assets each person surrendered to gain full membership in the commune. In addition to what he got from local folks, he has millions of dollars in accounts and real estate spread across the world. The last I heard was that Tom Bakken and Alissa Preston had offered a plea bargain that would put Palmquist in an out of state prison for the rest of his life if he returned all of the assets to the donors."

Conversation stopped when the coffee arrived. After the waitress left, CJ leaned forward. "Did Palmquist accept that offer?"

"His attorney was arguing about the money and real estate ownership."

Pam frowned and asked, "Why an out of state prison?"

"His attorney was concerned that the other commune members would kill him in prison once the information about his use of their contributions and his private surveillance of the women got out. His attorney was more interested in getting him somewhere he was anonymous than reducing his sentence."

"Did Palmquist explain why he poisoned the tax assessor?"

Floyd smiled. "Brother Palmquist was whining about the pressure he was getting from the tax assessor, who suspected the financial shenanigans. One of the women in the commune, who'd grown up in England, knew that undercooked kidney beans were poisonous. Brother Palmquist knew that Bob ate at the commune food booth at the horse show because he was paranoid about all the additives in the other food offerings. Although Palmquist didn't make the chili, or put the poisonous beans in the pot, he was an accessory before the fact."

Looking surprised, CJ said, "Palmquist personally served the bowl of chili with the poisonous kidney beans to Bob Olsen. I watched him go to a separate crock pot and dish up a non-spicy bowl of chili for the tax assessor. Bob commented on the beans being crunchy when he ate the chili. Palmquist is more than an accessory before the fact, he's Bob Olsen's murderer."

"You need to communicate that to the county attorney before the plea hearing."

CJ felt an adrenaline rush as she realized that all the pieces of the investigation were coming together. "How can we prove that Palmquist drowned the two boys?"

"The BCA found Arnold Dellwood's fingerprints inside the pickup that was abandoned at the museum and in the museum's van. He's one of the commune elders. When confronted with that evidence and the threat of being charged with Nick's murder, Arnold admitted to watching Palmquist drown the boys while giving them an extra baptism. The accessory to murder charges against Dellwood will be dropped in return for testifying against Palmquist and pleading guilty to tampering with a corpse."

CJ stared into her coffee cup. "Even though all the main suspects will be tried, I feel…hollow."

Floyd put his hand on her shoulder. "Three people died, so none of us feel elated. We need to find solace in knowing that the families will know the killers have been found and punished."

Pam changed the topic. "Floyd, you took the chief deputy position as an interim appointment. Are you really going to stay on past the election?"

"Assuming John gets re-elected, I'll stay as long as he'll have me."

Pam frowned. "Why? I thought you liked retirement."

"Despite Mary's wishes for me to re-retire, I missed being around the department."

Choking on her coffee, CJ wiped her mouth with a napkin. "You missed _us_?"

"I miss the job some but having coffee with you two and tossing around ideas is energizing."

CJ put her hand on Floyd's arm. "We were doing that while you were retired, Floyd."

"It wasn't the same. I wasn't part of the team. I wasn't there for the chases and arrests. I missed that."

CJ poked Floyd's shoulder with her finger to get his attention. "I'm planning to have a conversation with Mary about you throwing yourself on the kidnapper's back while I rescued the teen girl."

"Please don't. She doesn't want, or need to know, the details of what happens while we're working."

"You were being stupid," CJ whispered.

"It all worked out fine, didn't it?"

Pam shook her head. "You were in the line of fire. I had to hold my shots while you were riding that guy's back. It looked like you were on a mechanical bull ride."

"I had to stall him while CJ got the girl clear," Floyd explained. "As soon as I knew they were safe, I let go."

After a snort and headshaking, Pam pointed her finger at Floyd. "That's when the groom pulled his pistol. If the trooper and I hadn't been there, you and the sheriff might be dead."

"But you were there. And you did exactly as you'd been trained."

"Dammit, Floyd. We've got to stop ending these investigations with a shooting gallery," CJ protested.

Floyd turned to her. "Perfect! Next time, you and Pam are responsible for coming up with the plan. I'll keep the sheriff out of the line of fire, and you two can figure out how to deescalate the situation and rescue the girl."

CJ's mouth twitched. "I vote that we send Riley in to jump onto the bad guy's back. He did so well when he tried to disarm the woman wielding the potato peeler."

"No," Floyd said, shaking his head. "I need someone who's got self-confidence and…common sense. Give Riley time to grow into his uniform."

"What if I need someone to have my back? I'm afraid Riley will turn and run the first time he's in a tough situation."

"That's why Sandy is his Field Training Officer. Sandy will make sure all our backs are covered until we know that Riley's dependable. If he doesn't pass his field training, he's history."

CJ clenched her eyes shut. "I hate rookies. They're like puppies that follow you around, bumping into you, and peeing on the floor when they're startled."

"A lot of them grow up to be good cops. Look at you and Pam."

Nodding, CJ sighed. "I know, but it takes so damn long, and rookies keep doing stupid stuff for years."

Floyd put his hand on her shoulder. "Welcome to the legion of cynical veteran cops."

When her cell phone rang, CJ stepped away after seeing Eddie's phone number. "What's up?" she asked.

"Supper tonight. You name the place."

"We just went out. What's the occasion?"

After a sigh, Eddie said, "I saw a sanitized version of the commune raid on the news. I want the gory details."

"It's really not all that interesting."

"I'll be the judge of that."

"I'm tired of Mexican food. Let's eat at the Pizza Pub at the Sturgeon Lake exit." CJ noticed that Floyd was also having a phone discussion. He put up his finger to catch her attention. "Hang on. Floyd's trying to talk to me."

Holding his hand over the cell phone, Floyd stood next to CJ. "Mary wants to have supper with you. She's not buying my version of the events at the commune." He looked around, then whispered, "Keep in mind that she never wants gruesome details."

"Eddie is on my phone and he's looking for the same information. We're planning to meet at the Pizza Pub."

Floyd's eyes narrowed. "I don't see a dinner with the four of us going well. Mary wants a sanitized version of the events. Eddie usually wants all the gore and guts."

"It'll be okay," CJ replied. "We're meeting in a restaurant where blood and guts discussions would upset the other diners."

* * *

Eddie and CJ met in the Pizza Pub parking lot, where he gave her a brotherly hug. "We did the post-mortem this afternoon. The guy from the commune was dead before he hit the ground. The trooper's bullet ripped off the bottom of his heart."

CJ nodded. "I think every cop at the standoff was shooting 9mm ammo except the trooper."

"It's probably irrelevant because any of his wounds would've been fatal."

Walking past Floyd's personal pickup, CJ said, "Mary doesn't want gory details."

"No problem," Eddie said as he opened the door for CJ. "Tonight, I'm just another curious citizen."

"Bullshit," CJ whispered as they passed a group of children who were celebrating a birthday party.

Eddie slipped into the booth first, knowing that CJ didn't like being boxed because it limited her ability to respond to an emergency. "Hi Mary, it's nice to see you again."

The waitress arrived, delivering menus and taking their beverage orders.

Mary glanced at the menu, then handed it to Floyd. "I'd like a Hawaiian pizza. Are we splitting one half Hawaiian and half pepperoni?"

Floyd put his menu on top of Mary's. "I can pick off the pineapple and eat it later as dessert."

Eddie read through the options. "I'm partial to the house special pizza with all the toppings."

CJ smiled. "I'd gladly split a Hawaiian pizza with Mary. We can let Floyd and Eddie decide what they'd like."

Looking relieved, Floyd said, "A house special pizza sounds good to me."

After ordering, Mary asked Floyd to move to the inside of the booth, so it was easier to share their pizzas across the table. Once seated, she asked CJ, "How is your shoulder?"

Eddie turned to CJ. "What's wrong with your shoulder?"

"CJ didn't tell you she was stabbed at the commune?" Mary asked.

Glaring at CJ, Eddie said, "Somehow, she managed to skip the detail about her stab wound. Where was she stabbed, Mary?"

"It was minor!" CJ protested. "I got a band aid and a tetanus shot."

"Where were you stabbed?" Eddie demanded.

CJ grinned. "I was standing outside the barn at the commune."

"Okay, Sergeant Smartass, anatomically, where is your wound?"

Reaching up with her left hand, she touched her right shoulder. "My assailant found a spot between the top of my vest and shirt collar. It's nothing."

"I'll be the judge of nothing. How big a knife did he use, and how deep is the wound?"

"I was stabbed by a woman. The weapon was a potato peeler. I'm not sure how deep it went."

"Now I know you're yanking my chain. You weren't stabbed with a potato peeler."

Floyd nodded. "It was a potato peeler."

Eddie twisted CJ and rolled down her collar so he could examine her wound. "That's above your shoulder blade, near the axillary nerve. Are you experiencing numbness, or have you lost any strength in your arm or hand?"

Straightening her collar, CJ said, "There's no numbness or tingling in my hand. And my hand strength is just fine. Thanks for your concern." She paused for a moment, waiting for someone else to speak. Breaking the silence, she said, "Too bad the Twins didn't make the playoffs."

Taking the hint, Eddie looked at Mary. "I heard you have mixed feelings about Floyd continuing on as the chief deputy if Sheriff Sepanen is re-elected?"

Mary turned to Floyd. "What have you been telling people?"

"I tell them you prefer me being retired to working."

"Floyd Swenson, what ever gave you that idea? I was the one who suggested you to John Sepanen when I heard that Mike Smith was retiring." After taking a breath while CJ laughed, Mary added, "I'd be overjoyed if you continued on as the chief deputy."

"What if I don't want to?" Floyd replied.

"You're joking. All you talk about every evening is what CJ, Pam, and the department are doing. When you were retired, you moped around like a lost puppy."

"I did not mope!"

"You did too mope. The only days you were happy were when you went out for coffee with Pam or CJ. I hope John gets re-elected, and you stay on."

Floyd grabbed his Diet Pepsi with both hands. "I don't have a job description and…hell, I don't even know what I'm being paid."

CJ smiled. "I think whatever you're being paid is just whipped cream on top of the sheer joy you get from the job."

# Chapter 23

CJ had just pulled out of the doggy daycare parking lot when the dispatcher radioed her. "I had a non-emergency call. A woman left a phone number for you."

CJ parked behind the Pine City A&W and called the dispatcher on her cell phone. "Who called for me?"

"Fran Olsen asked that you call her. I didn't want to give her your cell phone number without speaking with you first."

Tipping her head back, CJ searched her memory for someone named Fran. "Did the woman say why she wanted to speak to me?"

"I guess Floyd suggested that she talk to you when he visited her husband in the hospital."

The pieces finally fell into place, and CJ realized that Fran was Bob Olsen's wife. "Please give me her number."

"Hello?"

"Hi, Mrs. Olsen, this is CJ Jensen. You asked me to call."

"Thank you for getting back to me. Floyd Swenson and I talked in the hospital before my husband died. He said you were the one who helped Bob at the horse show, and I wanted to thank you."

"I appreciate your thanks. I wish I could've done more."

"Um, Sergeant Jensen, could we have a cup of coffee together?"

"Sure. I'd be happy to sit down with you sometime."

"Actually, I'm sitting in the Whistlestop Café. Can you get away now?"

Staring at the barbecue restaurant across the parking lot, CJ searched for an excuse to meet Fran Olsen at a later date…or never. "I'm about fifteen minutes away. Perhaps we can get together sometime when you wouldn't have to wait for me."

"Sergeant, my world has come crashing down. I have nothing better to do than wait for you."

Taking a deep breath as she flashed back to the death of her own husband, CJ paused. "I'm on my way."

* * *

Downtown Hinckley was quiet with a few cars parked by the bank and other businesses, but no one on the sidewalk. A couple walked out of the Whistlestop Café as CJ drove past. She waved at them, then parked at the curb a half block north of the café. She picked a few dog hairs off her pants as she walked to the door.

The aromas of frying bacon, freshly baked cinnamon rolls, and coffee filled the inside of the café. The dining area was about half full of people eating breakfast. Most of the customers appeared to be contractors, people ready to go to work, or retirees. A lone woman waved from a table near the cash register.

Sitting in a chair across from her, CJ signaled the waitress for a cup of coffee. "I'm CJ Jensen," she said, offering her hand. "I don't believe we've met."

Fran Olsen clasped CJ's hand in both of her hands. "Thank you for making time for me. I wanted to thank you, but I know you're busy and…"

The waitress arrived with a steaming cup of coffee and a menu. "The breakfast special is an egg and sausage breakfast sandwich on an English muffin."

Having rushed to deliver Bailey to doggy daycare, CJ hadn't eaten anything. She handed the menu back to the waitress. "The breakfast sandwich sounds good."

Topping off the women's coffees, the waitress asked, "Are you ready to eat anything, Fran?"

"I don't think so."

CJ stopped the waitress. "Have you eaten anything today, Mrs. Olsen?"

Fran shook her head. "I haven't had an appetite."

"Bring two of the specials," CJ said, staring at the dark rings under Fran's eyes.

"I've known Floyd Swenson for years. We go to the same Lutheran church. I tried to be supportive when his first wife died, and when Mary was going through her breast cancer." Fran drew a breath and blew it out. "Losing Bob made me realize that I really had no idea what Floyd was going through. I'm so…lost."

"Losing a spouse is hard."

Fran searched CJ's eyes. "Floyd said you've lost a husband. How did you manage to…get over it?"

Their sandwiches were delivered, giving CJ a moment to compose her thoughts. Unfolding her napkin and setting it on her lap, CJ pulled the plate close to her. "I've never gotten over it. I think about Bobby every day. But there's more to mourning his passing than just his death. My future plans died with him. We'd planned to have children, to go on vacations together…to grow old together. All those dreams died with him."

After taking a tiny bite of her sandwich Fran asked, "How did you find the strength to go on?"

"Before you try to *go on,* you need to grieve. Talk to your family, pastor, and friends. Don't try to forget Bob. Remember all the good times and your life together. Ask people to share their memories of Bob and embrace them.”

“I’m not ready for that. I’d be a blubbering idiot.”

“It’s okay to be a blubbering idiot. That’s what widows do. We cry and express sorrow. You can act strong, but in reality, there will be things, sometimes stupid little things, that make you burst into tears.”

“That happened to you?”

“It still happens to me. I see or hear something, and memories flood back, bringing tears to my eyes.”

Fran swallowed a bite of her sandwich. “I’ve been drinking wine to fall asleep.”

“A friend reminded me that the answers to the world’s problems aren’t in the bottom of a Jack Daniels bottle. I quit drinking and dealt with my grief head-on.”

“You eventually went on with your life.”

“I had to go on. I dug deep inside myself and resolved not to give up. My name is Charlene, and I reinvented myself. I told people to call me CJ, and I dove into my job. I left my old police department and joined the Pine County sheriff’s department. I moved on from our old friends who were full of sadness and pity, to a new family in the sheriff’s department.”

“I can’t do those things. I have never been anything but a housewife.”

"When the time is right, get out of the house. Find a job. Volunteer at your church or the food shelf. Join the Sons of Norway. Find a way to fill your empty hours."

Glancing at her watch, CJ pushed the last bite of her sandwich aside and pulled out a business card. She wrote on the back. "This is my cell phone number. Call me if you want to talk again."

Fran took the card and read the number. "Thanks."

A pained smile creased CJ's face. "I'm not much of a therapist. I hope what I said helps."

Fran stood and wiped her mouth. "It does."

# Chapter 24

CJ checked her watch and realized she was supposed to meet Alissa and Paul in less than thirty minutes. She drove north on old Highway 61, crossing over I-35 before entering the town of Sandstone. She parked around the corner from Amy's Café. Checking the crowd, she was relieved to see that she'd beaten both of her guests to the café.

"All alone today?" the waitress asked as CJ checked Amy's small dining room for open tables and booths.

"I'm meeting two associates. Can we have a table?"

Taking out three menus, the waitress led CJ to a table set for four, still damp after being cleared. "Black coffee?"

"Yes, please."

Alissa arrived before the coffee was served. She spotted CJ and sat across the table. "This place is cozy, although it's a long drive from Pine City."

"The sheriff's department has a patrol station here, and the federal prison is south of town. You need to know where both of those are located."

Alissa ordered Mountain Dew when CJ's coffee arrived. "Tell me about the big shootout."

CJ had barely started the story about the commune confrontation when Paul Martin walked in. Spotting CJ and Alissa at the table, he introduced himself. "I'm Paul. You must be CJ's colleague."

Alissa smiled but gave CJ a knowing look. "I'm Alissa Preston. Yes, CJ and I are working on a case together."

"I heard about the big sheriff's department shootout on the news," Paul said as he signalled the waitress for coffee.

"I was just going to tell Alissa about being attacked by a woman wielding a potato peeler."

Alissa leaned forward. "What? Someone attacked you with a potato peeler?"

They laughed as the potato peeler incident was discussed, then they ordered lunch. CJ ordered a house salad having just eaten a breakfast sandwich. "I really can't get into any more of the details here." Looking around at the crowded café, she said, "There are too many potential jurors within earshot."

Paul's eyes got large. "Wait. You were at the shootout, CJ?"

"Shh. Yes, but I can't talk about it…other than to discuss my potato peeler injury."

Alissa nodded. "Paul, how do you know CJ?"

"I met her while she was having a discussion with Bailey, her basset hound."

"You've met Bailey, the farting dog!"

They laughed about the dog over lunch, then discussed Alissa and Paul's experiences as new Pine County arrivals. Paul looked at his watch as he finished his burger. "I've got to get back to the hospital." He put a $20 bill on the table as he stood. Pausing, he looked at Alissa. "CJ says Maxwell's has good barbecue. Would you like to go there for supper some night?"

Alissa took a card and pen from her bag and wrote on the back. "I'd like that a lot. This is my cell phone number." Smiling at CJ as they watched Paul walk away Alissa said, "This blind date was devious."

"Will you forgive me?"

"If Paul calls me and is as nice as he seems, you'll be forgiven."

Standing, CJ set another $20 on the table. "You can thank me by naming your first child Bailey."

Threading her way through the tables, Alissa struggled to catch up to CJ. "It's only a first date. And there is no way I'm naming a child after your farting dog!"

If you enjoyed this book, please leave a review.

The End

# Published by BWL Publishing

***Whistling Pines cozies***
Whistling up a Ghost
Whistling Pirates
Whistling Bake Off
Whistling Artist
Whistling Fireman (fall of 2023)


***Doug Fletcher mysteries***

Stolen Past
Washed Away
Dead in the Water
Death in Shifting Sands
Devils Fall
Prairie Menace
Down River
Burnt Evidence
Gator Bait
Grave Survey
Dead End Trail
The Last Rodeo
Peril in Paradise (mid-2023)


***Pine County Mysteries***

Killer Secrets
Deadly Mixture
Fatal Business
Taxed to Death

Dean Hovey is the award-winning and best-selling author of three mystery series. He uses his scientific background, travel, extensive research, and consultants to add reality and depth to his stories. One reader said his characters are like people he'd like to invite over for a beer and discussion.

Hovey's Fletcher mysteries follow U.S. National Park Service investigators Doug and Jill Fletcher as they solve crimes in a series of parks and national monuments, sometimes with a bit of humor and often with their evolving relationship. The Whistling Pines mysteries are humorous cozies set in a northern Minnesota senior residence, following Peter Rogers, the Whistling Pines recreation director, as he stumbles through the investigation of murders in his small town. The Pine County mystery series follows Sergeant CJ Jensen and Investigator Pam Ryan as they solve murders in rural Minnesota.

Dean and his wife split their year between northern Minnesota and Arizona.